Victoria Brownlee is an international food writer and editor, currently based in Victoria's Mornington Peninsula. She started writing about food over a decade ago, first as a blogger and then as the food and drink editor at *Time Out Shanghai*. She continues to write freelance articles on food trends across Europe.

For Jules, who loved this story before there was even a word on the page.

EAT YOUR HEART OUT

Victoria Brownlee

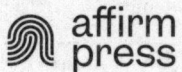

affirm
press

First published in Australia in 2025 by Affirm Press,
a Simon & Schuster (Australia) Pty Limited company
Bunurong/Boon Wurrung Country
28 Thistlethwaite Street, South Melbourne VIC 3205

Affirm Press is located on the unceded land of the Bunurong/Boon Wurrung peoples of the Kulin Nation. Affirm Press pays respect to their Elders past and present.

New York Amsterdam/Antwerp London Toronto Sydney/Melbourne New Delhi
Visit our website at www.simonandschuster.com.au

AFFIRM PRESS and design are trademarks of Affirm Press Pty Ltd, Inc.,
used under licence by Simon & Schuster, LLC.

10 9 8 7 6 5 4 3 2 1

A Cataloguing-in-Publication entry for this book is available from the National Library of Australia

 A catalogue record for this book is available from the National Library of Australia

9781923135604 (paperback)
9781923293793 (ebook)

Cover design by Andy Warren
Typeset by J&M Typesetting in Garamond Premier Pro
Proudly printed and bound in Australia by the Opus Group

Part One

Chez Duris

Paris

Chapter 1

The Invitation – CHLOE

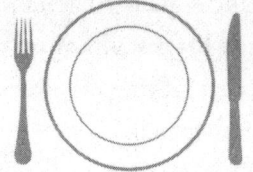

I walked into my fifth-floor Parisian apartment to find a small black card had been slipped under my door. Bending to pick it up off the creaky wooden floorboards, I read:

Invitation: Chloe Bridgers
Dinner
6 June 2023, 8pm
Chez Duris

Excitement bubbled in my stomach as I flipped the card over, hunting for more details. I'd been getting an increasing number of restaurant invitations from PR people lately, but generally they arrived via text or email, mostly with a little more notice – this event was tonight – and always with a lot more information. This one felt clandestine, exclusive. It felt sexy.

The embossed initials, *CD*, on the back gave little indication of who had left the invitation, or how they knew where I lived, but those small details quickly evaporated into irrelevance.

Tonight, I was going to Chez Duris, and that meant everything. *So much for a quiet night in ...* This was not an invitation I could turn down.

Chez Duris was the flagship restaurant of the one-and-only Carla Duris, daughter of the late restaurateur and cooking god, Jean Duris, and ultra-glam French model Catherine Voss. Jean Duris had opened his restaurant on the Place des Vosges in 1970, and it had been serving classic French food to Paris's most discerning diners ever since.

I wandered into the kitchen and grabbed my well-worn copy of *The Duris Family at Home*, a translated collection of Duris family recipes I'd found in a charity shop when I'd moved from Tasmania to study at the University of Melbourne. At the time, I'd been homesick and lonely, desperately trying to figure out if I'd made a terrible mistake.

That cookbook marked a turning point in my time in Melbourne. First, it made me fall in love with the entire Duris family, who became my fictional fill-in family during the long nights I spent at home alone. Second, it made my new friends fall in love with me, via Jean and Carla's famed boeuf bourguignon. Thanks to the Duris family, I found my people in a new city. I learnt how to bond with friends over food and wine. This knowledge helped me get through my degree, and taught me that the most important thing wasn't where I lived, but the people I surrounded myself with. And as long as I had the Duris family, I felt like I could be happy anywhere.

I opened the cookbook to a picture of Carla and her father in their home kitchen in the late 90s, around the time Carla was working as a commis chef at Chez Duris. She looked determined and serious, a woman on a mission. Given Carla's birthright, she could have coasted comfortably through her adult years doing little more than press appearances and managing the family's fortune. Instead, she followed in her father's footsteps, training in the very kitchen that she would take over in 2007, when Jean unexpectedly passed away.

I'd only eaten at Chez Duris once since arriving in Paris a year earlier – a birthday present to myself – and it had been a tour de force. I'd gone solo, to avoid being distracted by conversation, and the experience was almost transcendent. The menu was classically French, eschewing fads and trends in favour of seasonal vegetables from the restaurant's rooftop garden with carefully sourced French meat and seafood, all cooked to perfection.

As I mindlessly flipped through Jean and Carla's recipes – a comforting ritual – I wondered how I'd scored an invite to dinner. Chez Duris was definitely a special occasion place, and one that normally needed to be booked months in advance. It wasn't the kind of restaurant that even hosted press events, because Carla just didn't seem to need the extra press.

As I was fruitlessly searching for meaning in the recipe for *tarte à l'oignon*, I heard Drew's key in the door.

Drew had been in Paris for over a decade, and while he was also technically an Australian, his heart now firmly beat with French blood. His first day in Paris, he'd been walking the city in a jet-lagged haze and was shocked to discover that most of the coffee was awful and that nobody was cooking bacon and eggs. 'I couldn't go on starting my days with a bitter espresso and a croissant. I would have perished!' he told me. Finding this lack of a decent breakfast as sacrilegious as the French might regard filming TikToks in a church, Drew decided it was his life's mission to open a casual café serving hearty food and good flat whites. He'd wanted to teach the French a thing or two about the most important meal of the day. It was an instant hit. Since then, many so-called Australian-style cafés had popped up around the French capital, but Drew was still considered one of the pioneers.

I met Drew early in my own Parisian adventures when I went to his café to eat the good eggs and drink the good coffee. We got chatting. He needed a new housemate, I needed somewhere to live that wasn't an Airbnb – and so, our friendship began.

'Drew, you'll never guess what happened,' I shouted as he was slipping off his work clogs.

'Chloe, we've spoken about the French requirement to say *bonjour* before launching into whatever tirade you seem to be working up to,' he said.

'You're not even French,' I told him.

He shot me a look of faux-disdain.

'Now, off your high horse and get ready for some big news,' I continued.

'Go on then,' he said, cracking a tired smile.

'Well,' I started theatrically, 'here I was, minding my own business as I walked in the door earlier, when I almost stepped on this.' I handed him the card.

He flipped it over casually, and said, 'So?'

'What do you mean, "So"?'

'So, it's an invite to Chez Duris. I guess it's your lucky day,' he said, with a hint of sarcasm.

Drew was one of the few people in the world who *didn't* seem to admire Carla Duris. Perhaps because he wasn't one for fussy service, elaborate cooking or exorbitant price tags. Or perhaps because Drew believed the rumours about how Carla treated her kitchen staff. I'd tried to point out that she was innocent until proven guilty, but he remained unconvinced.

'It's not *just* an invite,' I explained. 'It's *dinner* at *Chez Duris*!'

'You've been getting loads of invites these days, haven't you? Your blog has kind of taken off. Just today somebody told me *your* post made them want to try *my* café,' he said, pulling a beer from the fridge and sitting on one of our bar stools.

My cheeks flushed. Until now, I'd tried not to get too excited about my increasing online readership. I didn't want to jinx it.

'So, are you going to go?' he asked, clearly not as intrigued by the mysterious invitation as I was.

'Of course!'

'Then what's the big deal?' he asked.

'I guess I'm just wondering why it's so last-minute. Why so secretive?'

'I guess when you're as famous as Carla Duris, you can do what you like.'

'Are you saying I'm *not* famous?' I countered, cracking a smile.

He ignored my question. 'You've got nothing to lose by

going – unless of course they make you pay for dinner,' he added with a laugh, taking a long sip of his beer.

Obviously, Drew was right. And I had plenty to gain: I'd get to eat Carla's food, I'd meet more people in the Paris dining scene, and I might even meet Carla herself. I *had* talked about her somewhat (okay, a lot) on my blog, but then, of course I had – I couldn't cover the city's dining scene *without* referencing Chez Duris.

'Right, well, I'd better go and get ready.'

I rummaged through my wardrobe, at a loss as to what to wear. I wasn't even sure what type of event I was going to. Dinner, yes, but was it dressy? I knew Chez Duris was relatively formal, but this was a private event. Did I want to look creative? Stand out? Blend in?

Usually, I wouldn't spend too much time picking an outfit, but then again, it wasn't every day – or *any* day, until today – that I was invited to Chez Duris. Nervous anticipation was building in my stomach, and manifesting as panic over what to wear.

French people always looked so effortlessly chic. They could make a bra and sheer dress work at a funeral as easily as they could rock a thousand-euro Chloe dress at an afternoon picnic.

My phone lit up and I glanced over to see who was calling. It was Mum.

As much as I would have loved to tell her about my

invitation to Chez Duris, I knew she'd immediately start asking questions about my blog, then about my plans for the future. All of which I'd struggle to answer, leaving me feeling flustered and her annoyed. I didn't need that right now.

She wasn't overly supportive of my choice to live in France, and she mentioned the possibility of me moving back to Australia *at least* once a week. Any time I complained to her about anything in Paris – the second-hand cigarette smoke, the smell of urine in the streets, the tourists – she would dutifully remind me that 'everyone' thought it would be best if I moved back home as soon as possible so I could get on with my 'real life'.

What Mum either didn't realise or refused to accept was that there just weren't the same job opportunities open to me in Tasmania. Sure, it was a beautiful place to live, but I'd tried cutting my teeth in the writing scene there, only to be rejected at every turn. The same thing had happened in Melbourne, where the number of people lining up to do unpaid copywriting internships was longer than the line for *les croissants* at Lune.

Since finishing university, I'd dreamt of living in the City of Light; and when a bilingual copywriting and translating job came up at the luxury hotel Hôtel Claris, that dream finally came true.

That had only been a year ago, but already the shine of working in a luxury hotel had worn off. I enjoyed the writing part of the job, even if my capacity for creativity had been limited to glamorous-sounding social media posts and promotional offers to valued guests. But the hours were awful, the pay even worse, and the glamour of the hotel completely non-existent in the back office – think dingy wallpaper, no natural light and cockroach infestations.

If it weren't for my blog, *Eat Me, Paris*, I might have even given up on life here entirely. Writing about French food had given me the sense of purpose that my day job had failed to provide, and over the past year, my blog had evolved into something that was part diary, part eating guide to Paris. It didn't make any money, but more and more people were reading it, particularly expats and tourists, thanks to my reviews of what I considered to be Paris's best restaurants.

Over the past couple of months, I'd started receiving invitations to soft openings and spring menu launches. This, I *loved*! Free food in exchange for a write-up and photos? What a blessing. I would hardly say that I was *in* with the inner circle of the Paris food-writing scene, but I felt like I was on my way. If only I had more time to dedicate to blogging.

I winced as I rejected the call, whispering a quiet, 'Sorry, Mum.' I needed to focus on the night ahead.

Outfit-wise, I settled on a black button-down silk dress and a cream blazer – unassuming, comfortable, safe – then added a colourful necklace from Parisian designer Bobo, who had a little studio near Bastille. It was a statement piece and always proved to be a good talking point – perfect for dinner with a group of people I didn't know. Putting it on, I wondered who else had been invited. Bloggers like me? Food writers? Australians?

I walked back into the lounge room where Drew was now sprawled on the couch. He lazily opened his eyes.

'Nice,' he said, appraising my outfit.

'Not too conservative?' I asked, doing an awkward little spin.

'You could afford to undo another button,' he suggested.

If Drew and I had one ounce of romantic chemistry between us, I'd view this as an advance, but given our strictly platonic relationship, I took it as helpful advice.

'Bring me a doggy bag,' he said.

'I think it's safe to say most people at Chez Duris polish off their plate.'

'I wish my customers would do that. It'd save on dishes,' he joked.

'Don't go too crazy while I'm out,' I said.

He just nodded and lifted a hand in a half-hearted wave.

'*Ciao*,' he managed to get out before appearing to fall asleep again.

I grabbed my bag, slipped on some black ballet flats and quietly shut the door behind me.

Walking from our apartment in the 10th to Chez Duris at Place des Vosges, my heart was thumping. As the streets got wider and the façades on the buildings got cleaner and brighter, I felt like I was walking towards a different, more opulent world. The clothing displays in the windows became more luxurious, the jewellery and watches more diamond-encrusted and expensive. The red-brick buildings that lined the square glowed in the evening sun, and the park inside was packed with people enjoying drinks and picnics, and children running out the last of their energy for the day. I looked at a group of friends drinking rosé from plastic cups and found myself envying how relaxed they looked.

It's just dinner, I told myself. *I'm a food blogger. This is normal ...*

But another part of my brain was wondering: *Could this be the start of something bigger for my blog?*

As I approached Chez Duris, I made a concerted effort to centre myself. I held the invitation card by my fingertips, not wanting it to touch my palms, which were – unglamorously, rather embarrassingly – slightly damp with sweat. I waved my hands discreetly by my sides to dry them.

Clasping the solid brass handle, I pushed the door open and nervously stepped inside.

I handed my invitation to a waiter, who inhaled sharply. *Why does he suddenly seem on edge?* He gave me the briefest look up and down, squinted almost imperceptibly, then ushered me through the colourful dining room, moving at such a rapid pace I almost had to trot to keep up with him.

Before I had time to wonder where he was taking me, he'd opened a massive wooden door, revealing a more muted private dining room with a single, large round table in the centre that was covered in the whitest tablecloth I'd ever seen. Plush green chairs and handpainted plates featuring different herbs and vegetables were the only pops of colour in the otherwise neutral space. The effect was striking. The room oozed elegance.

So distracting was the decadent feel of the rug underfoot that it took me a moment to properly register the people who were already seated around the table. I was the last to arrive. My face burnt. How could I have been so careless? But Parisians were generally ten minutes late to everything – clearly 'everything' didn't extend to an event at Chez Duris.

The room was silent as the waiter pulled out a chair and asked me to sit. My name was written in calligraphy on a little card that sat in front of a large decorative plate. Wine glasses lined up like soldiers gave me a hint of what was to come.

I sat as quietly as I could, placing my bag on my lap, grateful that I hadn't worn the bright pink top I'd been considering. The atmosphere in the room felt rather sombre. I attempted a smile, but was met mostly with stern or apathetic faces.

Once the waiter had left the room, I felt a little bolder. I looked around at my dining companions – seven of us in total – trying to work out if I knew any of them. I recognised a couple of faces from a few tastings I'd been invited to.

I forced out a little '*Bonjour*', but only got a couple of half-smiles in return. Everyone seemed to be busying themselves with their phones or staring at their plates. *Mon dieu*, I thought to myself, *what kind of evening am I in for?*

Chapter 2

The Arrival – HENRI

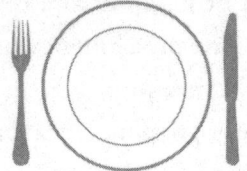

It is her. Be cool, Henri, I told myself as she appeared in the doorway.

I had met her before at the launch of some new bar – but which one? And when? The memory of her face was perfectly etched in my mind, but details of the evening in question were hazy.

Since taking over as food editor at *Le Cercle*, I had been eating out too much, drinking more wine than I should, meeting so many new people. The names, the details, they all blurred together. But in the weeks after meeting this mystery girl, I had found myself hoping to see her again. I had kept an eye out at press events and tastings – the Paris food circle was smaller than most people imagined – but she had never reappeared.

Until now.

The same waiter who had whisked me into this private area only minutes earlier led her to her seat. It was next to mine. My heart thumped.

She didn't look like the other food writers at the table. She didn't walk with that same arrogant familiarity. She was more understated, more reserved. Her curly hair fell gently around her face, and her dark eyes darted around the room nervously.

Henri, you imbecile! How could you forget her name?

Her nameplate was obscured by a wine glass, so I pretended to stretch my neck to see it.

Chloe. *Of course it is Chloe!*

A beautiful name. A beautiful woman.

But I had not been invited to Chez Duris to lose my head over a girl.

Honestly, I wasn't sure why we had been invited here at all, but I was not going to risk not finding out. If Carla Duris had her hands on something, or if she was starting something, I wanted to be a part of it. Or rather, I couldn't *not* be a part of it. Not that I was particularly close to Carla. In fact, I should probably call her Madame Duris. Uncle Michel would send me to the guillotine if he knew I was not paying due respect to one of France's best known chefs.

And … that had been the problem with taking over the food editor job at *Le Cercle* from my Uncle Michel. Although I had been doing the job for over a year, he was still finding ways to infiltrate my work, and even my social life. He was always there, omnipresent, either lurking in person or sometimes just in my thoughts. I could hear him telling me what to do, and how to approach certain situations. There were politics involved in the paper, and unfortunately my surname came with certain assumptions, a host of preconceptions and a dash of resentment.

Around me at the dinner table were mostly familiar faces.

I knew Juliette and Balthazar well (I liked the former and tolerated the latter, even though I knew he'd throw me under a bus as soon as the opportunity presented itself). They represented the French side of the dining table and I'd spent more than a few evenings with them at press dinners and soft openings. They were competitive – as hungry to write as they were to eat – and I had to work hard to keep up with them. But what I lacked in their mid-twenties energy, I made up for in experience. They were weaker writers than me, and the decade of additional practice I had on them had taught me a lot. I'd eaten at some of the very best restaurants around the world – *merci, Maman et Papa* – and I knew I brought a nuance to my reviews that theirs often lacked. Besides, my uncle was living proof that you didn't need to be young to be a leading food critic in this city. You just needed time, money and connections.

My phone buzzed in my pocket. The room was otherwise silent. I pulled it out as stealthily as I could.

Speak of the devil: a message from Uncle Michel.

'I hear you're at Chez D. tonight. Enjoy yourself but remain alert. M.'

By 'remain alert', what he really meant was don't drink too much. Solid advice that immediately made me want to do the opposite. But I knew the only person who would pay for my petulance was me, and I wasn't sure I could handle being punished by anyone at *Le Cercle* at the moment. *How on earth did he even know I was here?*

My uncle was suffocating me. Paris was suffocating me. I needed an escape plan.

This expectation to follow in my uncle's footsteps had hovered over me from the moment I'd shown an interest in food as a toddler, and was cemented when I'd chosen to study media and writing at university.

I'd graduated with good marks from a top international school in Paris. Happy parents.

Then I'd chosen to complete the majority of my degree in Melbourne, Australia. Unhappy parents. Unhappy uncle.

I'd stayed on the other side of the world until I'd run out of visa options.

My French father and American mother were baffled. They couldn't understand why I'd chosen to move somewhere they didn't have any connections. Maman could have got me into any of the universities in New York, she told me. Papa claimed he could have got me any internship or job I wanted in Paris. I'd told them I wanted to learn about a new culture and travel the world. In reality, I'd just needed to get as far away from my life as physically possible.

It sounds ungrateful to say that accompanying my parents during expensive meals was a burden, but I was young and just wanted to be with my friends, who wouldn't be seen anywhere near a Michelin-starred anything. They were eating falafel sandwiches in Le Marais, or Vietnamese Bò Bún near the Canal Saint-Martin. I'd wanted to explore things without being told how I was supposed to feel about them. Or without having to be grateful for the hundreds of euros my parents had just spent on my 'gastronomic education'. I'm grateful, now, obviously – this exposure to incredible food laid the foundations for what

I'm doing now – but try telling that to an eighteen-year-old enduring a four-hour degustation menu while his friends are drinking happy-hour beers at some dive bar.

Luckily, over the years, things had changed. And maybe tonight they were about to change again.

I looked across at Belle, who flashed me her winning smile. Belle was the west-coast all-American girl behind *La Belle Vie*, a YouTube channel about French food, fashion and culture. Her clips were so popular, she'd become the go-to girl for a lot of foreign media. We'd been at the same dinners a couple of times and she was a lot of fun.

Also at the table was Christopher, a mainstay on the Parisian dining scene, having started writing for *Luxury Travel* decades earlier, when expense accounts were still a thing and boring old English guys somehow got to rinse them dry. He wore chambray shirts and tweed blazers. Thankfully, he was on the other side of the table, because if anything was going to force me to drink too much, it would be listening to him drone on about, well, anything.

Then there was an older American guy – Chad? Chas? Chuck? – who I recognised but didn't know particularly well, and of course, sitting next to me was Chloe ... *Mon dieu*, she was a distraction. Her eyes were like inky pools in the moonlight that I wanted to dive into, naked.

Focus, Henri, I scolded myself.

Once Chloe had filled the last empty chair at the table, a man in a very sharp suit strode into the room.

'*Je m'appelle Max.* I'm Max,' he said in a brisk, hurried manner, as though he had more important places to be. 'I work with Madame Duris.'

I'd met Max once before, and from that interaction I knew he was all business. I *had* wondered if there was anything between him and Carla, which would explain why he seemed determined to scare everyone else off, but that wasn't any of my concern.

From what Uncle Michel had told me, Carla liked her staff to be devoted and determined. She didn't suffer fools, and had a great deal of respect for hierarchy – which meant, given that she was at the top of the chain of command, she commanded a great deal of respect.

'You might be wondering why you're here,' Max continued quickly, getting straight to the point.

'Chez Duris is one of France's most beloved gourmet restaurants. Since its beginning in 1970, it has been awarded the highest French accolades and is adored for its classic French cuisine, using only the very best ingredients sourced with the greatest care and attention. The food at Chez Duris is a veritable showcase of masterful cooking, pairing of ingredients and attention to detail.'

I felt like he was reciting the 'About' section of the Chez Duris website.

Max continued. 'Tonight: first course, you'll eat scallop carpaccio with Corsican clementine. Main will be Carla's signature rack of lamb with garden carrots, and for dessert, a *tarte fine aux fraises,* the perfect strawberry tart.'

To be fair, the menu sounded incredible.

Chad – or whatever his name was – flicked his finger in the air. 'So, we're just here for dinner?' he asked, in a loud, strong New York accent.

Clearly, Chas wasn't someone who enjoyed a preamble.

'Which brings me to my next point,' Max continued without a second look at the man who'd dared interrupt him.

The suspense in the room was palpable.

'Madame Duris would like everybody seated around this table to interview for a role working closely with her on a new writing project,' Max said, waving his hand around at us.

Parfait! I thought to myself. Just the pivot I'd been hoping for.

Chapter 3

The Opening Gambit – CHLOE

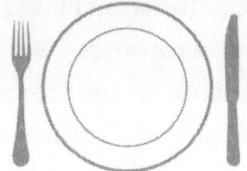

I felt like I'd entered an alternate universe.

First, the invite to Chez Duris; now, the chance to work on a project with Carla. I forced myself to breathe.

After pausing to let the idea sink in, the very intense, clipboard-carrying man named Max (who was also distractingly tall, dark and handsome) added: '*Alors*, here you have a decision to make, and it will be the first of many decisions you will make in the coming days. To note: we do not want anyone to feel locked into this job interview process. You are here of your own free will.'

His words hung in the air ominously.

I looked across the table at Christopher – one of the few people I recognised – to see his reaction to this news. His face remained surprisingly neutral. Aside from our native language, I got the impression we had very little else in common. He looked like he was in his late forties, probably from Cambridge. His parents had to be doctors, and undoubtedly lived in a giant house somewhere with ponies and staff. He'd been on the books at *Luxury Travel* for years, seemed to only write one new article every few months and would be the first to tell you he was very important.

Max continued: '*Alors,* let me first describe what Carla has outlined for the interview process. Tonight is merely a formality, an introduction of sorts. You are not being interviewed yet, but you will be meeting Carla at some point in the evening, and she will explain more about her project and her expectations.'

I held back a little yelp of excitement. *I am going to meet Carla!* Things were feeling more surreal by the moment.

'Following this evening, you will have one day to consider tonight's interview proposal and confirm with me your willingness to participate.'

I tried to piece together the timing in my head.

'You will be invited down to the Duris family villa in Antibes on the Côte d'Azur. I'm sure you've all heard of it.'

Heard of it? I'd all but drooled over its opulence in the pages of *Vogue*.

'You will catch the night train on Friday, arriving Saturday morning. You will be collected at the station and taken to the villa to participate in a weekend of activities, including a one-on-one interview with Carla, among other things.'

'Wait ... this coming weekend?' I asked quietly.

Crap! I was meant to be catching the Eurostar to London to see my friend Hazel. Wrong train, wrong direction.

Max dismissed my question with a curt nod.

He continued: 'You will sign a non-disclosure agreement. You shall not discuss any activity or aspect of the weekend, nor anything relating to Madame Duris, with anybody, regardless of whether you are successful in the interview process. You have been chosen from a long list of potential candidates based on who Carla feels is best positioned to accompany her on this project. It will be a long-term commitment, a one-year contract, renewable. The successful candidate will be on a retainer for Madame Duris during this time, and any other work they currently do shall be put on indefinite pause.'

My heart skipped a beat.

'Hold up,' said the same American man who had interrupted earlier. 'You want us to commit to writing some kind of puff piece on Carla Duris for a whole year without working on anything else? That's not sustainable,' he added, voicing what I could only assume everyone was thinking.

'With the proposed fee Madame Duris has disclosed to me, sir, I believe it is completely sustainable,' Max said sharply.

'I'm out,' he replied without pause. 'This sounds like some kind of set-up, not my vibe. Good luck to anyone willing to throw away the rest of their career for some random "project",' he said, making air quotes with his fingers. Then he stood up and ripped his nameplate in half, scattering the pieces with a flourish over the beautiful sprig of parsley that had been painted onto his plate.

'Anyone else?' Max asked, gesturing impatiently at the door.

We'd moved from a shortlist of seven applicants to six awfully quickly. The odds were increasingly in our favour. I wondered how many of the remaining shortlisted people would actually turn up at Carla's villa for the weekend. Max was doing a fabulous job of intimidating everyone.

I sat frozen on my seat. Obviously, I couldn't leave before finding out more about the project, and – perhaps more importantly – I wouldn't miss dinner at Chez Duris under any circumstance.

'Right then, onto dinner,' Max said, tapping his pen on his clipboard.

As if on cue, in walked several waiters clad in dark clothes, gliding effortlessly through the door. They delivered plates of immaculately presented scallop carpaccio, sliced so thinly that the segments were almost translucent, contrasting beautifully with the deep orange of the Corsican clementine wedges. The plating was, in itself, a work of art.

The chair and place setting of the departed American was whisked away and somehow, as if by magic, the table was made to look like he'd never even been there. How quickly he was forgotten.

With a theatrical '*Bon appétit*', Max sashayed out of the room, leaving us somewhat the wiser about why we'd been invited to dinner, but honestly, still pretty clueless. I was surprised nobody was talking about what this 'writing project' might be. Would it be a blog? A newsletter? Something bigger?

I turned to Juliette, who was sitting on my right. 'Well, wasn't that something,' I attempted. Juliette had a reputation for being the queen of food gossip in Paris, and I was pretty sure she could walk into any decent restaurant, bar or club in Paris and be recognised. I'd met her at a press lunch we'd hosted at Hôtel Claris once, but she gave me no reason to think she remembered me.

'*Absolument*,' she said in her high-pitched, thick French accent.

'Do you think you'll go for it?' I asked, right off the bat.

'Why of course,' she said without a moment's hesitation. 'This is a once-in-a-lifetime opportunity. Besides, I need a weekend away from *Paris*. The weather this month has been very depressing,' she added wistfully.

'It's short notice though, right? And kind of vague, too,' I said, fishing, in an attempt to work out if Juliette found this situation normal. Perhaps this was a commonplace approach in the food-writing world.

'When Madame Duris calls, you answer,' she said, picking up her fork and piercing a slice of scallop like she'd been born with cutlery in her hand. I smiled and followed suit, noticing the table had fallen silent.

An image popped into my head of Carla's most iconic paparazzi shot. It was taken when she'd been sunbathing topless on a yacht in the Mediterranean. On noticing the cameraman, she'd jumped off the stern, glass of Champagne in one hand, middle finger of the other fully extended, smiling coquettishly down the barrel of the lens as if to say: 'I see you, and this is the real me.' I found her take-no-shit attitude inspirational – and now, the closer I got to actually meeting her, rather intimidating, too.

I tried to pay attention to my scallops, but my nerves were messing with my appetite. I took a large sip of the Montrachet chardonnay we'd been served and then immediately had another, which helped calm me down. *My god, Carla Duris certainly knows how to look after her guests!*

Finally, I felt composed enough to actually taste our first course, and I revelled over the pairing of the salty scallops with the sweet-tart juiciness of the clementine. The food, the wine, the anticipation ... joy didn't even come close to describing how I felt in that moment.

Chapter 4

The Scene Is Set – HENRI

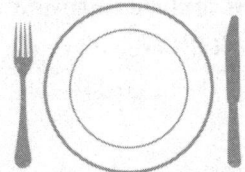

Before Max had even finished telling us all the details of the upcoming weekend, I sent him an email to confirm that I would gladly attend. I wanted this job, whatever it might be, and the prospect of quitting *Le Cercle* and committing to Carla for a year was thrilling.

While the waiters served our first course of scallops, I took a sip of wine, letting it linger in my mouth as I took stock. I'd gone to dinner secretly hoping for some kind of lifeline out of my current situation, but this offer felt almost too good to be true. An escape from the shadow of Uncle Michel handed to me on a plate alongside some succulent scallops. Did life get any sweeter?

Max returned as we were finishing our dish. 'I take it you all enjoyed your first course. Now, are there any further questions?' he asked, in a tone that insinuated if we had any questions, we'd be kicked out.

I looked around, wondering who would be brave enough to ask anything.

'Why do we need to give up our current job to work on this project? Couldn't we do both?' Juliette asked boldly while maintaining a look of doe-eyed innocence.

'This is a job working for Carla Duris,' Max replied sternly. 'She will require your full attention, your full availability and your full concentration. If that is too hard for you to understand, you may leave.'

Juliette went white. I assumed she wasn't used to being put in her place.

'And why a full weekend for the interview?' Balthazar questioned.

Max looked at him like he was an annoying bug he planned to squash. I stifled a chuckle. 'You will see in the fullness of time. But trust me, you will not be bored,' he said. 'Anything else?'

Others shook their heads, some looked down at the table. Nobody spoke.

The tension around the table was thick enough to cut. Perhaps that was what Carla had intended in gathering us together. Pitting us against each other as we competed for the one job.

Max strode out of the room as waiters entered to remove our plates.

As if attempting to even the playing field, Balthazar turned to me and asked: 'Did your uncle secure you a place at the interview?'

I rolled my eyes. I was used to people trying to discredit my work and attribute my success to nepotism, but he must have known it still stung.

'Will your *Maman* remember to pack your blankie for the weekend?' I retorted.

Balthazar scoffed but pulled his hands through his hair, obviously unnerved by my comment. I'd always had the impression he was self-conscious about his age, over-compensating for his youth as though he had something to prove.

'Maybe I should ask your little sister if I can borrow hers,' he said.

At the mention of Lucy, blood rushed to my face, but I played it cool. It wasn't a secret that Lucy and I shared an apartment. It wasn't a secret that we were very close, despite our age gap. Balthazar would have to do better than that to get under my skin.

'Lucy doesn't even know who you are,' I told him.

'*Ah, bon?*' he questioned.

Pretending to be the bigger person, I ignored his jibe, but despite my bravado, I knew I'd have to watch out for Balthazar. He'd played dirty tricks to get his way in the past, and as much as I hated to admit it, he put me on edge. I cringed at the idea of having to suffer through a whole weekend with him ...

I looked around the table at my other contemporaries – now my adversaries – and figured I had a good shot at getting this writing job, whatever it turned out to be.

I had a stronger knowledge of food and the French dining scene than Juliette and Balthazar, and I was pretty certain I was a better writer than Belle. After all, she was better known for being a TV presenter – but then, maybe that was what Carla wanted.

Christopher, I felt, wasn't Carla's type. He was too old and too pompous. I figured she'd realise this pretty quickly and he'd soon be sent home. Or maybe he'd be put off by having to compete against us, and would choose to leave himself. That felt very 'Christopher'.

But perhaps what worried me the most about this weekend was my capacity for concentration. As a food writer, the line between being professional and having fun often got blurred. At dinners where wine was being poured faster than we could drink it, it was hard to not get swept away in the excitement.

And then there was Chloe. The wildcard. The distraction.

I had to talk to her. I had to find out exactly where we'd met.

But as soon as I opened my mouth, I seemed to offend her.

Chapter 5

The Knives Come Out – CHLOE

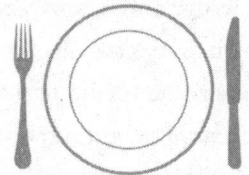

I'd just started allowing myself to imagine what a weekend-long interview with Carla Duris might look like when I realised the table had fallen silent.

I turned to Juliette to ask her how she'd found the scallops, in the hope it would lead to a bigger discussion. I still had so many questions.

'They were exceptional,' she said abruptly.

'Indeed,' I replied, trying to think of something more to say. Eventually, she leaned a little closer to me.

Here we go, I thought, prepping myself for a little insider knowledge.

'So, tell me, how did *you* get a place at this table?' she asked, picking up her wine glass and taking a very large sip.

'What do you mean?' I said, nerves bubbling in my stomach.

'You write a blog, *oui*?'

'Yes, and?' I asked, trying desperately not to let my insecurities make me defensive.

'It is just surprising, I guess,' she said. 'I'm just trying to figure out how everyone fits into the group, you know. Please don't take it personally, but I know everybody at this table well. Everybody except you.'

'Honestly, I'm not sure why I was invited either,' I said with a laugh, trying to lighten the mood

Sure, I loved my blog, and I took immense pride in my writing, but *Eat Me, Paris* was hardly *Le Cercle* or *Le Monde*. I didn't have clout like some of the other journalists around the table; I didn't even have the money to dine at the majority of the Michelin-starred restaurants around the city. I focused solely on flavour, not pomp – but perhaps that was what had landed me a place at this table. Or perhaps it was my gushing about the Duris family. Whatever it was, I had to remind myself that Carla felt like I deserved to be there. I bit back the urge to point this out.

I loved everything to do with food, and even if I didn't have one of the 'coveted' food media jobs in Paris, I knew I could write. I just had to hope Carla would agree.

While Juliette had been questioning my credentials, she had also managed to secure the attention of Henri de la Fontaine (does a name get any more French bourgeois than 'de la Fontaine'?). My nerves amplified as he looked at me with intent. I could only assume he, too, was wondering how I qualified for an invitation.

Henri was well known in food media circles for being as aloof as he was handsome – which is to say, very. He'd only been the food critic at *Le Cercle* for a year or so, having taken over the role from his uncle, but he'd already garnered a name for himself as one of the best known and most feared critics in

Paris. A bad review in *Le Cercle* could see bookings cancelled and some restaurants on the brink of closure.

'You're not from Paris, are you?' he asked me. It seemed an odd question, given this wasn't our first meeting.

'No, I'm Australian,' I said, blood rushing to my cheeks, embarrassed that he didn't recognise me. 'We've met before, actually ... At the launch of Bar Bisous. My friend Drew introduced us,' I told him.

A look of recollection appeared on his face, which was a relief, but still, the feeling of having been forgotten, even momentarily, was humiliating.

Unlike Henri, I remembered the evening we had met perfectly. I'd been having a wonderful time, riding high on the invitation and the free cocktails, until Drew had introduced us.

'Chloe writes *Eat Me, Paris*,' Drew had told Henri proudly.

'Ah,' he had said knowingly.

'You've heard of it?' I'd asked, excitedly, thrilled that somebody with his background had even heard of my blog.

But at that moment, Henri's phone had rung, and rather than replying, he'd answered it. Mouthing '*Attends*', he'd rushed off.

I'd waited around like a fool, but Henri never came back.

When I'd mentioned it to Drew later, he'd reassured me that Henri wasn't worth wasting any energy over. I suppose talking to a food blogger had been low on his priority list.

'Sorry, I go to so many events, they have a tendency to merge into one these days. Casualty of the job,' he said.

I nodded slowly. *Does he expect me to feel sorry for him?*

'And remind me, who do you write for?' he asked.

This was the icing on the cake. Forgetting my face was one thing, but forgetting my blog felt like a knife in my side.

'I write for myself,' I told him.

'Sorry?' he said, in a way that made me wonder if it was a statement or a question.

'I write the blog *Eat Me, Paris* ...' I clarified, hoping he would register.

'Of course, yes, I remember,' he said, his accent a charming mix of French, American and somehow Australian.

'You do?' I asked, again hopeful that we could turn this interaction around.

'Yes, you're the blogger,' he continued.

Was that a hint of superiority in his tone? *Here we go again,* I thought. Juliette had chipped away at my confidence and now it seemed it was Henri's turn. As if I needed any more reason to question why I was there.

Annoyingly, I took the bait. I had worked damn hard to carve out a name for myself in this city by writing about food. Henri, on the other hand, seemed to have been born into it. I hated that I felt the need to justify my writing.

'I *am* a blogger,' I said.

'*C'est bien*,' he said, encouragingly.

'It *is* great, actually,' I said defensively, not knowing if he was being sarcastic. 'I know my readers, they know me, it's all about building trust with them. They even help shape the things I write about. I guess you could say that blogging is less of a one-way relationship than traditional journalism ...'

'And do you find that you're able to get the access you need?' he asked.

'Access to what?' I asked.

'To PR, to the chefs?'

'Of course,' I lied. So often when I told restaurateurs that I was a food blogger, they lost interest, as if they only worked with 'legitimate sources'. It was my pet peeve.

'I'm sure there are also benefits to being a blogger,' he added. 'You can probably remain very anonymous. I am sure that no chef in Paris has a photo of you in their kitchen.'

I scoffed. 'Is that meant to make me feel better?'

'Sorry,' he said. 'It's just, the minute people find out that I write for *Le Cercle*, they are, how do you say, all over me.' His accent was incredibly sexy. It was striking. It was annoyingly seductive.

'Being treated well sounds awful,' I said sarcastically. The most I'd ever been gifted before this dinner was a free lunch and a glass or two of wine. And I'd been thrilled.

'Well ...' he said, and then paused, looking thoughtful. 'You must have done something right to be sitting here this evening.' He looked at Juliette pointedly, but she wasn't paying attention anymore. *Did he just stand up for me?*

I couldn't work out if Henri was suggesting I didn't deserve to be there, or if something was simply being lost in translation. He was clearly making an effort to be kind, but at the same time, he felt completely out of touch. And then there was the distraction of his handsome face, which I was trying very hard to ignore. It seemed he'd done very well from his looks so far in life, and I didn't need to get caught up in that wave.

Chapter 6

The Dressing Down – HENRI

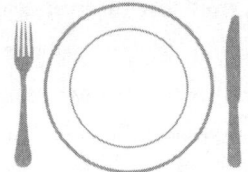

When Chloe had reminded me sternly that we'd met at Bar Bisous, my memories from the evening had started slowly piecing together. I'd been in a foul mood that night, and had drunk far too many glasses of Champagne. It had been an awful day – Uncle Michel had micro-managed the editing of every word of a restaurant review I'd just submitted. The humiliation had nearly broken me. That night, I'd wanted to rebel.

I'd just done a round of shots at the bar – out of character for me – when Drew had introduced me to Chloe. I'd been about to tell her how much I enjoyed her blog when Lucy had called me for help because her wallet had been stolen. The worst possible timing, but impossible to ignore.

I'd rushed off to take Lucy to the police station to make a statement. We'd waited for hours, and by the time we'd spoken to a policewoman, I was completely sober. A quick message to a friend confirmed that the party at Bar Bisous had moved on, so I begrudgingly called it a night. Paris certainly had a way of reminding you who was boss.

But that was all in the past. Surely the way I'd *met* Chloe didn't have to dictate our future. Perhaps I could still make up for our bumpy beginning. We hadn't even got to the main course yet. I just had to prove to Chloe that I wasn't the arrogant food writer she seemed to think I was.

In the time between courses, without Max's looming presence, the people around the table started to reveal whether they'd be attending the interview that weekend. First Christopher, which I must say surprised me slightly – wasn't he getting a little old for this kind of weekend? – and then Belle, who eagerly said she'd be going.

I knew Juliette wouldn't be able to resist a weekend of luxury, and Balthazar probably thought he was a shoo-in for the job. The thought of seeing his smug face all weekend was nearly enough to make me rethink going.

The only person who I wasn't sure would attend was Chloe.

I decided to make it my mission to convince her she should come. I wanted – perhaps even needed – to spend more time with her. Even though it meant we'd be competing for the same job, there was no denying that there was something intoxicating about her presence.

'So, Chloe,' I said, interrupting Juliette, who was talking about some hot English barman who'd just started working at La Dilettante, 'will you be joining us this weekend?'

She looked at me thoughtfully for a moment. *Progress?*

'Are you definitely going?' she asked, answering my question with one of her own.

'I wouldn't miss it,' I replied. 'I've already told Max I'll be attending. Good to show readiness.'

'What do you mean "already"?' she asked, nerves audible in her voice.

'I emailed him,' I explained, holding up my phone.

'Oh?' she said, seemingly taken aback.

I tried a softer approach. 'It should be an interesting weekend regardless of who gets the job. It is a shame about the non-disclosure, because I'm sure we'll all come home with plenty of stories to tell, but I suppose this sort of thing is to be expected.'

'Is it?' she asked.

'This *is* Carla Duris,' I said knowingly, even though I had no idea why Carla was insisting on an NDA. What kind of activities *did* she have planned?

'Has she done interviews like this before?' Chloe asked.

'Not that I'm aware of, but then, Carla doesn't always do things by the book, either. We're heading into uncharted territory. That's what makes it so exciting.'

'And I suppose that's the reason I'm hesitating,' she said.

'This is an incredible opportunity. You'd be mad to pass it up,' I told her.

'I'm just not sure it's the right fit for me,' she said with a diplomatic smile, as though that would end the conversation. But I was determined to convince her. She *had* to come, if only for my sanity. I knew I'd spend the weekend thinking about her regardless.

Chapter 7

The Guest of Honour – CHLOE

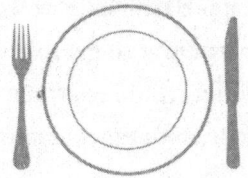

'Does the idea of a weekend-long interview scare you?' Henri probed.

Don't you underestimate me, I thought, even though a weekend-long interview was, by far, the most bizarre thing I'd been invited to since I'd started writing about food in Paris. (And that was saying something. Recently, I'd gone to an 'eight hands' lunch where we'd had to sample different dishes and then guess which chef had created them. It was chaos, and many egos got damaged in the process.)

Henri seemed determined to find out whether I would be attending the interview that weekend, god knows why. After a few more glasses of wine, everyone was talking about it like rushing off to Antibes at a moment's notice was a completely normal thing to do.

'I don't scare that easily,' I lied.

'Then maybe it is the work with Carla that worries you? Speaking French?' he suggested.

I looked at him, trying to work out if he was enjoying

himself, rattling off all my insecurities. But his attention seemed genuine, kind even.

'Nope – and besides, Carla's English is excellent. I'm just not sure if I'm free this weekend. It's very short notice,' I said, thinking about my weekend plans in London. Hazel would be crushed if she found out I'd bailed on her to swan around in the south of France in an attempt to get a job that would give me an even more compelling reason to stay in France.

'Best not to hesitate sometimes,' Henri said with a cheeky grin.

The door swung open, putting a halt to our conversation.

Six waiters swept into the room and delivered our main course in an incredible show of synchronicity. 'Lamb and a trio of carrots,' one of them announced in accented English before they all swept out just as nimbly.

People took photos, tasted, attempted to decipher ingredients, trying to figure out what gave Carla Duris's famed lamb dish such celebrity status. Still, nobody was hypothesising about what the writing project might actually be. There was plenty of talk about going down to Carla's villa for the weekend, but very little about the job we'd be interviewing for.

Maybe everybody was waiting for Carla to actually come and explain everything to us.

Finally, once we had polished off our mains – and I mean, cleared our plates without a drop of sauce remaining (Drew would have been proud) – Carla Duris appeared before us.

As she did, my stomach did a flip. It was one thing watching her on TV and reading her books, but in real life, her presence filled the room. She was in her mid-forties but looked younger. She was tanned, beautiful like her mother, but with her father's serious eyes. Her smile felt magnetic, and she looked around the room expectantly. I was on edge, unable to anticipate what would happen next.

She went around the table, welcoming us one by one, saying things like 'nice to see you again,' and 'hope so-and-so is well,' but when she got to me, she said, 'Nice to finally meet you,' which was a simple phrase I knew I'd spend hours attempting to decipher later. What could she have meant by 'finally'?

I was about to tell her I felt the same, but she'd already moved on to Henri. She looked at him as though she'd known him for years. Hell, she probably *had* known him for years, given his lineage.

'Henri, it's nice to see you so relaxed,' she said.

Carla spoke carefully, choosing her words and enunciating them clearly. I got the feeling that everything she was saying to us was calculated.

Once Carla had welcomed us all, she paused.

'Now, I hope you're all enjoying your meal,' she said with a light laugh, clearly knowing that everything was delicious.

I nodded enthusiastically but didn't speak, not wanting to interrupt her or draw unnecessary attention to myself.

'And I believe Max has filled you all in on the plans for our little weekend jaunt. I just want to reiterate that this interview process will be a little ...' she paused, searching for the right word, 'unconventional. But please know that there is always a reason behind my decisions, even if it is not at first apparent.'

She looked around the room, eyeing each of us carefully.

'I have decided to write a memoir,' she said. 'And would like one of you to join me on the journey.'

Somebody gasped quietly and my heart began to pound in my chest. Beyond the excitement I'm sure we all felt at the idea of reading Carla's memoir was the prospect of potentially helping to write it. This job was more than just a project; it would be life-changing.

Carla continued: 'Writing a memoir, or rather, writing somebody else's memoir, is a very emotionally taxing job, and I need to make sure I've got the right person with me for this undertaking. I'll be asking you to travel down memory lane with me and, as you might already assume, sometimes this will bring up things that I, myself, am not ready to deal with. Maybe you have your own triggers, too. Hopefully this weekend will help to establish where we stand with each other, but also, how you fit into my world.'

At this comment, I felt my cheeks start to burn. What did she mean, *how we fit into her world*? I'd never even stepped foot into her world. Did she perhaps get the wrong Chloe Bridgers? *Am I even meant to be here?*

'*Alors*, before I leave you to your dessert, make sure you bring a clear head with you this weekend. Pack for all scenarios, but also be ready to wow me and my team. Mostly we'll be having fun, but at the end of the day, you must realise that greatness is born out of more than just Champagne and caviar. This is your opportunity to really get a sense for what we could achieve together, perhaps even beyond this memoir ...' She paused again.

'But let me stop boring you,' she added, and we all laughed, because she was Carla-Frickin-Duris and she could never be considered boring. She then turned to leave, stopping as she clasped the door handle to issue one final statement: 'Good luck, *et à bientôt!*'

I sat there stunned. In all my time in Paris, I'd only ever dreamt of meeting Carla Duris. She'd been my idol for years, and she was, at least in part, responsible for me wanting to live in Paris. Now, to be meeting her in such an intimate setting, with the opportunity to potentially help write her memoir ... it was almost too much.

My mind was buzzing with excitement, and I was grateful that I'd have tomorrow to weigh up my options outside of this room. An element of competitiveness had been introduced among us – we would all be fighting for the role of memoir writer. Sure, we might not get our name on the cover, but with a memoir of this scale, everybody would know who had helped write it.

My first thought was what would happen *after* the year of working for Carla 24/7? Would I then need to go back to Hôtel Claris? Would they even hire me back? Of course, I wouldn't miss the paltry pay and sub-par conditions that came with working at the hotel, but a year without posting on my blog would pretty much run it into the ground. My readers were loyal because I went to huge lengths to keep my information and recommendations up to date. And I didn't feel like I could hand it over to anyone else. Who would voluntarily do so much work for zero pay?

But then my second thought was: would I even want to

keep writing my blog after spending a year working with Carla Duris? I could only imagine the doors this role would open for me. If things went well, the blog would pale in comparison to the experience of co-writing a memoir. Besides, a job with my French cooking idol would give me the perfect reason to stay in Paris, which, after all, was what I'd been longing for.

Our final course, the strawberry tart, arrived in front of us almost like magic. I drained what was left of my red wine and quietly asked the waiter for an espresso.

I admired the thin layers of sablé that separated the various forms of strawberry. As my spoon cracked through the towering dessert with a satisfying crunch, the smell of the fruit washed over me like a glorious wave.

'It's good, right?' Henri said, making me jump.

'Of course. I wouldn't have expected any less,' I replied.

'But this,' he said motioning to his dessert, 'is probably one of the best.'

'Carla is one of the best,' I said reverently.

'I guess we'll find out if that's true this weekend,' he said with an unexpected wink. My stomach jumped, a sensation that I quickly attributed to the prospect of the weekend ahead rather than the handsome man beside me.

Dinner finished, surprisingly without any fanfare, and I walked home slowly, grateful for the chance to clear my head. I watched people leaving restaurants and going to bars, drinking and smoking on the streets of Paris like they'd done for centuries. But that night, it felt different. I felt like I was a little more a part of this city than I had been before. Meeting Carla, being presented with this opportunity, it felt like the city had gone from being tolerant of me (but still aloof) to finally welcoming me a little, and that was thrilling.

I had to admit, Henri confused me. Hot yet cold, encouraging yet competitive, haughty yet flirtatious. He was almost as baffling to me as this whole evening had been, but there was something about him that had left me wanting more.

He hadn't even hesitated before accepting the offer to interview for the role. How could he be so willing to give up such a great job at *Le Cercle*? Then again, some people are much more trigger-happy than I've ever been. Besides, he didn't seem the type to shy away from intimidating situations. He seemed more likely to waltz through these with a glass of Champagne in his hand and a bounce in his expensively clad step. It wasn't that I was jealous of his money or family connections, but I was envious of the assuredness that came with them. He had his whole life planned out. He was comfortably seated in the chair his uncle had brought to the table for him. He had his shit together. Compared to his life plan, mine felt like jumping on unstable ground with slippery shoes while trying to hold onto a very full glass of cheap wine.

Get a grip, Chloe, I told myself. I mean, all that incredible food, a once-in-a-lifetime job opportunity, and all I can think about is Henri-de-la-blasted-Fontaine.

Chapter 8

The Night Cap – HENRI

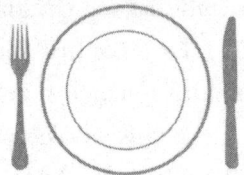

Dinner had ended rather abruptly, and while I would have been happy to go and get a drink with the other candidates, they'd all scurried off in various directions, probably keen to get home and start strategising for the weekend. It was a shame, because I rather enjoy fraternising with the enemy. What was wrong with a little fun between competitors?

Instead, I rode my Vespa back to the apartment I shared with my little sister in the 5th. As I parked the Vespa in the courtyard, Ren, our neighbour's cat, quickly came and curled up on the just-vacated seat. I gave him a little scratch behind the ears and asked him if his evening had been as unexpected as mine. He gazed at me with an exasperated look, then closed his eyes.

As I was about to head upstairs, my phone vibrated with another message from Uncle Michel, asking me about dinner. I felt like throwing my phone in the bin. He was always trying to get involved.

I knew there was a strong chance that if I told him about

the opportunity to write Carla's memoir, he would somehow interfere, either pushing for me to get the job or sabotaging my chances. The idea of him interfering was deeply embarrassing.

I replied, telling him that Carla was inviting a bunch of writers down to her house for the weekend to get to know us better. That it was a PR stunt, something to get her back into the papers. I said I'd let him know if I found out anything interesting.

Thankfully, he seemed to buy it and I breathed a momentary sigh of relief.

But then he started to type again.

'By the way, a new cocktail bar has opened up in the 16th. I walked past it the other night. Nobody has covered it yet. You really should get something on Instagram. Always good when we get there first.'

We! I thought. *He doesn't even work at the paper anymore.*

I briefly entertained the idea of ignoring the message, but I knew he was right. Our readers loved new openings. I ran through my schedule for the rest of the week and realised that every evening was already booked with a tasting or review dinner. I'd just go tonight and get it over with, I decided.

Cursing Michel one more time, I carefully removed Ren from my Vespa and jumped back on. Soon I was zipping through the quiet streets of Paris, wishing I was in my soft, comfortable bed.

The bar – called Boulevardier – was actually quite cool. I wandered into the dark room, wishing I'd dragged someone with me. It got lonely doing these things solo. I'd tried to talk to my friends about my work frustrations, but they struggled to understand. All they heard were the words 'food editor' and they assumed my life was perfect. 'Your job is eating and drinking,' they'd tell me, as if I'd somehow forgotten. But it wasn't just about the drinks and the food (which honestly, wasn't always good and was sometimes even downright bad), it was about always needing to be 'on', reviewing, assessing. Sometimes I just wanted to eat a pizza, drink some cheap beer and relax.

After taking a seat on one of the leather seats at the bar, I was handed a leather-bound menu. The review began writing itself in my head. *Lots of leather, blah, blah, blah.*

'You speak English?' the barman – wearing a leather apron – asked me in a distinct Australian accent. I couldn't help but smile. There was just something about Australians, about their twang, that made me feel at ease.

I nodded.

'Good,' he said, looking relieved. 'A few too many Frenchies in tonight. So, what'll it be?'

'What's popular?' I asked.

'The Boulevardier is good.'

'Named after the bar – or the other way around?' I asked, fishing for details.

'Dunno,' said the barman with a cheeky smile, not giving me much to work with. 'Tasty, though.'

'Right, one of those then.'

I watched on as the barman stirred bourbon, sweet vermouth and Campari together over ice, straining it into a rocks glass over an almost translucent ice cube and adding an orange twist.

I took a quick photo and then a long sip. Thankfully, the bartender knew what he was doing.

'So, where have you come from tonight?' he asked me.

'Chez Duris,' I told him. He made a whistling noise and looked me up and down. 'You've been?' I asked.

'Not on this salary,' he said, motioning to the bar.

'I was only there for a special occasion,' I said, not wanting to reveal my critic status.

'You know, Carla Duris is probably my ultimate celebrity crush. Talented, driven, rich *and* hot! Shame she's completely nuts,' he said.

I couldn't help a laugh at his honesty.

'Why do you call her nuts?' I asked.

'A guy I know mixed drinks for a while at Chez Duris. Ended up getting fired by Carla herself one night because he was wearing the wrong coloured laces on his shoes.'

'Well, she's a known perfectionist,' I pointed out.

'I also heard she's been known to wear a disguise to her own restaurant and then go on some kind of power-hungry firing spree if her meal isn't perfect,' he said.

This, I'd actually heard before. And apparently, heads usually rolled after these stunts of hers.

The barman busied himself with more drinks and left me thinking about Carla Duris.

I'd always had trouble matching the public version of her to the one from the rumours; it was hard to know which was real and which was exaggerated. Over the years, a few people had come close to doing a tell-all on Carla, but they'd all gone quiet at the last minute. Coincidence? Probably not.

It was easy to see why the prospect of her memoir would be so enticing. Very little about Carla had ever gone public. I wondered if all that was about to change, or if we were just going to get a glossed-over version of the events we already knew about.

Later, when I finally got home and crawled into bed, I couldn't sleep. I found myself watching replays of Carla's cameos on cooking shows.

The more I watched her, the more I began looking forward to the weekend ahead, if only to learn a little more about the mythical Carla. What would her house be like beyond what she'd shown to the press? How would she spend her time? Would we actually see her during this interview, or would she have Max do all the grunt work?

The only thing that still gave me pause was why Carla was choosing to publish her memoir now. For years, publishers had been desperate to release Carla's story because they knew it would be an instant bestseller. Her notoriety as one of France's most successful chefs, combined with her penchant for playing up to the paparazzi and her love of throwing extravagant parties were, dare I say, the perfect ingredients for a hit book.

But what kind of deal could the publisher have offered?

Carla seemingly already had everything. She was at the helm of one of the leading restaurants in Paris, and her villa in Antibes – featured in every French magazine that existed – was nestled among some of Europe's most expensive real-estate. Her terrace had hosted after-parties for the Festival de Cannes that were rumoured to have continued for days, her swimming pool was famous for the number of A-list celebrity skinny-dippers that couldn't resist jumping in, even her tennis court had been played on by the likes of Australian Open winner Chaz Franco.

So, what did she want? More money? More fame?

I guess only time would tell.

Eventually, hours into the replays, Carla's cassoulet started to meld into her crème brûlée and I finally fell asleep.

Chapter 9

The Great Debate – CHLOE

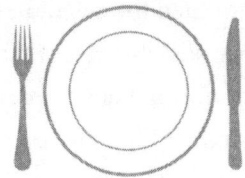

The next day, before heading to work, I was sitting at the bar in Drew's café, drinking a strong flat white and trying to explain the bizarre turn dinner had taken the night before.

Drew was making coffee for what felt like half of Paris, so perhaps his concentration levels weren't what I'd hoped, but I wasn't sure who else to talk to about all this. And at least Drew was in hospitality; he understood how people like Max and Carla worked.

'Are you sure you want to spend the weekend with these guys?' he asked.

I laughed, but he looked at me seriously.

'It'd be worth it if I got the job, right?'

'What does your gut say?' he asked.

'Mostly that I drank too much wine last night.'

'Ha, ha,' he deadpanned.

'I guess, even though it all seems like complete overkill for an interview, Carla Duris is an icon. If I don't go, I'll probably regret it my whole life,' I said dramatically, only half joking.

'You have to go then,' he said.

'It'll upset Hazel.'

'Just lie and tell her you've got gastro. Blame my cooking if you need to,' he said generously.

Drew made himself a coffee, got a staff member to take over and came to sit next to me. He seemed invested now, which was a relief. I needed a proper debrief. I wanted his advice.

'Are you worried Carla would prefer someone French?' he asked.

'I don't know who Carla wants,' I said. 'I can't even really explain why I've been invited to interview. I certainly don't have the connections that some of the other writers must have.'

'Anyone can make connections with time and the right introductions,' he said. 'You're a good writer, which is probably a pretty important aspect of writing a memoir, no?'

'Yes, but then Carla sort of implied that she wanted the writer to really get to know her, to fit into her life in order to do the book justice. I can't become a rich, French party girl, that's not my vibe.'

'No,' he agreed, and I didn't even bother pretending to be offended. 'Tell me about the others, then,' he instructed. 'Who will you be going up against?'

'Well, there's Henri de la Fontaine, who you already know because you introduced me to him at Bar Bisous,' I said.

'Hmm, I remember him being a little shit that night,' he said, 'which didn't seem too out of character.'

'He essentially ran off when he found out I was a blogger,' I said.

'That probably had nothing to do with you. Really, he's not so bad, just doesn't know how to handle his booze. He actually came in here for breakfast the other day.'

'Really?' I asked, surprised.

'Yeah. He brought his little sister – they ordered the pancakes. He said it was the best stack he'd ever eaten. He drank loads of coffee, too.'

'Aww,' I said, proudly. Drew deserved the praise, and it was nice to hear that an esteemed food writer was giving it to him. My mind lingered on the image of Henri sharing pancakes with what I could only imagine was an adorable little sister. I regretfully pushed the visual aside.

I continued: 'Well, obviously Henri is well positioned for the role. He has a famous uncle, works for one of the most revered papers in France, and he's handsome, which funnily enough seems like a requirement when working with Carla.'

Drew started to laugh, but stopped when he realised I was being serious.

'Plus, he's perfectly bilingual – he switches between English and French effortlessly,' I said.

'Eyes on the prize, Chloe,' Drew faux-scolded. 'Tell me about the other writers.'

'Christopher – an English gentleman who acts like he's the Duke of Paris.'

Drew shook his head with a snigger.

'He gives off old money vibes, and I feel like he's used to expense accounts and travel budgets,' I went on. 'I can't actually imagine Carla putting up with him, so I'm not sure he'll be any real competition.'

'Right, who else?' he asked.

'Juliette – French, perhaps too young to be serious, and too self-involved to actually get the job. Then there's Belle – tall, blonde, gorgeous American. She's probably in with a good chance, although she specialises in video content rather than writing, so that might not work in her favour. But she's incredibly charismatic. Did I mention she's gorgeous?'

'I know Belle,' Drew said with stars in his eyes.

'You mean you've hooked up with Belle?'

'Australians don't kiss and tell,' he said with a cheeky grin that told me both everything and nothing.

'And then there's Balthazar,' I said, pausing.

Drew raised his eyebrows. '*Le Monstre* from *Le Monde*?'

'I take it you've heard of him, then?' I asked.

'There's not a chef in Paris who hasn't.'

Until the night before, I hadn't met Balthazar in person, but he had a reputation for being cunning, and often cruel with his restaurant takedowns (I guess with a name like Balthazar, he was never going to be run of the mill). One time he even went undercover as a dishwasher to reveal that Jonathon Mercier added chicken stock to his 'vegetarian' *pot au feu*. Personally, I found his reviews unforgiving, never considering that a chef might just be having an off day. Balthazar stood firmly with the paying public, and didn't mind slamming a restaurant's reputation into the ground if the food wasn't perfect. He wasn't about second chances or the benefit of the doubt.

'So, he's your main competition?' he asked.

'I guess. Him, Belle and Henri,' I said.

'Three other people. You're in with a shot, I'd say.'

'A long-shot maybe. Who says I could even write a book?'

'Do you trust Carla?' he asked.

'I love Carla,' I said.

'But do you trust her?'

'Well, she's been my idol for years, but that doesn't mean I actually *know* her. The Carla I keep in my head is completely trustworthy, but the Carla I met last night wasn't exactly her.'

'Well, at least you'll get to find out what she's really like this weekend.'

Drew had moved back behind the counter, leaving me to fret. I knew I was overthinking this. I also knew that I was going to accept. I mean, how could I say no?

'Can I get another coffee to go?' I asked Drew.

He swiftly handed me a takeaway cup, having pre-empted my request. I passed over a ten-euro note. 'Keep the change,' I told him.

'Not sure this covers my consultancy fee,' he said with a laugh, waving away my offer to pay.

'I'll get you back when I'm a famous writer,' I joked.

'I'll hold you to that,' he said.

As I walked to work, I slowly sipped my coffee and mulled things over. By the time I arrived at the hotel, I felt like my brain was about to melt from the emotional rollercoaster of the past twenty-four hours. It was a relief to think about something other than Carla for the rest of the day.

On my way home that afternoon, I stopped by my favourite cheese shop, Serge's Fromagerie, because I figured nothing could cure indecisiveness like a good hunk of truffle brie, and at Serge's I knew I'd always get the best.

It had been years since Serge had worked there himself, but a framed picture of him and his family at their country property in the Loire Valley hung on the wall, smiling down at customers.

A very sexy young man named Guy now worked behind the counter. He was as welcome a sight as the cabinets full of cheese.

'*Bonjour*, Guy,' I said as I walked in.

His smile widened when he saw me.

'Chloe, it's been a while. I was almost beginning to worry,' he said, a hint of concern in his voice.

Thankfully Guy's English was excellent, but he'd maintained his French accent. It was *beau* to say the least.

Guy wrapped me up a piece of his best truffle brie and motioned towards a slice of comté with a little French shrug. 'You look like you need this.'

I laughed and nodded, because apparently, Guy understands what will help me to make good life decisions: cheese.

'Anything else?' he asked.

'That should do it,' I said.

Before handing me my bag, Guy threw in a little round of goat cheese.

'To cheer you up, on the house,' he said with a wide smile.

'Oh, you didn't need to do that,' I tried to protest.

'Do any of us need to do anything?' he said, leaving the philosophical question hanging heavy in the air for a moment before starting to chuckle.

'Well, *merci*,' I said.

'And Chloe, don't be strange,' he said.

'Huh?' I asked, wondering what I'd done to warrant that advice.

'Wait, that's not it, is it?' he added hurriedly.

'It's not?' I asked.

'*Beh non*, silly me. Don't be a stranger,' he said, correcting himself. 'I've been practising my idiots.'

'Idioms?' I suggested, supressing a giggle.

'That is the one,' he said.

'You're doing a great job, Guy,' I told him.

I walked a few doors down to the bakery to get a baguette and was excited to find it was still warm from the oven. It was shaping up to be a delicious night in and – life-changing-decision-making aside – I was looking forward to it. Nothing helped me concentrate more than a decadent selection of cheese.

It turned out, overindulging in truffle brie was the final push I'd needed to accept Carla's offer.

Before even finishing the cheese, I opened my email and sent a quick message to Max, accepting the offer and thanking him for considering me.

Max replied immediately – had he already known that I

would accept? – with booked tickets for the sleeper train and a brief warning: 'Carla does not appreciate tardiness. Good luck.'

And that was when I began to quietly panic.

I had agreed to the interview. And judging by the lack of information in Max's email, I'd be going into the weekend relatively blind.

Rather than worrying that I'd made the wrong decision, I decided to get organised. I rushed to my room to pick some suitable clothes and make sure they were clean. I packed for as many scenarios as I could anticipate. I tried on my bathers to make sure they still fit. I started to feel calmer.

Once I was relatively sure of my wardrobe, I reluctantly got my phone out to email Hazel and cancel our plans for the weekend.

Just as I hit 'send', my phone started to buzz with an incoming call.

'Oh, hey Dad,' I said.

'Ah, it's my long-lost daughter, finally not too busy to answer the phone when her parents call.'

He must have spoken to Mum.

'What's been keeping you so occupied?' he asked.

'Oh, nothing much,' I replied, trying to sound casual, not wanting to tell him about the potential job opportunity.

'And how is *le* work?' he asked, laughing at his joke.

'Fine. It's fine,' I replied, a little too quickly.

Dad went silent for a minute, probably trying to work out why I was acting weird.

'So, your Mum and I were wondering if you'd be home for Christmas?' he asked.

'If I can get the time off, sure,' I said. Swapping French winter for a few weeks of summer in Tasmania was perhaps the easiest decision one could ever make.

'What do you mean, time off?' he asked.

'Oh, you know, I'm just not sure what things will look like work-wise at the end of the year,' I said.

'I assumed you'd try and wrap things up in Paris by the end of the year,' he said. 'Especially given that you don't love your job.'

I wanted to tell him that I was completely devoted to Paris – the church bells on a Sunday morning, the wine with lunch, the literary history woven through the bookstores and cafés. I wanted to explain how I'd come to love the freedom that came with being an expat, the lack of expectations, the otherness of living and speaking in French. Even the work–play balance was more aligned with what I wanted from life. Plus, the whole of France (and Italy, Spain and Germany) was a mere fast train ride away (and the trains served wine ...).

Instead, I said: 'It's just hard to know what will happen in six months. There are so many great opportunities in Paris.' I thought of Carla and my heart fluttered.

'Better than being in the same country as your entire family?' Dad asked. The disappointment in his voice almost made me want to email Max and cancel.

'Dad, don't be like that,' I said.

'Chloe, your life, your choices. But, if I can say my piece ...' he said, then paused, like I'd be able to stop him. 'It does feel like it's the right time for you to move home. You've had your fun. And you're certainly not getting any younger.'

I rolled my eyes, relieved he couldn't see me. Dad had never understood my love of France. I'm not even sure he liked the French. I think he was actually kind of embarrassed to tell people that his daughter wrote a food blog in Paris. He'd always referred to my move to Paris as a gap year, or a flight of fancy.

'Okay, Dad, I'll keep my old-maid status in mind.'

'No need to be dramatic, Chloe,' he said.

'I'll look into flights for Christmas,' I promised. 'Both one-way and return.'

'As you wish,' he said. 'Talk soon.'

I hung up and burst into tears, the gravity of decision-making weighing heavily on my heart.

After a good cry, and knowing I was destined to annoy my parents no matter when I returned home, I cemented my commitment to Carla. It was time to get serious. It was time to do my research.

I pulled out the extra goat cheese Guy had gifted me and got to work.

By the time I'd polished off all the cheese, I realised there was a lot more to Carla Duris than her fabulous family and her cooking. Sure, I'd heard a few bits of gossip about her, but the reason I loved her was her food. It was easy to ignore the negativity, especially when I hadn't lived in France or followed the French papers.

The deeper I went, the more I learnt.

After unexpectedly quitting on her father when she was twenty-five, Carla had gone through what the press called her *enfant terrible* stage. Finding Paris and her weighty family name 'too restrictive', she'd left France to try her luck cooking in New York City. During those years, her lust for life had been notorious. She'd dated movie stars and bankers, only returning to France for pleasure – lavish parties, clubbing on the Côte d'Azur and walking the red carpet in Cannes.

Since returning to France to take over Chez Duris following her father's death, many people had wondered where she'd hidden her wild side. She'd surprised everyone with her loyalty to his legacy and her faithfulness to his menu.

But it turned out Carla had been involved in plenty of legal proceedings – from unfair dismissal to sexual assault in the workplace. She was no stranger to scandal, but any claim against her had always petered out. She'd never actually been charged for anything beyond driving her yacht while being over the limit. Was the world out to get her because she was a successful woman, or were her misdemeanours pushed under the rug because of her name and fortune?

What have I agreed to? I asked myself as I dug deeper into the rumours.

Maybe I was in over my head.

Chapter 10

The Blue Train – HENRI

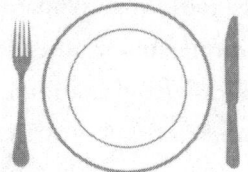

Friday night rolled around and I was relieved to finally sit down and have dinner at Le Train Bleu before catching the night train down to Carla's.

Honestly, I was surprised not to see any of the other food writers there. I didn't know how anyone could contemplate starting a weekend on the Côte d'Azur *without* first eating at this iconic bar and restaurant. It's probably the best part of catching a train from Gare de Lyon (beyond the part where you get out of Paris). I had fond memories of dining there with my parents when I was younger and they insisted on going camping on the Côte d'Azur because they believed it would teach me resilience. What they didn't realise was that by taking me to such a star-studded area, with all the glamour on show, and then making me sleep on a fold-out bed, my sights became firmly set on making sure I would never have to pitch a tent again.

Stepping inside Le Train Bleu felt like stepping back in time (that was, if you managed to block out the groups of wealthy foreigners talking incessantly about how everything is better at 'The Blue Train' ...).

My order was always the same: a seafood or seasonal vegetable starter, followed by the roast lamb (served *à table* from their carving trolley), and to finish, the rum baba with vanilla whipped cream. A simple set of dishes, yes, but with perfect execution. What more could you ask for? It was perhaps a little heavy for a pre-train dinner, but dining there was so infused in my memories that to stray from tradition might ruin my trip, which I wasn't prepared to risk. Not this weekend. There was too much at stake.

Plus, I couldn't miss watching the waitstaff carve the lamb with unrivalled finesse, using a theatrically sword-like knife. Fragrant roasted garlic cloves were then sprinkled on the meat before a jus was ladled over with a flourish. It was spectacular in all senses of the word.

To accompany my dinner, I planned to have a modest couple of glasses of wine to relieve any lingering anxiety I was feeling. It wasn't like me to pander to the whims of a chef like Carla, but the job of writing her memoir felt like an easy road out of my current role, and it just happened to be one that had the potential to be paved in gold.

While I ate, I tried to avoid overthinking how the weekend would play out.

I had a game plan for the interview and I was determined to stick to it: I would go on a very discreet charm offensive, showing Carla and Max that I was destined to write this memoir, and gently letting the other interviewees know that they should just go home and accept defeat. I would prove that

I was better than the competition; or rather, I would let the other interviewees prove that they weren't up to the task. Let them self-destruct if it came to that.

The only thing that had the capacity to railroad my plan was Chloe.

The curveball.

Would she even show up?

In preparation for the interview, I'd quickly stopped obsessing over Carla and turned my attention to my adversaries. Even though I knew I should focus on my own application and on how I could improve my chances, I couldn't get Chloe out of my head. I rationalised this as being normal because she was part of 'the competition'. I'd spent hours reading through her old blog posts and comparing our write-ups for restaurants we'd both covered.

Reading *Eat Me, Paris* had made me better understand why Chloe raved about writing for a blog. Because she was her own editor and didn't answer to advertisers or PR departments, she could be selective about what she covered, and as such was almost exclusively positive. She wrote about all the amazing things people were doing across Paris, instead of writing cutting reviews that lured readers in. As a result, she appeared to have a readership that respected her. And she described food beautifully. Her tasting notes and descriptions were poetic while being incredibly evocative. Sure, she had a tendency to put chefs on a pedestal, but then again, there weren't many food writers who didn't.

Going off Chloe's writing alone, I might have been nervous

about competing against her – she had a way with words – but I knew that in terms of industry connections in Paris and knowledge of the French dining scene, I had her beat.

Why couldn't she have just agreed to the weekend at Carla's on the spot and saved me some angst? Perhaps she'd declined, and I'd spend the entire interview pining over her, unable to concentrate, and blow any chance I had at getting the job.

Finishing the last of my rum baba, I basked in the glory of the boozy cake and ordered a coffee. I pulled out my phone to update the paper's social accounts with some pictures from dinner. It was astonishing, people's seemingly insatiable appetite for French food – but then again, here I was enjoying it, why shouldn't they? I was mid-post when I saw Juliette arrive and sit in the bar lounge. I contemplated trying to hide, but I had little at hand to use as a good disguise, and I felt a napkin over the head would set the wrong tone.

She spotted me almost immediately, and swanned over.

'Henri, how wonderful to see you,' she said in French.

'*Bonsoir*,' I replied, professional but unenthused.

'I must say,' she continued, sitting opposite me, uninvited, 'I'm surprised you agreed to come this weekend.'

'And why is that?' I asked.

'We all know you have the best job in the city,' she said.

'If that's what you think, you could always apply to be my replacement when I get the job with Carla,' I told her.

'Well, who can say which will end up being the better deal? Unfortunately I don't have any well-connected uncles who would put in a good word for me.'

She waved over a waiter and ordered a glass of Champagne.

I wasn't in the mood for her mind games, so I raised my coffee cup and said, 'May the best food writer win.'

I asked the waiter for my cheque and indicated that I would also pay for Juliette's drink, something I'm sure she was intending when she came to sit with me.

Getting up to leave, I wished her luck and a safe train ride.

'Hold up,' she instructed.

'Hmm?'

'Look, I've got to tell you something about Balthazar.'

'Go on,' I said, intrigued. Annoyed.

'I feel like I should tell you, even warn you – he made a joke about wanting to take your little sister to dinner at Chez Duris when he gets the job,' she said.

'When he gets the job? Dinner with Lucy?' I confirmed, surprised beyond comprehension.

'*Oui,*' Juliette said.

'But he's not going to get the job. *And* Lucy is hardly out of high school! What is he thinking, wanting to take her on a date?'

'I'm not sure age difference matters much to Balthazar,' Juliette said.

'*Typique,* he thinks he cannot beat me so he goes after my sister to annoy me. Well, more fool him; Lucy would never agree to go out with one of my competitors. She may be young, but she isn't stupid. She probably knows more about the sordid side of the Paris food-writing scene than I do.'

'Well, I just thought you should know,' she said lightly.

I could tell she was delighting in telling me this little piece of news. I forced myself to appear unbothered, but the thought alone had me seething with anger. Had that been Juliette's intention – to throw me off my game?

She flashed me a bright smile and took a large sip of her Champagne. 'Thanks for the drink,' she said, raising her glass.

I wanted to reply, 'Like I had a choice,' but figured it was best to keep Juliette on side lest she have any gossip on me that she hadn't owned up to. Scheming and scamming unfortunately came with the journalistic territory at times, and Juliette was very good at doing her research. All I knew is that I'd be watching my back around her.

I meandered through the train station, stopping to pick up the latest edition of *GQ*, then boarded the train to find my two-berth cabin. Thankfully, it was empty for the time being. I hoped it would stay that way. Knowing my luck, I'd probably be bunking with Balthazar.

Chapter 11

The Sleeper Cabin – CHLOE

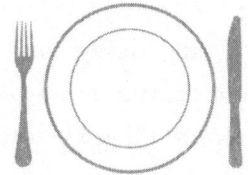

'What are you doing in here?' I asked, horrified to find myself face to face with Henri de la Fontaine at the door to my cabin.

Henri was wearing jeans and a blue knit jumper that made his eyes sparkle like the sea. It was annoyingly distracting. As was his smile, which was broad and seemed genuine. He almost looked relieved to see me – I couldn't imagine why.

'Nice to see you, too, Chloe,' he replied as I struggled to put down my epically over-packed 'overnight bag' so I could check the number on my ticket.

'This is *my* cabin. Only one bed, see?' I said, flashing the ticket on my phone with one hand and motioning around the tiny space with the other, wondering if Henri had gone mad or if he was just taunting me.

'Have you never been on a sleeper train before?' he asked.

'Um, no,' I said, pausing. *Why?*

'There are two beds in here,' he said.

Blood rushed to my cheeks. 'Wait, does this mean we're

sharing a cabin?' I asked, trying to conceal the horror that was evident in my voice.

'There could be worse things, *non*?' he said. 'I do not bite.'

He smiled warmly, but my mind was spinning. Could I change cabins? Surely this had to be some kind of a conflict of interest or something.

'Of course not,' I said, trying to keep this interaction professional. 'Besides, I actually have some work to do this evening, so once we set off, I'll just put some headphones on and get on with it.'

'No need for headphones,' he said with a grin. 'I'll be quiet as a mouse.'

I sat down, hunting in the depths of my bag for my laptop.

Henri followed suit, rummaging around in his Louis Vuitton bag, which I noted was beautifully packed.

As I pulled out my computer, he pulled out a bottle of wine and two plastic wine glasses.

'Fancy a little drink?' he asked, offering me a glass.

'Do you always come prepared with wine to woo your cabin mate? Or are you just trying to numb your senses because the train isn't your usual five-star accommodation?' I asked. I hadn't meant to insinuate that he would be interested in wooing me, but it just slipped out.

'Woo?' he asked, and I hoped he was asking because he'd never heard the expression, even though he was completely bilingual.

'Never mind,' I said, hoping he'd let it slide.

'I feel like the only way to sleep well on a night train is to ensure you have the right amount of liquid sedative,' he said.

Looking around me, I figured he was probably right. I hadn't slept on a bunk bed since school camp, and to do so with a competitor felt a little uncomfortable.

I contemplated his proposition for only the briefest moment longer, and decided to see it as a peace offering of sorts. It would have been rude to decline.

'Sure, why not,' I said, with a smile. *When on a train to the Côte d'Azur,* I figured. Perhaps I could make an ally out of Henri yet. We hadn't gotten off to the smoothest of starts, but the weekend was young. It was daunting enough going into this whole interview process solo. If I at least had a friend by my side, perhaps everything would feel a little easier.

Henri filled our glasses, we clinked them together and I took a long, slow sip. I could feel my shoulders soften as the wine slipped past my lips and warmed me from the inside out.

'Do you think all the other people interviewing are on the same train?' I asked.

'I assume Max booked us all on here together,' he replied.

'I didn't notice anyone else when getting on,' I said.

'I did see Juliette at the station, so I assume she's boarded. As for the others, maybe they've pulled out. It will most likely be a very intense weekend. Not for the faint of heart,' he said, still with that sparkle in his eyes.

Had Henri received some kind of agenda for the weekend that Max had forgotten to send to me? I'd spent hours imagining what Carla had in store. Had I been naïve thinking that it wouldn't be too intense? That there would even be a few moments for fun?

'What do you think will happen?' I asked, trying not to sound nervous.

'With Carla, nobody knows,' he said, as the train lurched into motion. No turning back now.

I thought about the requirement to sign a non-disclosure agreement and my heart skipped a beat.

'But nothing weird, right?' I asked, remembering some of the rumours Carla's staff had obviously spread about her.

Henri shrugged, drained his glass, and then topped us both up. 'If you're asking if this is going to be like a culinary edition of *The Hunger Games*,' he said, 'I don't think it'll go that far.'

'The Hungry Games?' I suggested, trying to lighten the mood, or rather trick my brain into believing we were in for a weekend of light-hearted fun.

Henri laughed so hard he snorted wine out his nose. It was the first time I'd seen him lose his composure, and honestly, it was kind of charming.

When he'd recovered, he looked at me earnestly and said, 'So you're funny. Is that your thing?'

'And you're observant. Is that your thing?' I joked, and he laughed again.

Perhaps this weekend wouldn't be so bad after all. Watching the lights outside, seeing the centre of Paris slip further away, my anticipation for the interview ahead was growing.

'I must say, I'm surprised you're willing to give up your job to work for Carla,' I said, knowing that if I were in his shoes, I'd be quite content to keep writing for the paper forever.

'Well, sometimes change is good, right?'

'But you'd be giving up a lot,' I said, not wanting to push him but desperate to figure out if there were more to his decision to come to the interview.

'*C'est la vie,*' he said, pouring the remainder of the bottle into our glasses.

I was surprised at how quickly the wine had gone down. By that point, I was feeling a little more than tipsy. I'd hardly eaten anything all day and we'd made quick work of the wine. Luckily I'd grabbed a sandwich from PAUL on my way to the train. I was embarrassed not to have brought something more elaborate, but eventually I fished it out of my bag and offered to share it with Henri.

'You want to break bread?' he asked.

I laughed. 'Would you like some?'

'I've actually already eaten,' he said, with a hint of remorse in his voice.

Secretly, I was grateful. I needed the sustenance.

Soon after, the conductor passed by and offered to set up our bunks.

He eyed the bottle of wine and gave us a grin.

'*Ahh, l'amour,*' he said in French.

I went to correct him but Henri just laughed and said, '*La vie est belle,*' giving me a little wink.

My cheeks burnt.

I stood back and watched as our beds were made, trying not to think about the fact that I'd be sleeping in such close proximity to Henri. A few days ago, he didn't even remember me and now here we were sharing a room, and apparently polishing off a bottle of wine, too.

'Do you prefer top or bottom?' he asked, motioning to the bunks.

I think it was a combination of the stress and the wine, but his question gave me the giggles.

Henri looked at me, confused, and I forced myself to take some deep breaths and think of sad things, like that time I dropped an *éclair au chocolat*, icing side down, onto my new white Sézane pants.

'Top bunk is fine,' I eventually blurted out.

I was clearly tipsier than I realised.

Henri wished me '*bonne nuit*' and I crawled ungracefully up into my bed. Unsure of the pyjama etiquette on a sleeper train, I didn't bother changing out of my clothes, hoping I'd fall asleep quickly.

But, despite the gentle rattling of the train, I was wide awake, replaying the evening's conversation with Henri in my head.

Any intention to do work had been quickly forgotten. Instead, I pulled out my phone and scrolled Instagram, trying to distract myself.

Chapter 12

The Like/Not Like – HENRI

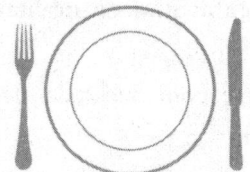

With Chloe in bed above me, I had zero chance of falling asleep.

I wondered if she was feeling the same. I would have happily stayed up with her, probably all night, if she hadn't already climbed into her bunk, essentially ending our little tête-à-tête. It was frustrating, because things had gotten off to a relatively good start. At least, once she accepted the idea that we'd be bunking together.

Chloe had seemed surprised when I'd pulled out the bottle of wine. To me, it was just common sense. Uncle Michel had instructed me to always travel with a bottle (or hipflask) where possible. To this day it has remained one of the best pieces of advice I've ever been given: 'You never know what situation you'll get yourself into, but there are very few moments in life that a bottle can't make better. A bribe? Wine. A potential date? Wine. An intruder? A heavy glass bottle filled with wine.'

I'd been worried that Chloe was going to make me drink it alone, but she'd eventually accepted a glass and we'd had what I would say was our first 'normal' conversation.

We'd talked about Carla, and I'd tried to put her mind at ease about how the weekend would go, but from what I knew of Madame Duris, I knew to expect the unexpected.

Chloe had asked me about my accent. 'So, why is it that you mostly sound American when you're speaking English, but say some words with a distinct Australian twang? It's an odd combination.'

'American Mom, French Dad, Australian university experience,' I told her.

'You lived in Australia?' she gasped excitedly. 'What uni did you go to?'

'Melbourne. How about you?' I asked, trying to fill in the gaps from what I'd learnt about her from her blog.

'Oh my gosh, same!' she said. 'When were you there?'

That led us to talking about our favourite Melbourne cafés and places to hang out. To think we could have been at the same place at the same time without knowing each other was thrilling to me.

'So you loved it?' she asked.

'It was incredible, but the best part had to be the food ...' I paused, trying to sum up how the experience of eating in Australia had been so different to what I'd grown up with. 'It was multicultural and diverse, and it didn't come with the weight – both in terms of richness and in terms of expectations – of French food. There was so much authentic flavour to be found. I'd spend my weekends travelling to different suburbs in search of good food – from the Chinese yum cha restaurants in Box Hill to the Vietnamese restaurants that lined Victoria

Street. Even the meals in the pubs were surprisingly good. Plus, the coffee ... God, the flat whites ... perfection.'

'So why did you come back?' she asked.

'I ran out of visa options, so I came back and Uncle Michel coerced me into interning at *Le Cercle*.'

'You must have been glad to come back, though. Paris will always be Paris,' she said.

'The only thing I missed about France was the bread, the wine and the cheese,' I said.

She laughed and held up her glass, saying, 'Cheers to that.'

'And what brought you to France?' I asked.

'I came for the bread, the wine and the cheese,' she said without skipping a beat.

I snorted, and then felt my cheeks burn. I didn't normally snort.

'And has France lived up to your expectations?' I asked.

'And then some,' she said. 'And now I'm hoping this job with Carla will give me a reason to stay a little longer.'

'You're planning to leave Paris if you don't get it?' I asked, a ball lodging itself in my throat.

'Eventually, maybe. I don't love my current job and my family has been telling me it's time to come home,' she said, taking a long sip of wine.

Then she asked me why I was willing to give up my job at *Le Cercle* and I froze, unsure about how honest to be, how much I should tell her.

I had lost count of the number of times I started a new week, promising myself I'd look for a new job. I needed a way out of Uncle Michel's shadow, that much was certain, but there was no clear exit that wouldn't have me severely offending my uncle and creating some kind of war-worthy feud in my family. My aversion to drama meant I was stuck.

Plus, I loved writing about food – it was the rest of the job that bothered me. The schmoozing, the desperation for the scoop, my uncle breathing down my neck, telling me who to talk to, who to avoid. The job at *Le Cercle* just wasn't me. I wanted to celebrate good food, not to try to take anyone down, or ruin reputations. Unfortunately, those reviews were some of the most successful among our readers.

Ideally, I'd just find a new food-writing job where I could forge my own path. But that would require some careful manoeuvring, and honestly, taking a job with Carla felt like the perfect escape path.

But I couldn't burden Chloe with the truth, could I? So instead, I'd brushed off her question, telling her that change was good.

I pulled out my phone and unlocked it, almost dropping it when my screen opened to Chloe's blog. *Merde*, I thought, thanking the gods that Chloe hadn't leant over the edge of her bunk and seen that I'd been looking her up.

In the name of research, I'd been reading her review of Le Train Bleu over dinner and, stupidly, I hadn't thought to close the page. I scanned through the comments, surprised at how thoughtful and gushing people were about her writing. It must be nice for her to have that kind of feedback on her articles. Sometimes, writing for a paper felt like screaming into a void. *Is there anybody out there? Is anybody reading?*

And then I saw a link to her Instagram account.

I felt a flutter of excitement, while simultaneously feeling annoyed at myself that I hadn't thought to look at it earlier. Because, while Chloe's writing unveiled a lot about her preferences and sensibilities, photos often told a different story.

Is it weird to be stalking her socials while she sleeps above me?

I pushed the thought aside.

Her account was mostly food photos, and nice ones, but very little of anything else. It was a professional page, linked to her website, but I couldn't help thinking that it wouldn't hurt to have a few pictures of her, at least to break things up a little. I settled for looking at the tagged photos of her.

Seeing the grid, I snapped to attention, feeling like I'd just been given access to something a little more personal. There were photos of Chloe on a boat, brooding skies behind her, with a fishing rod in hand. Even with windswept hair and a big rain jacket on, she looked cute. It was strange to think of her outside of Paris, but judging by these photos she was in her element on the water.

And then there was a photo of her with some big dudes, which made me want to destroy my phone until I saw the caption: *'Little sis finally returns from France for a visit.'*

Thank god for siblings, I thought, breathing a sigh of relief.

I hovered my hand over the follow button, then wondered

if Chloe would find it a strange thing to do while we were on the train together.

Figuring that yes, she absolutely would, I went to my own account.

I uploaded an old picture of me that a friend had taken down south, and drafted a caption saying I was going to Antibes for the weekend, insinuating that I would have something to celebrate when I got home.

Thankfully, Uncle Michel wasn't on Instagram, otherwise he probably would have chased down the train to stop me.

Posted.

The notifications came rolling in because, thanks to my job, I had a decent number of followers.

Just as I was about to put on a podcast and try to sleep, my heart skipped an actual beat when I saw that the account *Eat Me, Paris* had liked my photo.

My palms went sweaty and I inhaled sharply, immediately trying to pass the sound off as a cough. Should I say something? Should I just follow her?

I stared at the screen, frozen by indecision.

And then, just as suddenly, the 'like' notification disappeared.

I lay there stunned.

Obviously, Chloe had seen my photo.

And she'd *liked it*.

But then she'd unliked it.

What did it all mean?

Chapter 13

The Accidental Like – CHLOE

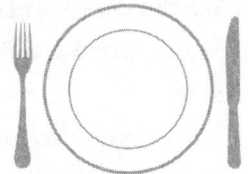

Oh god, I just accidentally hit 'like' on Henri-de-la-blasted-Fontaine's Instagram picture. *Shite, shite, shite*, I thought to myself, blood pumping through me like a jackhammer through cement.

Clearly the stress of the weekend ahead was messing with me.

I'd been mindlessly scrolling Instagram and had suddenly found myself wondering if Henri was on there.

Before I'd been able to stop myself, my fingers were suddenly on the search bar. It had been easy to find his profile photo, flutters in my stomach betraying any false sense of innocence I'd been trying to convince myself of.

Pushing those feelings away, I'd clicked on his name, opening his grid. *So much for him keeping a low profile*, I said to myself. He had thousands of followers. His most recent picture showed him in tight swimming shorts, standing on a beach somewhere. I'd checked the location – Baie des Milliardaires – then opened the map and realised it was in Antibes. The caption read, *'Back to Antibes this weekend on a secret mission. Put the Champagne on ice, as I plan to come back with news worth celebrating.'*

How bloody arrogant, I thought. Was there any point in us other writers even going? Not in Henri de la Fontaine's world, clearly. Oh no, in Henri de la Fontaine's world, he was getting this job.

The image already had hundreds of likes.

And then all of a sudden, without quite realising what I'd done, I'd added one more ...

I panicked and hit unlike as quickly as possible.

Could he have seen the notification? Did he know I was lurking on his page? I could only imagine how that would feed his ego.

In the bed below me, Henri coughed, which only fuelled my embarrassment. Should I say something?

This is why I shouldn't have shared a bottle of wine with the man! Would I ever learn?

I closed Instagram and this time, forced myself to sleep.

I woke up to the sun creeping through the window and slowly it dawned on me that the train had stopped.

My head pounded with the realisation that I'd drunk too much wine too quickly the night before, and then I remembered stalking Henri's Instagram account. I massaged my temples, bemoaning my decision-making.

It took me another moment to register where we were.

I looked over the side of the bunk to see Henri, completely

dressed, looking as sharp as he did when I'd boarded the train, standing by the cabin door.

'Sleep well?' he asked. 'The wine helped, yes?'

If he knew about me liking his photo, he didn't show it. Maybe I'd gotten away with it.

'Where are we? Why have we stopped?' I asked, panic rising in my voice.

'We have arrived, Chloe.'

My heart skipped a beat as I jumped out of bed and started to get changed. 'Why didn't you wake me? We're going to be late,' I said, panicking.

'I won't be late,' he said, picking up his bag to leave.

'Oh my god, was that your plan all along? To get me drunk so you'd get the upper hand this morning?'

He gave me an innocent smile. 'The wine helped you sleep, no?' he asked.

'Well, yes. But it's certainly not helping me now!' I snapped back.

'I should leave you to get ready,' he said.

I looked down, horrified to realise I was still standing in my bra. Heat rising in my cheeks, I quickly pulled on my dress, angrily wondering if Henri would have left me on the train if I hadn't woken up when I did. *Is he trying to declare some kind of war?* I asked myself. I'd thought we'd made inroads on a friendship the night before. We'd bonded over our mutual love of Melbourne; we'd laughed over what was in store for the weekend. Why did he suddenly seem competitive, like he wanted to get the upper hand? Did it have something to do with my Instagram gaffe?

He looked me up and down before pushing a strand of my dishevelled hair behind my ear. The gesture made me shiver, then left me frozen on the spot.

And then he turned and walked off the train.

I was so furious with him that I was able to completely ignore the tiny frisson that went coursing through my body. Almost completely.

I smoothed down my hair and rushed out to the platform to join the group, who were all waiting for me. Max looked at me, tapping his watch.

Damn, I thought as he turned and walked briskly towards a very luxurious black mini-van with heavily tinted windows. On each of our seats was a bottle of water, a box of mints and a notebook and pen.

'First things first,' instructed Max. 'There is a non-disclosure agreement in your notebooks. Please read it, sign it and return it to me before you enter Carla's villa.'

What could be so pressing in the agreement that we needed to sign it *before* arriving? If we didn't sign it, would we even be allowed in the inner sanctum?

Around me, I heard pens scribbling on paper. I was surprised that most people weren't even taking the time to read the agreement. After a quick scan through the dense text, with nothing untoward jumping out at me, I signed the agreement with a shaking hand.

I was already too committed – in too deep – to turn back now.

Part Two

Carla Duris's Villa

Antibes

Chapter 14

The Bad Wake-up – HENRI

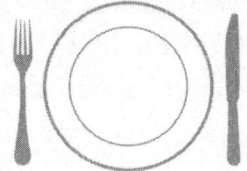

I hadn't meant to *not* wake Chloe when we'd arrived at the train station, but she'd looked so beautiful sleeping on that damn bunk bed that I couldn't bring myself to do it. I wasn't sure what to say, either – Hello? *Bonjour*? It all sounded so wrong in my head – so I'd quietly gotten ready to disembark, hoping she'd wake naturally. Besides, the Instagram snub from the night before was weighing on me, and at risk of sounding petty, had made me feel like perhaps she didn't want anything to do with me.

And then suddenly, the peaceful image of a sleeping beauty had been replaced by a furious awakening. Chloe had leapt out of her bunk, ripping off her T-shirt, her panic apparently making her oblivious to my presence. Meanwhile, I was left with my jaw hanging on the floor.

Her skin was the most perfect pale pink, creases from where she'd been sleeping making a beautiful pattern along the side of her torso, the sight of her bare skin against her black lace bra making me want to rip my own shirt off and wrap my arms around her.

But I could tell she was mad, and I couldn't make my brain function properly, not with her standing there without her top on. When she'd interrogated me as to why I'd offered her wine the night before, I'd mumbled something incomprehensible in my defence and had randomly tried to smooth down her hair. Before the conversation could swerve further out of my control, I'd left her to get ready and had gone to meet Max. One last glance back at her face had told me everything I needed to know. *Bad idea, Henri!*

Seeing Balthazar on the platform, I was tempted to interrogate him about Lucy. Juliette's words from the night before had been weighing heavily on my mind, and I was desperate to find out his intentions for my little sister.

But I didn't want to give him the upper hand, so instead I merely said a polite '*Bonjour*'. I would call Lucy when I got a free moment and warn her off him. For now, I just needed to keep everyone on side.

Chloe arrived shortly after the rest of us, looking frazzled but still gorgeous.

Getting into the van, I gave her a smile but she seemed to be avoiding my gaze. Could she actually be angry with me? She'd only been a minute late. No harm done.

I forced myself to refocus. We had an interview to get to, plus non-disclosure agreements to sign. This last step *did* worry me slightly, but not enough to make me back out of the weekend. Carla probably made all her staff sign them. Was this the reason nobody has ever been able to prove the rumours about her? One certainly could wonder.

While we drove and I pretended to read through the non-disclosure agreement, my mind came back to the question of why Carla Duris had finally agreed to write her memoir.

During the week, I'd found out through a publishing friend that Avantage Publishing House had won an eight-way auction for the rights to Carla's memoir. Apparently, the advance was seven figures. It was hard to believe that money could be the motivating factor, but perhaps I was wrong.

Carla certainly didn't live a quiet life, but she'd somehow managed to keep her record mostly clean, despite her fair share of negative press. That said, there was one area of her life that hadn't received much attention in the media, and that was her relationship with her father.

Carla had worked under Jean Duris as a commis chef, and it was well documented that Jean had been harder on her than on any of his other cooks. This hadn't deterred Carla. She had kept her head down and pulverised suggestions that she was little more than a pity project, creating her own signature cooking style that had many people predicting she would one day outshine her father.

Her sudden departure from France and from her father's kitchen had come as a surprise to the culinary world. Monsieur Duris hadn't been getting any younger, and everybody had anticipated that he would soon hand the reins to his – by then, well-deserving – daughter.

Whatever it was that had driven Carla out of Paris, when

she'd announced that she would be opening her own restaurant in New York City, backed by some big finance group, the news was generally well received. People had wanted to see her succeed, and were excited to see what she could do for France's image on the New York stage.

What happened next, however, could be considered a disaster on all fronts. Chez C – Carla's new restaurant – had been avant-garde, overly theatrical; in some cases, diners had even feared for their lives (eating live octopus!).

Carla had been given full creative control, and after years of falling in line under her father's strong and steady hand, she'd abused her new-found liberty, quickly running the restaurant into the ground. It had only been open a total of six months. I remember Uncle Michel telling me later that her publicity team had done a fabulous job of pretending Chez C had always been destined to be a pop-up – somewhere ephemeral, only opening for a short period of time. Surprisingly, this narrative appeared to be accepted and Carla's reputation remained intact, with very few people knowing the truth about her business dealings.

Carla had then gone to work for some of New York's elite as a private chef. She'd become known for hosting lavish parties, and given her client list – actors, bankers, socialites – she had quickly established a name for herself, and a price point, that had made many of her critics' eyes water. She'd turned things around and come out on top – a feat that had almost seemed as daring as her croquembouche recipe.

When Monsieur Duris had died of a heart attack (that many people attributed to how much butter he used in his mashed potatoes), people were shocked when Carla announced she would be taking over as head chef. Everybody questioned whether she could maintain Chez Duris's legacy as one of Paris's finest dining institutions, or if she would turn it into something new. Perhaps to everybody's surprise, Carla had opted to keep her father's menu, tweaking only the seasonal degustation menus, all while preserving a flavour profile reminiscent of the late Monsieur Duris.

And yes, there were rumours about her private life, and yes, there had been claims of mistreatment (bordering on '*psychopathique*') from her staff, but none that had ever been proven.

It was also rumoured that Carla had one of Paris's top legal firms on retainer, but the accuracy of even this information was almost impossible to confirm. Ultimately, all this was what made the prospect of Carla's memoir so thrilling. What was she willing to tell the public now that she has previously refused to divulge? What might *we* discover this weekend that would shed light on the real Carla Duris?

I had to admit I was intrigued, even a little excited. I signed the form without hesitation.

Chapter 15

The Dreamy Weekend Begins – CHLOE

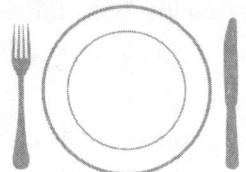

The drive to Carla's villa passed in silence. I personally couldn't have maintained a conversation even if I'd wanted to – Antibes and its surrounds had left me speechless. And as we drove out towards the cape, there really was nothing to say beyond 'wow'. On either side of the road, the views were breathtaking.

It felt like the farther south we went onto the cape – and the closer we got to Carla's – the larger the houses became. By the end of the drive, it wasn't even houses we were looking at; rather, it was large gates the size of my entire apartment whose sole purpose was to shield out the riff-raff and act as an entry to whatever sumptuous mansion lay beyond.

The prospect of soon arriving at Carla's villa was nerve-racking. How on earth was I going to pretend it wasn't a big deal for me to be there? This was not my crowd. To be honest, I hadn't realised a crowd like this even existed beyond royalty.

I stole a look over at Henri, who seemed completely unfazed by his surroundings. God, for all I knew, someone in his family probably lived next door, or at least had a house nearby. My parents' holiday shack on Bruny Island looked like a doll's house compared to these estates.

I closed my eyes to escape the opulence for a few seconds. *I can do this*, I said to myself. *This is a completely normal thing to be doing ...*

Entering the grounds, making our way up the driveway, walking through the towering front doors; I suppose these could be considered normal activities, but at Carla's villa, each step felt like an occasion. Manicured gardens, opulent staircases, marble, the smell of jasmine floating through the air, not a fleck of dust or a household item was out of place.

I found myself wishing I'd brought more glamorous clothes, or rather, wishing that I owned more glamorous clothes that I could have packed.

Max explained our room allocations.

He'd positioned me next to Henri.

At least tonight, there would be a wall separating us. At least tonight, we wouldn't be sleeping in bunk beds.

Looking around, I was more than happy with the upgrade from the sleeper train.

Henri and I walked down the corridor to our rooms in silence. The realisation that I'd stripped half naked in front of him in my panic to get ready had settled somewhere in my throat, apparently stopping me from being able to form normal sentences.

Henri stopped at his door and slipped in the key, pushing it open effortlessly. He turned to me before entering. 'We should really stop meeting at our bedrooms like this,' he said with a raise of the eyebrows.

I forced myself not to smile by wondering if he'd rehearsed the line or if cute little quips just came naturally to him. Before I could think of something to say in response, he was gone. I fumbled with the lock and entered my own room.

If there was an upside to all the unknowns about the weekend, it had to be that I'd get to spend it here, with a view over the glistening Mediterranean Sea, in what looked like the fluffiest bed I'd ever seen.

I put my bag onto the luggage rack and quickly went to lie down, confirming that the bed was in fact as heavenly as it looked.

I admired the ornate cornices of the room, the intricate panelling of the doors and wardrobes, and the beautiful chandelier. It all felt so out of reach.

I turned my head and spied a pretty little tea table. On it sat a small folded piece of paper with my name on it.

I rushed over.

It felt strangely like a clue – the first clue of the weekend?

Tennis breakfast at 10am
Wear whites

I chuckled at the instruction. This wasn't Wimbledon – I hoped. A friendly hit of tennis didn't scare me, though. My brothers had taught me to play at the ripe old age of three, mostly by throwing tennis balls at me until I got good enough to return them, which curiously put a stop to their enjoyment. My mother, noticing some kind of skill, or at least my enthusiasm for the game, found me a local coach. Coach Gayle helped me to learn to play gracefully rather than competitively, which meant that I never did very well at a competition level, but I could certainly hold my own on the court.

I hadn't thought to bring a tennis outfit – how senseless of me – but I did have a white linen skirt and a silky, light beige top that could pass. I also had white trainers, which wouldn't quite match the ensemble, but would have to do.

I made myself a long black from the pod coffee machine, cursing the lack of decent coffee, and went to sit outside on my private terrace.

As I stepped into the crisp morning air, I could hear Henri talking to someone, presumably on the phone. Figuring it was the perfect chance to get some intel on him, I slipped back behind the curtain, making sure to remain hidden as he stepped out onto his own terrace.

'There are only five other people ...' Henri said, drifting off.

'How hard can it be?' he said after a pause.

Silence.

'Honestly, we haven't been given much information. I know there's a tennis breakfast this morning, though. Shouldn't be too hard to show a bunch of writers a thing or two about sport. I doubt most of them even know how to break into a run ...'

Harsh.

More silence.

'Anyway,' Henri continued, 'I was wondering if you'd spoken to Balthazar lately, or if he'd tried to contact you?'

Silence.

'On Instagram? Right, well you leave it to me. I'll put him in his place,' Henri said.

Hearing my own phone vibrating, I crept away from the window, wondering what was going on between Henri and Balthazar. Could a possible feud be enough to get them both sent home?

A text message from Drew: *How is it? Or have you given up your phone? Are you sure it's not an escape room kind of scenario? Anyway, I'm worried, so shoot me a text to let me know you're ok.*

All going well. Perfectly civilised except for the lack of decent coffee.

Let me guess, pod machine? At least your outrage confirms nobody has hijacked your phone. Good luck. Message me later.

Now that we'd arrived, I could feel myself starting to relax a little. Everything seemed – dare I say – normal, or I guess I should say, relatively normal, considering the location. I found myself actually looking forward to playing tennis and discovering a little more about Carla's life.

Once I'd made a vague effort at unpacking – in other words, hung up some clothes in the hope that the creases would magically fall out – I threw on my 'whites' and, with some time before the tennis breakfast was due to start, decided to walk around the gardens and clear my head.

Chapter 16

The Villa – HENRI

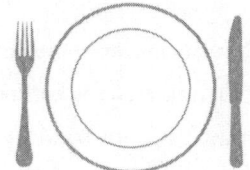

We'd arrived early at Carla's villa. I'd been hoping to get a break from thinking about Chloe, but unfortunately our rooms were adjacent, so I just had to sit there, trying not to picture her changing into her tennis whites mere metres away.

Instead, I called Lucy.

'Hey big brother, what's up?' she asked.

Since she was old enough to no longer be my 'annoying little sister', Lucy has gloated about the fact she's a decade younger than me. I got my revenge by reminding her she was an accident, a truth our parents took no care to conceal.

'Just checking in on you, making sure you haven't burnt down our apartment,' I said, knowing that with age did *not* come responsibility – at least not in Lucy's case.

'Of course not. I haven't cooked anything, just to be safe.'

'Probably smart,' I told her. While I loved all things food, Lucy found cooking to be one of the most onerous of human requirements and was happy to live off baguettes and coffee.

It was my life mission to get her to enjoy food, but I knew I had a long way to go.

'So, what's it like?' she asked.

'As you could imagine,' I told her.

'Oh, don't be cruel. You've got to give me more than that,' she said.

I went on to explain the extravagance of my room, the view over the garden and onto the water, the bathroom. My descriptions were met with appropriately jealous-sounding murmurs.

'And do you think you'll get the job?' Lucy probed. She was the only person in my family to whom I'd disclosed the actual interview part of this weekend. I knew I could trust her to keep quiet if Uncle Michel questioned her. She was strong willed, that much was certain.

'Honestly, I don't know at this point,' I replied, distracted by thoughts of Chloe. 'There are only five other people ...'

'That sounds like good odds,' she replied.

'How hard can it be?' I asked, half-joking.

And then I made some dumb joke about the other interviewees' lack of athletic ability and Lucy forcefully told me to get my head in the game and not waste this opportunity. If anyone knew about my desire to leave *Le Cercle*, it was Lucy. She had become my makeshift therapist after many hard days in the office with Uncle Michel 'popping by'.

Eventually she forced me off the phone by saying, 'Right, well, I have to go to the bakery before I starve. Good luck!'

I went to make myself a coffee and re-read the note we'd been given about our first activity.

Tennis breakfast with whites. I'd expected something along these lines, knowing that Carla is a tennis fan and plays quite well. It was harder to imagine her actually playing against us, though. I figured she would appear later that afternoon, maybe even on Sunday morning. She was Carla Duris, after all; she probably had more important things to do than play tennis with a bunch of food writers, even if she *had* asked us to be there.

After showering, I pulled on some shorts and a Lacoste polo.

I could hear Chloe pacing around her room, and then I heard her door open and shut. It was an effort to stop myself from running after her like a lost puppy. We weren't due at the courts for a while yet. I wondered where she was going.

I made another coffee to pass the time, even though I knew it would do nothing to help calm my nerves. Fingers crossed it would make me extra alert on the court.

Eventually, I headed outside to find the others.

On my way, I ran into Christopher.

'Hello old chap,' he said.

Has he forgotten my name?

'It's Christopher, right?' I replied, knowing full well that questioning his notoriety would ruffle his feathers.

'Indeed! So, why on earth do you think we are about to play tennis?' he asked.

'A little competitive fun?' I suggested.

'Or a way to make us sweat?' he retorted.

'From what I've read, Carla is quite good at tennis. Maybe

99

she wants a strong competitor during memoir-writing breaks.'

'I hardly think sporting prowess should be a condition of employment,' he said.

I couldn't help a laugh, because even though I agreed with Christopher, we were talking about employment with Carla Duris. I imagined the contract would look unlike any other we'd seen before.

'In any other job interview, I'd agree, but I'm not sure Carla Duris does things by the book,' I told him.

He snorted, whether in agreement or disgust, it was hard to tell.

'How is your room?' I asked, changing the subject.

'Salubrious. Yours?'

'Almost as nice as the George V,' I said, even though I'd never actually stayed there.

'I am surprised by all the cameras outside, though,' he said. *Huh?*

'I hadn't actually noticed any cameras,' I admitted.

'Pretty much on all the exterior light poles. And on my little terrace,' he said. 'I assumed this place would be secure, but it seems like someone is being particularly cautious. Is Carla worried about people breaking in, or is she just keeping an eye on us, do you think?'

'Probably a bit of both,' I said, standing a little taller. If there were cameras watching, I needed to be on my best behaviour.

Christopher continued, more quietly now: 'I did hear one story about Carla when she was in New York. Apparently, she had cameras in her dining room. She would re-watch the service every night, and if any waiter made even the slightest error, or strayed from Carla's script, they would be fired.'

I nodded, unsure of how to respond.

Maybe Christopher had an edge to him that I hadn't given him credit for. It forced me to rethink how much he knew about Carla. He was certainly more astute than I'd realised. I cursed the fact; I'd need to keep an eye on him, too.

Chapter 17

The Tennis Breakfast – CHLOE

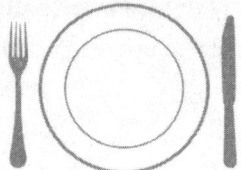

Carla's garden was just as elaborate as her villa. As I was reaching what appeared to be a rose garden – all the while feeling very heroine-in-a-Victorian-period-drama – I saw a head bopping about behind a hedge. Blonde hair, long, elegant neck – it had to be Belle. I contemplated rushing the other way, keen to avoid any distractions that might throw me off my game, but she saw me before I could make my move.

Her big smile immediately drew me in.

'Chloe! Imagine seeing you here,' she said with a laugh in her light and breezy American accent. We'd hardly spoken at dinner the other night, and suddenly I was grateful for the opportunity to get to know her a little better.

'How's it going?' I asked, sounding more Australian than ever.

'I'm so nervous, I just had to get out for a quick jog to reset.'

Her hair looked immaculate and her make-up was perfect. Not a drop of sweat had dampened her tennis whites (did she get a packing list, or did she just travel with athletic gear for all scenarios?). She certainly didn't look like someone who had been exerting herself.

'I'm doing the same thing,' I said. 'Well, the trying to shake off the nerves part. Max hasn't been particularly forthcoming with information about the weekend, has he?'

'I was thinking the same thing,' she said, nodding. 'But I'm just trying to go with the flow, I guess. I feel like I'm a pretty outside shot to get the job, so I plan to try and enjoy myself this weekend. I'm not even technically a writer, other than my scripts and some interview work.'

'We're a diverse group, aren't we?' I agreed.

'Do you think that was the plan?' she asked.

'If Carla has a plan, it's hard to decipher.'

'Time will tell, I guess,' she said with a smile.

We walked for a few moments in silence, me rushing slightly to keep up with Belle's long stride.

'I love your YouTube channel, by the way,' I told her. 'I've been catching up on it since we met the other night.'

'Aww, thank you, that's so kind. I've been checking out the competition, too,' she said candidly. 'Shall we compare notes?'

'Oh, I don't really know much about any of the other interviewees,' I said. 'Other than some gossip. Plus, I was forced to share a cabin on the train down with *Monsieur Henri de la Fontaine*.' I said his name in the way he would, with a pompous French accent.

'Tell me more,' she said. 'And then I'll fill you in on what I know. I've been going deep!' she said lightly, laughing.

I looked at her, with her wide smile and her perfect, white

teeth, and I could totally understand why she'd been invited for the weekend. She was infectious, the type of person everyone wanted to have at an event or party thanks to her mystical ability to make everybody else feel good.

At that point, I figured it was safer to try to make her a friend rather than an adversary, so I said: 'Let's do it.'

I got the feeling that this weekend would push me so far out of my comfort zone, I may as well get an early start.

Belle went first. 'Shall we kick things off with Henri? Tell me what you know, beyond the fact that he's probably the best-looking of all the guys here.'

I grinned. 'Sure, we can start with that. But I should warn you, with great beauty comes great arrogance. At least, that seems to be the case with Henri.'

She laughed. 'Love it.'

'From what I can tell, he's well connected,' I continued. 'He walks the walk, if you know what I mean, but he doesn't speak particularly highly of his job at *Le Cercle*. Sure, he's a good writer, but who knows what hand his uncle plays in *rewriting*,' I said. This was probably a little harsh, but then again, Henri had stitched me up on the train this morning. I was in no mood to be generous with him.

'And do you think he's going to try and flirt his way into the job? That's the one area where he could have a distinct advantage with Carla.'

I laughed. With Henri, anything could be possible. He'd made me swoon when he'd pushed my hair behind my ear on the train, even though I was pissed off with him. It was easy to imagine he could turn his charms onto Carla to try to get the job; I just had to hope he had more integrity than that.

'And what about the others?' Belle asked.

'Honestly, I've spent more time looking into Carla than the rest of us, although I have been at a couple of dinners with that English man, Christopher. Until now, he's mostly ignored me because I'm not posh enough for him.'

'You're not *posh enough*? What?' Belle asked.

'It's an Australian versus English thing,' I told her. 'Goes back to convict days ...'

'Right. Well, I don't buy into all that,' she said in a breezy way that made me envious. 'I think he'll be out of here pretty quickly once the weekend gets going.'

'Really?' I asked.

'I'm not sure Carla really agrees with the whole "age before beauty" thing,' she said.

Judging by Carla's overtly beautiful staff, this seemed to be true.

'How about you? Do you know everyone well?' I asked.

'Where should I start?' she asked.

'Start with Balthazar. What's his deal? Seems like he's quite the lad about town.'

'Oh, trust me, you don't want anything to do with that spoilt French *bébé*,' she said dramatically.

'How come?' I asked.

'Well, I met him last year at this flash truffle dinner. He was so sweet, all roses and compliments. Now don't tell anyone this,' she said, looking at me conspiratorially, 'but we actually went on a couple of dates just before Christmas. Anyway, it didn't take me long to realise that he is an awful human and I ended things fairly quickly, but still, it wasn't my finest moment. He spent more time looking in the mirror and loving on himself than he actually spent talking to me. I don't even think he's a good writer. Have you read his stuff?' she asked.

'A little, but it's not really my vibe,' I said, thinking about his scathing reviews. Although popular with readers, they just didn't sit right with me. I agreed with his point that too often chefs are treated like gods (when clearly Carla was the only one who should ever claim to have attained god-status), but a chef's work was also their livelihood, and Balthazar's reviews rarely seemed to take into account the actual person pouring their heart and soul into making the food.

'Can you imagine building a name for yourself in this industry by being an asshole? I don't even know why Carla would want him here,' she said.

'Better to have him on her side than not?' I mused.

'Probably. Also, I *have* wondered if he and Juliette might have a little something going on.'

'Seriously? That guy is getting more action than he deserves.'

Belle laughed. 'Couldn't agree more! But then, I think Juliette has had her fair share of good-looking, rich boyfriends. She's the ultimate Parisian. Uber gorgeous, fashionable, a French It Girl, even though it pains me to say it.'

'And her writing?' I asked.

'It's pretty gossipy, which is why people love it. But then, she's young and she's well connected. She hasn't really figured out her own voice yet, which is perhaps why she's here. Carla probably thinks she can mould Juliette into whatever she's looking for in a memoir writer,' Belle said.

We reached a natural lookout point that had sweeping views over the sea, and lapsed into silence. I was in awe of how beautiful Carla's property was. It was hard to imagine that one of us would soon get the job, and then spend weeks, maybe months, with Carla down here. What a dreamy place to write a memoir.

'What about you? How do you feel about this whole mad mission?' Belle asked me.

'Um, good, I guess. I don't really know,' I said.

'Do you think you can take these other idiots down?' she asked.

'Umm,' I stalled, a little taken aback.

'In the tennis,' she added with a laugh, although I wasn't sure her comment had been as innocent as she made out.

'I guess time will tell,' I said.

Belle clapped her hands together and started walking even faster. 'Yes, let's get over there.'

Thankfully, she seemed to know the way.

Just when I was thinking Carla's villa couldn't surprise me any further, we arrived at the tennis court. The red clay contrasting against the deep blues of the ocean it overlooked was a sight.

'Jesus,' Belle said. 'That's one hell of a court.'

'Absolutely.'

And then I saw the breakfast spread. A large wooden table had been laid with all sorts of breakfast foods – croissants, waffles, berries, yoghurts and charcuterie. Everything was just so beautiful, so sumptuous, it made me wish my life looked like this all the time. Even the cheese board was over the top, with at least eight varieties of cheese, in slices and quantities so large I couldn't imagine how anyone could think we'd ever get through them. But I don't think Carla cared about budget, or probably even food waste. She was hosting us for the weekend, and she wasn't going to let us forget it.

A drinks trolley sat beside the table, boasting a large ice bucket filled with bottles of Champagne, fresh juice and San Pellegrino. Drops of condensation caught the sunlight, sparkling like diamonds.

There were Lacoste logos everywhere. Shorts, polos, tennis shoes. I wondered if Lacoste were somehow sponsoring the weekend and I'd just forgotten to check my cupboard. But then I reasoned with myself that a lot of my fellow interviewees were French, and simply couldn't help themselves when it came to dressing the part. I did a quick head count; everybody was already here.

The boys were standing around, sipping from delicate, little espresso cups, and Juliette was sitting on one of the plush yellow deck chairs, typing something on her phone.

Once Belle and I arrived, a waiter started handing out glasses of Champagne, which everyone else eagerly accepted but I regretfully turned down. Given my sleep-in on the train this morning, I wanted to remain as clear-headed as possible. I told myself I would probably be getting quite drunk once this was all over. For the time being, I needed to focus.

We were invited to help ourselves to food and I served myself a modest pile of waffles, fresh yoghurt and berries. (I didn't want to embarrass myself by getting a stitch from overeating.) And then I drowned my plate in maple syrup that smelt so fragrant I wouldn't be surprised to find it had come straight from a maple tree in Carla's garden (because I am only human).

Beyond what I could fit on my plate, I saw perfect little stacks of eggs benedict with quail eggs, and mini bagels with salmon and cream cheese. Everything was presented with such beautiful precision, I felt like I was on the set of a cooking demonstration and we were the lucky chumps who got to eat the leftovers.

Eventually, Max strode over the grass towards us, signature black clipboard in hand.

'Let us start the weekend with a little competition. You are going to be playing a few friendly mixed-doubles sets. See what you are all made of,' he said, his serious expression indicating that this was more than a 'friendly' game of tennis.

'As you all should know, Carla is a dedicated tennis fan. She has created the menu many times for La Brasserie Des Mousquetaires at Roland-Garros, and attends the Open every year. She will probably invite you to play against her if you get this job, so it'll be easier for everyone if you know your way around a court,' he said.

Well, that settles that, I thought to myself, resolving to play the best I could, and hopefully send a ball or two whizzing past Henri or Balthazar. It wasn't that I wanted either of them to look the fool – well, actually, I kind of did. Henri, because he'd let me sleep in on the train, and Balthazar, because he had resting arrogant-smug face.

We finished eating while Max outlined the schedule of play. One set per pairing, winners get one point each. The two people with the most points will play each other in a final singles game.

First up was me and Balthazar vs Henri and Belle.

I wasn't thrilled with the match-up, preferring to spend as little time with Balthazar as possible, but what could I do?

We won the toss.

'I'll serve first,' he said, probably assuming that I couldn't hit a ball.

'As you prefer,' I said, figuring resistance was futile.

He double-faulted.

'Next one's an ace,' he said, changing sides.

It wasn't, but at least it went in. He was serving to Henri, who actually made a pretty good forehand return, seemingly aimed directly at my head. I wondered if he was trying to take me out with a concussion. Instead, I volleyed, returning the ball hard and fast down the line. Our point. I squealed with joy.

And then it was game on. From the conversation I'd overheard earlier on the balcony, Henri had clearly thought he wouldn't have much competition on the court, and he seemed thrilled at the prospect of serious play. I smashed another ball across court just outside of his reach, hitting away my nerves with each shot.

I wouldn't say that Balthazar was good at tennis, because his strokes were easy to return, but once he got his eye in, he had solid aim, which helped things along. As I'd expected, Belle could *play*. I assumed she was just good at everything. She got on top of the ball easily and with force. Henri, it seemed, couldn't believe his luck; not only was Belle gorgeous and wearing a short tennis skirt, but she was also very good. I played well. Perhaps not as consistently as Belle, but I got in a couple of fast ground shots that I know surprised everyone.

Henri and Belle took out the first match, our four games to their six. I wasn't too worried about losing, but Balthazar didn't seem impressed. I heard him say to Henri that he hoped for a better partner next time, and I couldn't suppress a smile when I heard Henri reply under his breath: 'Not sure your partner was the problem.'

The next match was Juliette and Henri vs. Belle and Christopher. I found it fun to sit back and watch them battle it out on the court.

Balthazar took a seat as far away from me as possible, looking agitated. Clearly, he was itching to get back to being the centre of attention.

Belle once again dominated, and it looked like the game against Henri and Juliette would be quickly won. Christopher was surprisingly good, given he was several years older than his opponents. He was strong and steady – boring to watch, but effective. Henri put up a decent fight, but unfortunately Juliette, while adorable in her whites, was useless on the court. Playing up in an effort to conceal her ineptitude, she stopped constantly to clarify the rules and prance about. I could tell Max was getting irritated with her behaviour.

It was mid-prance while trying to return Christopher's serve that she was hit in the head by the ball.

She crumpled to the ground soundlessly and we all rushed over.

After a few moments of panic, she opened her eyes, batted her eyelashes and said: 'Well, I guess that puts an end to my tennis career.'

Max gruffly declared Belle and Christopher the winners, and Juliette was escorted to the sidelines by a thrilled-looking Balthazar. I wondered if their flirting might actually lead to something, and found it odd that they could even consider the distraction of romance when they'd come all this way for a job interview. Some people wouldn't know a good thing if it hit them in the head, apparently.

I'd hardly had time to finish my orange juice before I was up playing again.

The next game was meant to be me and Christopher vs. Balthazar and Juliette, but because Juliette was 'in recovery', Henri stepped in for her.

It was the Commonwealth vs. France, and we smashed them.

To be fair, Balthazar and Henri made a terrible doubles pair. There was no communication between the two, both of them reaching for the same balls and running into each other constantly. It was more slapstick than I would have expected, and their clear dislike for each other quickly cost them the game.

This meant that Belle and Christopher would go head-to-head in the 'final'. The rest of us took a seat on the sidelines to see who would win.

Henri sat next to me and, once the game was underway, whispered, 'Who taught you how to play?'

'I learnt in self-defence,' I told him, laughing at the memory of my three older brothers.

'Sorry?' he said, not following.

'I had to learn to hit so my older brothers would stop throwing balls at me,' I explained.

He smiled warmly, which took me by surprise.

'I have a little sister, although I'm not sure I can beat her at much,' he said with a laugh.

'I hope you're nicer to her than my brothers were to me,' I said.

'I am now, obviously. But when she was a kid, I mostly ignored her. Big age gap and all. Now I adore her. I'd do anything for her.'

I wasn't sure what to say. This conversation felt very personal, out of place even. I'd been under the impression that Henri and I were set to be rivals, at least for the weekend. Finding out that he was kind and sweet at this point in the game would be trouble.

'What's with you and Balthazar?' I asked, changing the topic.

'What do you mean?' he asked.

'You guys seem to have beef. And not in the bourguignon way.'

'Sorry?' he asked, my attempt at a joke landing flat.

'You don't get along?'

'Oh, he's not my favourite,' he said. 'As you Australians like to say, he's a snake in the long grass.'

'Interesting,' I said, wondering if something had happened between them or if it was just Balthazar's personality that seemed to rub people the wrong way.

A few games into the set, Christopher began to tire, and Belle dominated the rest of the game, meaning she'd won the 'casual' tennis tournament. One point to Belle.

Max announced her victory and said a terse, 'Congratulations.'

It was hard to ignore Carla's absence as we all applauded Belle and she looked around bashfully. We'd established that most of us could return a ball – except for maybe Juliette – but what did that mean for the rest of the interview?

'Now, you all have an hour to change before lunch. One pm sharp on the front terrace,' Max said with a clap of his hands, dismissing us.

But I had questions for Max. Where was Carla? When would we be conducting the actual interviews? When would we be going back to Paris?

Before I had a chance to speak to him, he walked away. Who knew what would happen at lunch? I just hoped that it would be Carla in the kitchen feeding us. I found her absence slightly unnerving.

I went ahead to the house, wanting as much time as possible in my room before our next scheduled activity. I had a date with the claw-foot bathtub that took up a good portion of my perfectly delightful bathroom.

Just before I entered Carla's villa, I turned back to see Juliette and Henri discussing something. She looked animated and he looked serious. I couldn't help wondering why. I knew better than to get involved in other people's affairs, and doing so on a weekend like this felt even more dangerous. And yet, even when I lowered myself into that beautiful bath, I found myself still thinking about Henri.

Chapter 18

The Casual Hit – HENRI

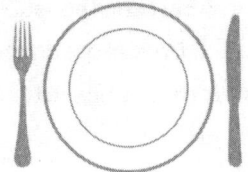

I was in a pretty good mood after we'd finished tennis. The endorphins from the matches coupled with the beautiful location, and topped off by my exchange with Chloe about our siblings, had made me almost joyful.

That was, until Juliette took me aside as we were heading back to the house.

'Henri,' she purred. Immediately I could tell she was flirting with me, but it didn't feel anywhere near natural; it felt like she wanted something. 'You were very good out there on the court.'

'Not really,' I said.

'I think you would have won against Christopher if the games had been organised in a better way,' she said.

I didn't bother to disagree, because I didn't feel like she'd have cared if I did.

'Did you enjoy yourself?' I asked, although I'd gotten the impression that Juliette hadn't enjoyed the tennis at all.

'Oh, you know, sport is something I prefer to leave to the professionals,' she said. She laughed, and it wasn't a stretch to imagine her sitting in a corporate box at Roland-Garros, sipping Champagne and delicately clapping her perfectly manicured hands together at somebody else's expense.

I may sound jaded, but PR people had tried to win me over almost too many times to count. While they would act like they were your best friend, their motivation always felt so obvious. I didn't want to feel obliged to write rave reviews just because somebody had given me a branded set of wine glasses or offered me a plate of complimentary caviar. It was a whole scene that I didn't want to be part of.

As Juliette took springy steps beside me, I was distracted by thoughts of Chloe. Her chasing down the ball with unwavering determination. Her sitting and watching the other games while sipping orange juice. The smell of her rose perfume, enchanting. I shook the images from my head, willing myself to stop obsessing.

'So, what can I do for you, Juliette?' I asked, frustrated at my inability to concentrate on the task at hand.

'Oh?' she said questioningly, pretending to be taken aback.

I gave her a smile to try and soften my directness, and she seemed to relax slightly.

'Look, I've heard on the down-low that Carla just fired a bunch of chefs from Chez Duris. I wanted to get your take on the news.'

'Where did you hear that?' I asked, trying to conceal my surprise.

'One of my many sources,' she said with a light laugh. 'I assumed you would have known about it.'

'Well, I haven't had my phone on me. Perhaps I got a

message while we were playing tennis.' I was relieved that she'd told me. Even if it wasn't true, it was better to know that something might happen than remain in the dark.

'What do you think it could all mean?' Juliette asked.

'Not sure,' I admitted.

'Do you think it is related to the memoir?' she asked.

'Hopefully Max will tell us more at lunch,' I said.

'Do you think Max has the authority to do that?' she said.

'Max has made it pretty clear that he's in charge in Carla's absence,' I replied.

She looked thoughtful for a few moments.

'Anyway,' she continued, 'until Carla *does* get here, and for the remainder of the weekend, I was thinking maybe you and I could make a truce. Share any information we pick up during the interview or from the other interviewees ...'

'And why would I do that?' I asked.

'Because if you help me, I'll help you. The more we know, the more we can control. Just think about it,' she said, and then sauntered off, turning only to add: 'I'm guessing the knives will eventually come out.'

I assumed most guys found Juliette charming, but I wasn't in the mood for her mind games.

Then again, I knew better than to entirely dismiss a rich Parisian girl. Once, I'd broken up with a senator's daughter because she was an absolute bore, and the next thing I knew, I got a call from my father with a list of things I'd done in the past month (with said ex-girlfriend), and ended up grounded for the next two months. My summer had essentially been destroyed, all because I'd suggested to this girl that I wasn't looking for a serious relationship.

Maybe I'd make more of an effort with Juliette at lunch, try and edge my way back into her good graces.

As soon as I got back to my room, I messaged Uncle Michel. I figured if anyone were to know about the change of staff at Chez Duris, it'd be him.

'Have you heard about any staff changes at Chez Duris?' I texted, getting straight to the point.

Within seconds bubbles appeared to show he was typing, not missing a beat.

'Nothing concrete, but some rumours of a change-up of her kitchen team. Maybe that means Carla is planning a new iteration of Chez Duris. Exciting stuff. See if you can find out more while you're down there. Get an exclusive. It'd be quite the scoop for Le Cercle *if you could pull it off.'*

If Carla actually bothers to show up this weekend, I felt like replying.

Instead, I was left wondering if the news had anything to do with her memoir, or if the timing was just a coincidence. Was she actually writing a memoir or were we just here to create PR buzz for her possible new restaurant idea?

Chapter 19

The Long Lunch – CHLOE

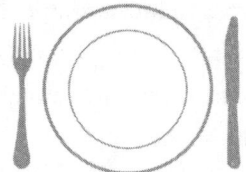

Walking out onto the terrace for lunch felt like being transported to a different world. Sweeping views over the sea, plush cushions lining the seats, colourful flower arrangements adorning the table, all sorts of glassware and cutlery hinting that we were in for a feast.

And I was hungry. The waffles at the tennis breakfast had been so light and fluffy that they hadn't kept me full for long, and I was looking forward to a proper meal. *I am Australian, for crying out loud, don't mess with my coffee or my breakfast!* My mind went to Drew and I laughed.

A few people were already seated, so I found my nameplate and joined them. I was at the end of the table, next to Balthazar – groan – and opposite Christopher – double groan.

The men in question arrived seconds after, blocking me from the rest of the interviewees. Balthazar started talking to Juliette, who was opposite him, in quick French, using plenty of jargon. I did my best to listen in. They were hypothesising over when Carla would arrive this weekend, and Balthazar was betting that something really weird would go down tonight. When Juliette questioned him on it, he simply said: 'I've heard things about her. Keep your wits about you.'

Juliette seemed to carefully process this information, and then changed the subject.

Christopher and I talked about the weather – because apparently, we were small-talking clichés – and then we slipped into silence. I twisted my napkin through my fingers, wishing I could at least sit with Belle.

Unfortunate seating plan aside, I shifted my focus to the prospect that we'd be eating soon. I was sure Balthazar and Christopher could ruin many good things, but nobody could stand between me and a good meal; food and I were in the ultimate romance.

When I saw Max come outside, my heart sank a little. I'd been hoping to see Carla, and Max's stupid clipboard had turned into an ominous sign that Carla wouldn't be making an appearance.

'Today's lunch will be a little different,' Max said as six waiters marched out and stood behind our seats, each holding plates covered with silver cloches.

Max paused while the waiters placed them in front of us, my heart racing as their hands clasped the silver ball on top of each cloche, awaiting further instruction.

When Max gave a sharp nod, the waiters lifted the cloches in unison and we let out a collective gasp.

Blindfolds.

Blindfolds?

I looked at Max, feeling a mixture of confusion and panic.

'Today, Carla has designed for you a menu that she would like you to taste using all your senses – except, of course, your sight.'

Oh god. I felt any chance of having a normal experience here at Carla's villa slowly slipping out of my grasp.

'It will be a blind degustation. You're invited to use the cutlery provided, or your hands. Nobody will judge you, because nobody will see you,' he said.

I found that hard to believe. I knew for a fact that Max wouldn't be eating with us, because there were only six places set. Therefore, it was safe to assume he'd be watching from the sidelines, probably laughing at us as we attempted to eat complex and delicate dishes with our fingers.

'Your waiters will introduce each dish, and I will tell you when you can chat to your neighbours between courses. The only thing I would *not* recommend is removing your blindfold.'

I didn't know if something had been lost in translation, but Max's last statement felt unnerving. I mean, what would happen if we didn't obey him? Would we be asked to leave?

Across from me, Christopher mumbled something about whether all this was necessary, and Max shot him a look so fierce that Christopher actually reddened in the cheeks.

Balthazar picked up his blindfold and said, 'Okay, shall we?'

I hesitated, wondering why nobody else seemed to be questioning the absurdity of this 'job interview'.

We were served a glass of Champagne – or so we were told – and everybody laughed as they fumbled around the table, bumping their hands into things and clattering cutlery. If anybody spilt their drink, they didn't mention it, because why would they?

'Let's all raise our glasses to Carla Duris,' someone said in a French accent that sounded like Balthazar's. 'For this unexpected weekend of bliss.'

I questioned the motive of the toast, but joined everyone in saying, 'To Carla!' while raising my glass (noting that nobody seemed confident enough to try and clink their glasses together).

I carefully took a small sip, bubbles exploding on my tongue as the crisp, fruity flavours hit my tastebuds. As much as I wanted to drain my glass, I decided it was best to stay sober. I didn't want to dull the senses that I still had at my disposal.

I carefully returned my glass to the table, struggling to not remove my blindfold, struggling to relinquish control. There was something about Max, something about the set-up of this whole weekend that just felt a little too far outside of my comfort zone. Normally, I felt confident pushing myself – hell, I'd moved to live and work in a foreign country on the opposite side of the world – but somehow Carla's villa just seemed like a step too far.

I pictured Belle and Juliette loving this activity and tried to ward off any apprehension I was feeling and just enjoy myself. This was easier said than done.

'Your first course ...' a waiter announced, and I sat back so he could safely deliver the plate. 'Oysters.'

I waited for him to elaborate, but we were given no further details.

Okay, I thought, perhaps this is a test of our ability to discern flavours and ingredients. This was actually one of my favourite things to do, but I normally had the satisfaction of confirming my deductions with a waiter, which was now off the cards.

Max's voice rang out: 'Everybody has been served. You may begin. Please refrain from discussion until I say,' he instructed.

We descended into silence. I could hear Max walking laps of the table, his shoes clicking on the terracotta tiles. I tried to convince my imagination that with our blindfolds on, we could be anywhere. I was back at my family dining table and my brothers were just playing a good-natured prank on me. I took a deep breath to steady myself.

I felt around my plate gingerly, nervously, finding three oysters in their shells, cold and slippery. But what were they topped with? I could feel little flecks of something crunchy – perhaps fried onion, a crushed nut, maybe even a breadcrumb – and a chopped herb or something soft to one side.

I decided to forego cutlery and picked up an oyster shell, bringing it to my lips. I could smell something citric; was it yuzu? I tipped the oyster into my mouth, feeling the crunch of the fried shallots, tasting the rice wine vinegar. It was delicious.

I couldn't think of a Carla recipe that combined these ingredients, so assumed this was something different to the food she'd normally serve.

I could hear the sound of clinking cutlery – brave – and somebody clinking a wine glass into their plate as they tried to pick it up.

Eventually, Max spoke. 'How was it?' he asked.

Everybody murmured their enjoyment. It had been an excellent dish.

'And now, I have a few questions. Raise your hands if you tasted lemon ...' he said, and it dawned on me that this was indeed establishing our ability to taste.

I remained still. It had been yuzu, I was almost certain.

'Raise your hand if you tasted onion.'

No, I really believed that they were fried shallots.

'Shallots,' Max said, again pausing.

There we go. I raised my hand.

'White wine?'

No.

'Rice wine vinegar?'

Yes.

I waited for more, but was met with an extended silence.

'You'll have a short pause between courses. Leave your blindfolds on, but you can chat among yourselves,' Max said.

I was desperate to talk to somebody about how any of this related to our ability to co-write a memoir, but given that I didn't know where Max was standing, I hardly felt comfortable questioning the interview process.

So, I took a sip of water and listened to everybody else.

'This is great,' I heard Belle say. 'Reminds me of the time I went to a restaurant in the dark for a travel segment I was filming. OMG, you should have seen the state of my dress when we walked outside. I looked like a wild animal.'

'It's such an interesting way to eat,' agreed Juliette. 'It forces you to really focus on what you are consuming.'

Was I the only person finding this all absurd?

Thankfully – or perhaps annoyingly – I heard Christopher mutter that this was all ridiculous. I wanted to agree with him, but again, was unnerved by the knowledge that Max could be standing right behind us.

Balthazar got chatting to Juliette about how he'd gone on an Ayahuasca retreat and had seen the story of the origins of humanity play out in front of him through the forms of flashing lights, and then he himself had transformed, taking the form of an owl, all of which was to say the whole experience had essentially changed his life. Or some rubbish like that. I'd stopped listening.

Henri had been awfully quiet. This surprised me; I thought a meal like this would have been entertaining for him. I got the impression that he really knew his ingredients, and that he had a good palate, but perhaps he just had a nice way with words.

The more I focused on the sounds of people's voices, the more I began to struggle to differentiate between them, and, just as abruptly, I began to feel flustered, muddled. Flavours, thoughts, sounds all started to blur in my head, backed by the soundtrack of my thumping heart.

I needed to get this blindfold off, if only for a minute.

I needed to ground myself.

Suddenly, I felt my hand shoot up.

Max quickly grunted a questioning 'Hmm' in my ear, confirming my suspicion that he might be lurking behind us.

'Bathroom,' I whispered to him.

'Leave your blindfold on,' he instructed.

'Seriously? To go to the toilet?' I asked.

'Just until you leave the table,' he said, perhaps trying to reassure me.

He held my arm after I stood up, and ushered me around the other side of the table. Through the tiny gap at the bottom of my blindfold, I noticed that Henri's chair was empty.

How strange.

A waiter took over from Max and, when we rounded a corner, told me I was allowed to take off my blindfold. Light rushed in and a wave of relief broke over me. I was still outside, just around the corner from the terrace. I could still hear voices, but the table was out of sight.

I was shown to a bathroom and, with some relief, locked the door behind me to regroup.

By myself, I could relax. I wondered how long I could remain in there, hiding from everything, before it began to look suspicious.

Chapter 20

The End of Lunch – HENRI

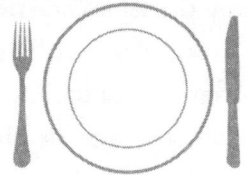

Lunch had gotten off to an intense start.

So intense, in fact, that I'd asked Max if I could go to my room to get something for a headache. I told him blindfolds were problematic for me because I didn't want him to think I was prone to headaches, which I was. The less he knew about my private life, the better. Besides, I'd needed a break from that table. It was a strange feeling being in a social setting with a blindfold on. I wasn't enjoying it.

I'd remained pretty quiet during lunch up until my escape. I'd raised my hand regarding the ingredients, of course, when instructed, but had otherwise avoided any conversation. Who knew what was going on? I wasn't going to risk exposing myself when I literally couldn't see who was watching. Christopher's comment about the cameras earlier that morning had made me cautious.

When I'd arrived back downstairs, I waited where Max had told me to.

'You need to fix microphone two,' I heard someone say quietly in French.

'Again?' someone else asked.

'Apparently nothing is coming through on it,' the first man said.

I froze, trying to get more of the conversation, but that was it.

I stuck my head around the corner to glance at the table. It looked normal enough, considering it was occupied by blindfolded people. I did, however, notice that Chloe was missing. Had she been excused? Did she leave?

I figured it was only a matter of time before we lost our first person in this crazy weekend-long interview. But *mon dieu,* I hoped it wasn't her. I talked myself down by reasoning that she knew her flavours, she knew her ingredients.

Which led me to my second – perhaps more pressing and problematic – question: why were the waiters worried about a microphone not working?

As a waiter returned and handed me my blindfold, I placed it back over my eyes with apprehension. Part of me wondered when the real interview would begin, part of me wondered why there were microphones and NDAs. But I kept quiet. I didn't say anything or ask anything. Best not to ruffle any feathers until I could find out more. I'd just be more careful about what I was saying. I needed to play things smart.

When I was seated back at the table, Max announced the next dish: 'Spaghettini.'

For once, I wished that Max wasn't a man of so few words.

At first, I was uneasy about attempting to eat this dish without a spoon and fork, especially considering we were dining in one of France's most beautiful villas, but quickly realised I needed to get over myself.

I hesitated before clumsily feeling around the flat bowl with my fingers.

Okay, I thought to myself. *Prawns. I could de-shell and eat prawns in my sleep.* I ripped the head off one and sucked out the juice.

The prawns had been seared in butter, garlic and lemon juice. The flavours felt like summer in my mouth. I ate them quickly but with reverence, and soon realised I had no idea where to put the shells. Also, my hands were now a mess.

'Excuse me,' I asked, hearing someone walking softly behind me. 'Is there a napkin? Also, something for the shells?' I questioned.

A delicate hand encircled my wrist and manoeuvred it to an empty bowl, and then to a little waxy packet that contained a wet wipe.

'*Merci*,' I murmured, although I wondered if I was allowed to be talking. Once my hands were clean, I felt around my place setting and my hand landed on exactly what I'd been looking for. A glass of white wine, Chablis, chilled to perfection. I took a greedy sip before remembering that I was in the middle of an interview and should practise some restraint.

There was a strange vibe among the group as everybody ate in silence. I felt a foot kick me under the table but had no idea who it had been, or if it had been intentional.

And then I went in for the spaghettini. I swirled the pasta with my fingers, stupidly attempting to replicate the job only a fork should do, which resulted in an avalanche of pasta when bringing it to my mouth.

I felt a few strands land on my shirt, in my lap – it was a disaster, like I'd gotten myself into a food fight, except the fight had been with my own clumsiness.

The only thing I was grateful for was that the dish wasn't tomato based. I'm not sure my shirt, or my dignity, would have recovered.

Max's voice returned: 'Raise your hand if you tasted lemons.'

I did.

'Raise your hand if the lemons came from Menton.'

They did; the lemons tasted like sunshine. These questions were almost too easy.

'Raise your hand if you tasted chilli.'

Nope.

'Raise your hand if the garlic was preserved.'

Hmm, on that specificity, I wasn't sure. The garlic had been sweet, it tasted young, but I didn't think it was preserved. I had to hope it was a trick question.

Of course, we didn't get to find out if our palates had obeyed or betrayed us, because after that question, Max informed us our main course was now complete.

Our plates were removed shortly after, and we were given permission to start talking again.

I listened out for Chloe's voice. Had she even come back to the table? I wished I could have stolen a glance at her seat, but I didn't want to risk getting in Max's bad books, so I sat and waited for this particular part of the interview to be over.

Dessert was thankfully a simpler affair, a sugared chestnut tart with whipped cream. More questions from Max followed. I put my hand up like a good schoolboy, and bided my time. I wanted desperately to move on with the weekend.

'Lunch is now finished. Please remove your blindfolds,' Max said eventually.

I did so swiftly, inspecting the damage to my shirt. Thankfully it wasn't too obvious, but still, I could feel my cheeks burning.

And then I looked around and realised that I wasn't in the worst state. I was almost elated to see Balthazar and Christopher had made quite the mess of themselves.

Belle joked with the other guys about their appearance, but was not much better off herself. Juliette, on the other hand, pulled a napkin gracefully from her low-cut blouse as if she'd done blind tastings a hundred times before. *How hadn't I thought of doing that?*

I looked over at Chloe, who had thankfully returned to the table. Her clothes appeared to be pristine. She was the picture of elegance, quiet and steadfast, trying to adjust to the light like a deer in headlights. I noticed she was taking slow, deliberate breaths. Was she panicked?

When a waiter circled the table with espressos, Chloe asked for a cup of jasmine tea. He gave her a dirty look but said he'd be back with one shortly. I had to fight back a chuckle, but I admired that she stuck to her guns.

As we drank our coffee, the talk turned to our favourite restaurants in Paris.

I found this piece of personal information rather telling. Generally, I tailored my response to this question depending on who was asking. Some people loved hole-in-the-wall places, others loved high-end. Suggesting something expensive to a couple of college kids was never going to end well, in the same way that recommending Lucy's favourite dive bar to a couple of well-heeled oldies wouldn't fly.

When Belle asked me my go-to place, I told her it was *Les Enfants du Marché*.

'In the *Marché des Enfants Rouges*?' questioned Chloe quickly, surprise lacing her voice.

'Mm,' I said. 'It has never disappointed me, not once, in terms of flavour, seasonality, quality of the produce.'

'That's my favourite place to eat, too,' Chloe said quietly.

I shouldn't have been surprised, knowing that Chloe was all about flavour over fuss, but I knew she hadn't written it up on her blog. I had checked.

She continued, as though reading my mind: 'I just try not to tell too many people. In their opening months, I could always get a table, but recently, it's been packed.'

'So how come I've never seen you there?' I asked her.

'Perhaps you have and you just forgot. Like how we first met,' she said.

'I never forgot meeting you, only the circumstances under which we were introduced,' I said truthfully.

Chloe looked at me as though she wanted to say something more, but Belle interrupted: 'What *I* want to know is why haven't I eaten there if it's so damn good?'

'We'll have to go together once this weekend is over and we're back in Paris,' Chloe said.

Considering we were all interviewing for the same job, things were still remarkably friendly between us. I wondered when the real competition would begin.

Chapter 21

The Yacht – CHLOE

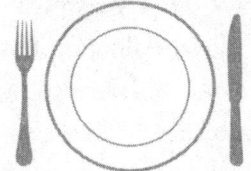

Max drove to the Antibes Port in the black mini-van, zooming through the streets at an alarming pace, narrowly missing walls and pedestrians alike.

There was a whiff of competition about the outing, because at the end of lunch, Max had returned, clapped his hands and instructed us that we were heading out for an afternoon of boating with the aim being to 'catch our dinner'.

In more concrete terms, this meant that we had to fish something out of the water that was delicious, and then design a dream menu to accompany our catch.

The best menu would then be selected and used to make dinner. We had no idea of the activity's significance in the grand scheme of the interview, but it seemed to have taken on some importance among the interviewees, perhaps in the absence of anything else for us to focus our attention on.

I looked around the van and noticed that most people had undergone a costume change. Gone were the frilly dresses and white button-downs from lunch, and in their place were Breton stripes and – conveniently – boat shoes.

I, once again, hadn't got the boating-dress-code memo and was wearing canvas shoes, jeans and a T-shirt. Luckily, I had nothing to prove to these people. Or so I kept telling myself.

Making our way, thankfully more slowly now, along the port, I tried to pick out Carla's yacht among the rows of gleaming white and chrome floating fortunes. These vessels were nothing like the one I'd learnt to fish on. Hell, most of them looked as though they hadn't even seen the open seas. There was a huge discrepancy in sizes, with some yachts taking up huge berths, and others squished in rather insignificantly between them.

When we finally pulled over and were ordered out of the van, we saw a strikingly handsome man wave us over to what must have been one of Carla's yachts. Compared to what I'd been picturing, the yacht was understated, but my god, she was beautiful – all wooden, sleek lines, plenty of light green cushions placed on the seats. The name, *La Présidente*, was written on the side in flouncy gold letters.

There was probably space enough for ten people on board, but there was very little room to hide. A couple of cooler boxes sat on one of the seats and I could spy the fishing equipment on the bow. Very lightweight, not industrial like I was used to. More hobby-level fishing rods. That was okay, I could adapt.

The captain who helped us aboard was, like his vessel, gorgeous. All tanned, sleek lines, wearing a perfectly tight white polo shirt with dark blue short shorts. He introduced himself as Gregorio, and I did a little internal swoon. He was perfection.

I imagined recounting all of this to Drew and wondered if he'd even believe me. And then I remembered the NDA.

Gregorio removed the dock lines deftly and we were off. The boat was on the smaller side, which amplified the movement of the sea beneath us. I hoped that everyone aboard had strong stomachs – they should, they were all food writers – but I knew that not everyone had sea-legs. The last thing I felt like witnessing was a reappearance of our three-course lunch floating on the Mediterranean.

Before long, we were out of the port and all that lay ahead was the vast expanse of the Mediterranean Sea, glistening like a jeweller's window. The afternoon was beautifully sunny. A light breeze was blowing across the water and the sun was still hours off setting. Other boats and yachts were out on the water – who wouldn't want to be on such a gorgeous day? – and I felt a little pang of homesickness for my family's boat in Tasmania. Living on the sea was the sweet life.

Looking around at our group, I began to think some people just shouldn't be allowed out on the water. Juliette had nearly fallen in while taking a selfie, Christopher was looking utterly green around the gills, and even Max himself was focusing more on the horizon than on any of us.

To his credit, Gregorio, in all his glory, did a deft job handling the yacht. He seemed like a good captain. Assured, secure, blooming nice to look at.

When we finally dropped the anchor, much further from the shore than I'd anticipated, the silence on the water and the warmth of the sun on my bare skin had lulled me into a much calmer state. I had to keep reminding myself that I was there on a job interview. It would have been rather easy to relax into holiday mode.

But then the fishing started.

Max separated us so that the boys were fishing on one side of the yacht, and Juliette, Belle and I were on the other. The set-up suited me perfectly, because it meant that I could laugh my way through things with Belle, and also help her set up her line, because – as she confessed – this was her first time.

'I thought you Californians lived on the water,' I whispered to her.

'Yeah, we do, but fishing isn't really the go-to activity on Venice Beach, now is it?' She sounded slightly panicked.

'Isn't it?' I asked. I had no idea what life was like on Venice Beach.

She laughed loudly and Max shot us a frosty look. For what was meant to be a fun activity, he was certainly taking things very seriously.

Juliette turned out to be as bad at fishing as she had been at tennis, however she did manage to flirt her way into Gregorio's good graces, and he was very accommodating when she asked for *un peu d'aide*. Perhaps I should have known better than to worry about her capacity to get by.

I snuck a glance over at the boys and was surprised to see Henri deftly casting out. He had good technique. It was nice to watch. *Damn him!*

But then Balthazar followed suit, crossing his line over Henri's and making them both look like amateurs. I couldn't suppress a little giggle. When Belle caught me watching them, she raised her eyebrows.

I cast both Belle's and my lines out while everyone was preoccupied, and we began the relaxing wait for bites.

'Over here, Gregorio,' Christopher said, motioning the captain over to him. Although Christopher didn't do himself many favours, I did feel sorry for him at that moment. The poor guy was the only one without a line in the water at this point, and after Henri and Balthazar had sorted themselves out, unfortunately Christopher's inability to touch the bait and get it onto his hook became quite the spectacle.

'Just don't think about it,' encouraged Gregorio in his thick Italian accent.

'It is really not so bad,' agreed Juliette, although she hadn't even come close to doing it herself.

'Normally I'd have someone do this part for me,' Christopher said, clearly frustrated.

I winced at this obvious show of entitlement.

'I will help you this time,' Gregorio muttered, clearly annoyed at having to remove himself from Juliette's side.

Christopher physically squirmed as Gregorio attached his bait, showing him how to hook it on.

I looked over and noticed Max was watching Christopher carefully, but his facial expression was hard to read – surprised or disappointed?

And then Belle said quietly, 'Ooh, ooh, I think I've got something!'

I turned to see a sharp tug on her line.

'Yeah, you do!' I said. It was hard not to be excited by the prospect of the first fish of the day. And judging by the bowing of her rod, it looked to be a fairly big one.

'What do I do? What do I do?' she asked me, nervous excitement audible in her voice.

'So, you want to start reeling in your line, giving it a little tug every now and then,' I instructed. 'But gently, so you don't lose your fish.' I was whispering, because it was so ingrained in me when out on the water.

One of my earliest memories of fishing with my brothers was of them whispering to each other almost inaudibly, which was wildly out of character for them. They were not the type of guys to whisper. Out on the water, the rules were different.

Belle looked at me with a mix of fear and excitement. Nobody else had noticed her line yet, which meant that I could help her as much as she needed without being accused of interfering. We hadn't been instructed *not* to help each other, but I knew better than to anticipate the rules.

I showed Belle the motions with my own rod – slowly pulling and reeling in the line – and being a quick learner, she brought the fish in with relative ease.

It was a cod – quite big, too. Once it hit the deck, chaos ensued.

Belle was jumping up and down in excitement, Juliette was standing back, sheltering behind Gregorio, and the boys had finally turned around and noticed the action.

'Oh my god,' said Christopher, clearly uncomfortable at the sight of a live fish.

While Belle had done an excellent job at bringing the fish in, she had no idea how to get it off the hook. Henri and Balthazar looked on nonchalantly, waiting for Belle to prove she was capable of the next step. Juliette was pulling a face.

The fish made one last gallant attempt to get back into the water, launching itself towards the boys.

Christopher gasped and inched away.

The fish flapped some more.

Christopher stepped back further and, in his panic, lost his balance and fell into the water with a loud splash.

He made a noise that sounded somewhere between a piglet squealing and a Chihuahua barking – in other words, a sound almost impossible to attribute to the pompous man who'd been complaining about putting bait on a hook only moments earlier.

The whole scene felt surreal; almost too ridiculous to believe. One second, Christopher was on board, terrified *of a fish*, and the next he was overboard, seemingly terrified for his life.

Gregorio launched into action, flinging a floatation ring into the water. Oblivious, Christopher continued to struggle, flapping about in a similar way to the fish, seemingly unable to even grab the ring that would keep him afloat.

After a few long seconds, I wondered: *Can he swim?* My heart started racing at the realisation that he might actually be in trouble. I rushed over to his side of the yacht and called out: 'Christopher, do you need help?'

His head kept slipping underwater while his arms punched the surface ineffectively. More splashing, more flailing, no response. *Is he too proud to call for help?*

Before I even realised what was happening, Henri pulled off his blue striped-shirt, diving in towards Christopher.

It was hard to tell if he'd gone to Christopher's aid out of virtue or out of competitiveness. He must have known that Max was watching and would be reporting back to Carla. Was that the reason behind his good deed, or was he actually just gorgeously gallant? I mean, who would be that desperate to save Christopher?

Henri swam out effortlessly, securing the life ring under Christopher's arm and dragging him back to the boat. It was a calm day and the sea was still, but it was probably a good thing Henri had beaten me to it. Although I was a strong swimmer, Christopher was a big guy, and he'd required a lot of assistance. Henri and Gregorio managed to haul Christopher back onto the boat, where he sprawled on the deck, gasping for air.

But my attention was drawn to a more pleasing sight: Henri's perfectly sculpted torso. There are some moments in your life that just etch themselves into your brain, and I got the feeling that Henri's abs would be hard to forget.

Once Christopher had stopped coughing and panting, embarrassment seemed to radiate off him, and soon enough, his embarrassment turned to anger.

'What the hell are we even doing out here on a yacht?' he demanded, looking at Max furiously. 'I came here to interview for a writing job, not to catch a blasted fish. If this is Carla's idea of a joke, I think it needs to end here.'

Nobody spoke.

I looked at Belle's fish, which had long given up the fight and was resting peacefully on the deck.

Gregorio gave Max a loaded look before he swiftly removed Belle's fish from its hook and slid it into a cooler box. After leaning over the deck to plunge his hands in the water, he then handed Christopher and Henri a towel each, and said, 'Right, let us get back to fishing.'

I turned to face the sea once more, chancing a look at Belle, who was doing some deep breathing, seemingly trying to supress a laughing fit at the string of events that had just taken place. I had to remind myself of the seriousness of the sea to stop myself from joining her. Considering we were on a beautiful boat in the sun in the Mediterranean, there was an awful lot of tension in our little group. Perhaps now that we'd caught the first fish, and had survived our first man overboard, things would settle down.

Time slowed and calmed, and the return of silence on the boat was welcomed. I think Christopher questioning the purpose of this fishing trip was playing on everybody's mind. Why hadn't Max answered him? What *was* Carla playing at with all these activities? Meanwhile, Christopher sat looking furiously back at the shoreline, refusing to take up his rod again.

The calm didn't last long, and soon enough both Balthazar and I had bites.

I slowly reeled in my line, getting a sense of the weight and drag of the fish, happy that it felt like something we'd be able to take back to Carla's rather than something we'd need to throw back. Gregorio and Max came to watch, with Gregorio applauding loudly when the fish hit the deck. I couldn't help a smile – it had to be one of the biggest sea bream I'd ever caught. And on this flimsy little rod! I couldn't wait to tell my brothers and Dad, knowing they'd be both thrilled and jealous.

But then, as I was removing my own fish from the hook, I looked over to see that Balthazar had reeled his in. It looked smaller than mine, but it was a decent size.

I watched Henri quietly remove the hook and slide Balthazar's fish back into the water.

'Hey,' I called out in surprise, 'what are you doing?'

Everyone turned to face Henri, and his cheeks immediately flushed pink.

'It was far too small,' he replied.

'Are you sure?' I asked, knowing I had a pretty good eye for these things. 'You probably should have checked.'

'*Certain,*' he said in a tone to match.

I looked to Balthazar for backup, but he watched on from a distance, flipping his hair away from his face in a way that told me he found the act of fishing quite repulsive.

I gave Henri a questioning look and he just shrugged that classic French shrug. Had he intentionally tried to sabotage Balthazar or had it been an honest mistake?

Our lucky streak ended with my fish, it seemed. Not long after, Gregorio announced that we'd soon be hauling anchor and heading back to port.

The sun was still shining. I'm not sure who first floated the idea of having a quick swim, but as soon as the rods were packed away, everyone was in the water (bar Christopher, of course, and Max and Gregorio).

After diving in, I was almost able to forget the rivalry that was intensifying around me and just enjoy the feeling of the cold, salty water on my skin. It was almost like a reset. I swam away from the boat for a few strokes, clearing my head. We'd probably be meeting with Carla on our return to the villa, and then the serious part of the interview would begin. For the umpteenth time, I told myself that it was time to refocus.

Chapter 22

The Open Water – HENRI

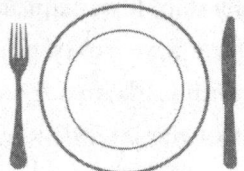

Treading water out there in the middle of the Mediterranean Sea made me want to throw the whole interview process away and just swim off with Chloe.

I could picture the scene unfolding like an old French film. We'd emerge from the sea on a nearby beach, droplets of water streaming off us, gleaming in the sunlight. We'd grab a burger and some chips at a beach club, maybe even share a bottle of rosé. We'd walk hand in hand along the beach and watch the sunset. We'd sit for the final few moments before the sun disappeared into the sea and then we'd kiss. Cheesy, maybe, but *mon dieu*, it sounded good.

I swam over to Chloe while she was floating on her back, basking in the beautiful sunshine.

'You're a woman of many hidden talents,' I said, immediately regretting my choice of words, worried they sounded weird.

'Not hidden,' she told me.

'Really?' I asked.

'I make no attempt to mask my capabilities,' she said.

'Then how do you keep surprising me?' I pressed.

'In life, I try not to pigeonhole people based on preconceptions. It's a fun way to give people the benefit of the doubt,' she said, only half-jokingly. 'You should try it.'

'I feel like I am a pretty good judge of character,' I told her.

'Really?' she asked, sounding surprised.

'For example, I could tell as soon as we got on this boat that Christopher was not an outdoors man,' I said.

'That much was obvious,' she said, starting to swim away from me again.

'And what do you make of me?' I asked, desperately trying to keep our conversation going.

'Honestly, I'm not sure yet,' she said, grabbing onto the boat. 'You seem competitive, but also confident. I'm guessing you feel like you have a good chance of getting this job, and you're just waiting for the rest of us to mess up. Sound accurate?' she asked.

I looked at her with a hint of a smile. 'Why do you think I'm competitive?' I asked.

'Well, the fact that you threw Balthazar's fish back in the sea when I'm pretty sure it would have surpassed the minimum size requirements, seems a little – dare I say – fishy,' she said.

I couldn't fault her observations, but what I didn't want to admit to was that I, like Christopher, struggled with the concept of fishing. Not because I was squeamish, but because I cared for the damn fish, and biting into a hook seems like an undignified ending for any life. And then the poor fish is forced to flap about ingloriously on the deck like an inebriated burlesque dancer until it gives up and dies. I knew it was almost hypocritical of me – especially as a food writer who enjoyed seafood – but watching the whole spectacle broke my heart a little. That was why I had vowed to only ever keep a fish if it looked old and was large enough to feed a good amount of people. I accepted that perhaps my logic was flawed, but it was how I chose to make peace with the aquatic world.

So, when Balthazar caught a fish that, to me, looked probably too small to cook – in the prime of his life, really – I quickly removed the hook and slipped it back into the water. It wasn't that I wanted to mess up his chances of glory (although perhaps this was part of my subconscious thinking); I just didn't want that fish to have to die for our dinner. And I would have got away with it if Chloe hadn't called me out, but how was I to know she could measure the size of a fish with her eyes?

'It was an honest mistake,' I said. 'I'd rather err on the side of caution and let a fish live another day.'

'Which tells me that you're compassionate. Similar to the way you didn't even hesitate to jump in after Christopher when he fell.'

'I was a lifeguard one summer,' I told her. It was the truth. That training had really stuck with me. And even though Christopher had embarrassed the hell out of himself by: A. being scared of said fish; and B. falling off the side of the boat in an attempt to get away from it, I still didn't want to let him drown.

'Well, lucky for us,' she said.

'I'm sure you would have done the same thing,' I said.

'I can swim, but I'm not sure I'd have the strength to rescue someone.'

'Do you think you could make it all the way back to shore?' I asked, wondering if Chloe might be keen to play out my fantasy.

'Swimming? Maybe ...' she said. 'But I'm not sure Max would approve. *You* can if you want, though. Perhaps you were already considering dropping out of the interview because you've realised we're all not as hopeless as you first imagined.'

'I never thought you were hopeless,' I said.

'Oh?' she said. 'Then off you go.' She motioned to the shoreline, which admittedly looked quite far.

'Only if you join me,' I told her.

'Ah ... no,' she said with a nervous chuckle. 'But tell you what, I'll happily play you at tennis again any time you like. It's a shame we didn't have a one-on-one game.'

'One-on-one does sound fun,' I said with a look that I hoped implied I was talking about more than tennis.

She looked vaguely amused and then got back on the boat, where she accepted a towel from Gregorio – who was beyond handsome, almost a crime to the rest of us – and dried herself off.

I had to wait a few more moments before getting out myself, because the sight of her had got me all hot and bothered.

We'd only been out on the water for a couple hours, but I was feeling pretty drained from all the action.

I sat alone on the mini-van ride back to Carla's villa, trying to reset my game face and refocus my energy on my reason for being there.

So what if Chloe had turned down my offer to swim ashore and my ego had disappeared into the depths of the water faster than that fish I'd released?

So what if I'd attempted to compliment her tennis and fishing skills and my words had seemingly fallen on deaf ears?

Unfortunately, Chloe continued to be wary of me, and her mistrust had only been made worse by Balthazar's damn fish. I could have told her the truth about how I felt about fishing, but what if she told Max? Carla needed someone pretty ruthless to write her memoir, and I'd worked hard to show that I was competitive while still being a good team player. Now wasn't the time to show any weakness. I really wanted this job and would do whatever I could to get it.

Arriving back at the villa, Max instructed us to return to our rooms and write up our dream menu for the evening, based on the fish that had been caught.

'The cod and the sea bream will be barbecued,' he advised. 'Please come up with what you believe would best accompany the fish, as well as any marinades or cooking instructions. Carla will choose her favourite menu to be prepared for you this evening. You have until 7pm.'

Did that mean Carla would be joining us for dinner?

I put aside thoughts of everything else and began to plan my menu. I'd been brought up on sea bream and cod. This should be easy.

But back in my room, I struggled to make any food decisions.

The most obvious menu would involve grilling the fish with lemon and butter, but after the prawns we'd been served at lunch, that felt too similar.

And then I thought about a dish I'd had in Nice with my parents, cod with a chorizo and parmesan crumb. It had been the perfect mix of salty, fleshy and sharp. I added it to my menu.

For the sea bream, I continued with my spice theme, recommending that it be rubbed in *Piment d'Espelette*, olive oil and lemon before barbecuing it. To accompany everything, something simple: boiled potatoes with lots of butter, salt and parsley. Green beans with lemon and garlic. Let the fish take centre stage.

To drink, something sparkling – Champagne/pét-nat – and chenin blanc with the fish.

I added a note suggesting the evening begin with a cocktail – a Serendipity: calvados, apple juice, Champagne and mint.

I knew from Chloe's blog that she adored calvados, so this cocktail would be my little nod to her.

Slipping my menu under my door as instructed, my mouth was already watering.

Chapter 23

The First Departure – CHRISTOPHER

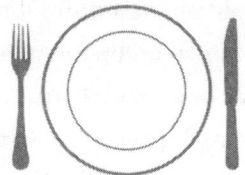

Requested to leave because I couldn't swim, or because I was asking too many questions? Christopher asked himself as he was packing his bags.

Whatever the reason, he was relieved to be returning to Paris. This whole expedition had been a waste of his time. He should have known that trying to get a job with Carla Duris would only result in drama. For the longest time, he'd been wary of even writing about her restaurant, acutely aware of her reputation for being unreliable and erratic.

That Carla hadn't even graced him with her presence before he'd been asked to leave said a lot. He knew better than to trust her, or any of her lackeys, ever again.

He had only agreed to come on this ridiculous weekend because he'd imagined the job of writing a memoir to be quite relaxing. He'd sit around, listening to stories and writing them up. It had seemed preferable to the constant deadlines he'd faced over the years. He'd even convinced himself that a year down in the south of France would do him good. A little rest by the seaside was how he'd built it up in his head.

But the weekend had proved that what Carla Duris wanted and what he wanted could never possibly align.

Better now than later, Christopher reasoned with himself, making his way downstairs and leaving the villa promptly. The thought of a barbecue with the imbeciles he'd been lumped with for the weekend would have been enough to make him want to leave anyway.

Fishing disaster or not, these were not his people, and he was happy to be getting away from them and back to his real life.

Chapter 24

The Casual Barbecue – CHLOE

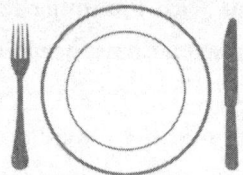

Coming downstairs for the evening, I was greeted by a waiter holding a tray of cocktails. I accepted one, taking a small sip. Calvados, my favourite.

I sighed and felt my shoulders relax.

Being the first downstairs, I took a seat on the terrace and waited for the others, trying not to think about whose menu would be selected for dinner.

I was pretty certain it wouldn't be mine. When trying to plan it, I'd felt rushed and uninspired, drained after what had already been an eventful day.

In the end, I'd planned for a simple *sauce vierge* to accompany both varieties of fish – olive oil, lemon juice, chopped tomato and basil. I'd added coriander seeds for a little more depth of flavour, but still, I knew it wouldn't be impressive enough for Carla.

Belle and Balthazar arrived in quick succession, followed by a rather overdressed Juliette, who was wearing an ankle length, strapless black dress. And then came Henri, who looked like he'd just stepped out of the shower into a perfectly ironed shirt and snug-fitting chinos. Water beads clung to his well-coiffed dark hair, and somehow, amid all the action of the weekend thus far, he managed to look calm and peaceful.

He accepted a cocktail from the waiter, took one sip, smiled and then looked at me, almost as though we now had a shared secret. I gave him a puzzled look in return and he winked at me. Winked! Was the calvados cocktail his doing? And did this mean that his menu had been chosen for the evening? A little bubble of nerves bounced around in my stomach.

'Where's Christopher?' Belle asked, interrupting my train of thought.

A few people shrugged but there were no conclusions until Juliette said, without a hint of feeling, 'I saw him out my window with his suitcase. I'm quite sure he is gone.'

'He's gone?' I asked, my voice wavering an octave higher than normal. It wasn't as though I'd been desperate for him to stay, but I was still surprised. He was the first of us to have officially left. I guess it had to happen eventually, but it made things feel a lot more real.

The question of whether Christopher had been asked to leave or had left of his own accord hung in the air. I waited for somebody to hypothesise about what might have prompted his departure.

Before we could, however, a beautiful chef came out and stood behind a beautiful barbecue, tongs at the ready.

Where does Carla find all these incredible-looking employees, and is it a prerequisite for getting hired? I asked myself.

Max appeared and I stifled a groan. Once again, I'd been hoping we'd finally see Carla.

'Tonight, Carla has instructed me that you will be dining on Henri's menu,' he said.

Our small group began to applaud, and I quickly joined in. I couldn't help feeling a pang of disappointment as another string was added to somebody else's bow. *I'll need to do some serious catching up if I'm going to stay in this,* I told myself.

I shot Henri a look and was surprised to see him blushing, looking at his hands. I was momentarily distracted by what I could only assume was an act of bashfulness, and then something clicked in my brain. *So, he did plan the calvados cocktail! But was it the act of a friend or foe?* He must have known that I couldn't help myself when it came to indulging in 'calva'. I'd been stupid enough to write about it plenty of times on my blog, and he'd clearly done his due diligence. Perhaps he was even more competitive than I realised.

Regretfully, I placed my drink aside. I needed a clear head to go into battle with these people.

Max went on to describe Henri's menu, which I had to admit sounded delicious, then told us all to have fun. I hesitated momentarily before raising my hand to ask a question. 'Will Christopher be joining us tonight?'

'He went home,' Max reported.

'Right,' I said. 'And that was his decision?'

'The feeling was mutual,' Max said, and then strode off.

I mulled this over while listening to how readily the other interviewees just accepted that Christopher had gone. Didn't they realise that one of us would be next? Sure, Christopher was an idiot, but now he was out of the running for this job because he couldn't put bait on a hook. Or was it because he fell unglamorously into the sea and needed to be saved like a child?

The fish was cooked on the barbecue, we were invited to eat, and it was all wonderfully flavoursome. Henri had opted for a spicier menu that I would have ever planned, but it worked. He paired the fish with beautiful white wines from the Loire Valley and Alsace. His accompaniments were simple, which I loved, and allowed the ingredients to shine. I should have been more annoyed that dinner was such a success, but my stomach was singing, and instead I felt joyful.

After dinner, everyone else seemed fairly jolly, too. The wine had been poured with no restraint, and the absence of Carla had gradually made everyone relax, even me. There were rumours circulating that she wouldn't arrive that evening at all, but rather that we'd be seeing her the following day. There was talk of the interviews taking place after breakfast. I think this prompted us to all let our guards down a little. I even risked an extra couple of glasses of wine.

At some point, somebody put on some music, and when Brigitte Bardot started playing over the speakers, Belle pulled everyone up to dance. I had to admit it was a relief let loose, to shake away the anxieties of the day.

I noticed Balthazar and Juliette slip off into the garden at one point, him grabbing her hand as they walked down the stairs, laughing like teenagers. The prospect of them getting together was in equal parts hilarious and stupid. They were here for a job interview, not a singles retreat. I could only imagine Max's reaction if he found out. Their actions seemed so short-sighted to me – Max had been watching all of our movements closely since the moment that we stepped off that train. But maybe their egos were like shields to them. Maybe they felt invincible.

It was at this point that I stopped drinking wine and switched to water.

Seconds later, a searchlight lit up the sky above and I heard a whooshing-thumping noise getting louder and louder above us.

At first, I felt scared, confused by the intense change in vibe. My heart started to race and my mind sobered up with the flick of a switch.

And then I realised what was going on ...

It was a helicopter. Landing in the gardens beyond the terrace.

But who could be arriving via helicopter so late at night?

I was actually surprised how long it took for my brain to register.

Carla Duris. It had to be Carla Duris.

When the rotors stopped their violent spinning, out Carla stepped, looking impressively poised and elegant in her chef's jacket with tight black jeans and high heels. Had she flown directly from Paris? Had she just finished work? She floated across the lawn towards us, her smile lighting up the evening sky.

Max intercepted her and whispered something into her ear.

Meanwhile, Juliette and Balthazar reappeared on the staircase, still giggling, although more discreetly now.

The music was cut, leaving us in complete silence.

Carla and Max approached the terrace where we waited, dumbfounded, shifting about and eyeing each other as if to say *did you know about this?*

Carla's sudden appearance seemed to have reminded us that we were here to compete against each other for the same job. The general consensus had been that she would arrive the next morning, and I was left wondering if perhaps somebody had started this rumour to throw the rest of us off guard. The drinks had been flowing and waiters had been topping up our glasses all night. Had this been intentional? I tried to get my racing thoughts in order, but the task felt near impossible.

Instead, I stood as still as possible, trying to match Carla's poise and confidence. I noticed Belle wobbling slightly beside me and felt some relief that we were in a similar state.

Carla finally broke the silence: 'I'm so sorry I have missed the start of our fabulous weekend together. I trust you've been in good hands.'

We nodded.

'So far,' Carla began, and then paused for a moment ... 'through the eyes of my trusted Max, I've tested your stamina, your adaptability, but also I've got a sense of who you all are as people.'

Another pause.

She has been watching!

'Now, it's finally time to get to the fun part. I want to discover how *you* see *me*, if you understand what I'm all about. Not because I'm vain and want a polished version of myself portrayed in my memoir, but because I want to see if you really know me. It is important that this book is a true reflection of my life so far, but also of how things are changing for me here in France. There has been a lot of gossip about me over the decades and I think it's time to set the record straight. I have big plans for the coming years, and this memoir will be the beginning.'

As Carla spoke, a nervous excitement grew in the air.

'So, let us get to work making up for lost time,' she said, rubbing her hands together.

We looked on, unsure of what she meant.

Max clarified: 'Carla will now be conducting interviews with you all individually.'

There was a collective gasp.

He continued: 'Juliette, your presence shall not be required. You can pack your bags and I'll arrange for you to be taken to the train station this evening.'

'What?' she squealed.

'I won't embarrass you by detailing why. Please leave before I have you escorted out.'

Carla gave a coquettish laugh and raised her eyebrows at Juliette, somehow looking completely unsurprised.

'Best of luck in the future, *ma belle*,' Carla called out as Juliette walked unsteadily towards the bedrooms.

Carla turned back to us. 'Right, I will see the rest of you one at a time in my office, please. Max, I will leave you in charge.' He gave her a nod.

Carla strode off, leaving us staring in her wake. Leaving us to fret. Leaving us, once again, in the hands of Max, who had magicked up his clipboard from somewhere and was about to guide us to our fate.

Chapter 25

The Second Departure – JULIETTE

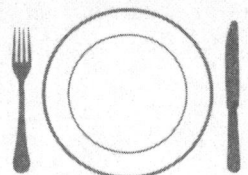

Oh mon dieu, how will I ever live this down? Juliette thought to herself as she was packing her bags.

And just when Carla had arrived at the villa – the timing was awful! She hadn't even had the chance to properly interview for the role.

Alors, so what if she'd peed behind some bushes? Balthazar had done the same thing.

Juliette couldn't be sure, however, if it was the public urination that had led to her dismissal, or the fact that she'd been kissing Balthazar only moments prior to the helicopter's arrival.

Juliette knew that Carla demanded loyal men. Loyal, *handsome* men. What she hadn't realised was that Carla would remove the threat of another woman before removing the handsome man.

When mulling this over, Juliette convinced herself that the only reason she had been asked to leave was because Carla was either jealous of her, or threatened by her.

Juliette hadn't realised until that moment that Carla was so old-school. She had expected her to lift up the women around her, not tear them down.

After coming to the emotional conclusion that Carla was just a jealous old crone, Juliette felt less embarrassed, and more empowered. 'Women like me are going to rule this scene in the coming years, and people like Carla will have to watch their backs,' she said aloud to no one in particular.

With her head held high, Juliette left the villa in a cloud of delusion, feeling wonderfully positive about her future.

Chapter 26

The Chef's Arrival – HENRI

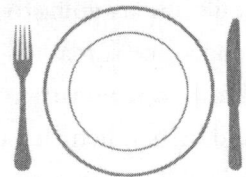

I wasn't completely surprised when Carla showed up in a helicopter. Well, I guess I was a little thrown, but I had half expected something like this from her.

Carla Duris loved to keep people on their toes. She had a habit of arriving in her kitchens unannounced, or of visiting her dining rooms in disguise. I had been lulled into a false sense of security, thinking that we were at least safe to enjoy ourselves for the evening.

Et, non!

After Carla went inside to her office, we were left, once again, with gatekeeper Max, unsure of how the tête-à-tête meetings were about to unfold.

I wished I hadn't created such fantastic wine parings for the dinner that evening because, despite my best intentions, I'd probably overindulged. At least I knew I wasn't the only one who was a little over their limit.

Max announced the order of the interviews, and a little hope returned to my body.

'Balthazar ... Belle ... Henri ... Chloe.'

The order had apparently been chosen at random, but still, I was relieved that I wasn't up first, particularly after Juliette's sudden departure. I didn't want to go into that room without finding out what she'd done wrong. If I could at least learn from her errors, she'd have given me something concrete to work off. That, and the knowledge that Carla had just fired some chefs from Chez Duris. That *had* to mean something, although I hadn't yet figured out what.

Balthazar strode gallantly with Max into the house. Rather than looking nervous, he looked primed for action. His confidence had me questioning if he hadn't suspected Carla might arrive at any moment. Come to think of it, I wasn't sure I'd seen him drinking much that evening. He actually appeared relatively sober. Maybe he was smarter than he looked.

He left me, Belle and Chloe on the terrace.

We made quick work of ordering coffees from the lingering waitstaff and gulping down water.

I was tempted to sit apart from the girls to try to get my thoughts in order before my interview, but I couldn't resist spending time with Chloe. She looked anxious. If there was any way that I could ease her fears, even if just slightly, I wanted to try. Plus, I felt guilty. I had designed a menu that included a strong cocktail I knew she would love. If she felt in any way inebriated, I had been partly responsible.

Belle didn't seem put out by Carla's abrupt arrival, she just took it in her stride. *Damn those laid-back California girls*, I thought. Despite having an American mother, I couldn't adopt the same carefree attitude towards life. You can take the man out of Paris, but not Paris out of the man.

'What the hell happened with Juliette?' Chloe asked eventually.

'Wasn't it wild!' Belle exclaimed. 'Okay, so don't quote me on this, but I think a security guard or someone busted her peeing down in the gardens. I heard a waiter talking about it just before. Honestly, it seems like they've got eyes everywhere in this place.'

I almost choked on my coffee, thinking about my conversation with Christopher.

'You really think that's why she's gone?' Chloe asked, sounding equally entertained and horrified. 'I can't imagine Juliette peeing in the garden!'

'Doesn't really fit that pristine image of hers, does it? But honestly, I think she'd had more cocktails than all of us put together, and she's only a tiny little thing. Balthazar was with her of course, but I think he managed to escape unseen. The joys of being able to pee standing up, lucky boy,' she said.

'We could be back in Paris having this exact conversation,' Chloe said. 'At least here, the smell of urine is masked by the fresh sea air.'

The girls looked at each other knowingly and I wondered if they'd forgotten I was even sitting there. I cleared my throat, just in case.

'Do you think this will be the only interview?' Belle asked.

'I hope it's just a preliminary interview,' Chloe said. 'She can't expect too much from us at this hour, right?'

'It's very Carla to swoop in at the last minute and make an entrance. She's the queen of the stealth attack,' I said.

'Is that what this is?' Chloe asked. 'An attack?'

'No, that's not what I meant,' I said.

'Should we be nervous?' Chloe asked. 'Or rather, should I be *more* nervous than I already am?'

'No point fretting, now,' said Belle. 'Besides, I'm pretty sure I left my nerves in my cocktail glass hours ago,' she added with a twinkle in her eye.

'Oh god,' said Chloe.

'Just be yourself and you will be *parfaite*,' I told her.

'That's easy for you to say, Henri,' she replied. 'It was your dinner menu that landed us in this predicament.'

'I am sorry that I have good taste,' I said, attempting a joke, but it fell flat.

We waited quietly, a sense of foreboding in the air. Balthazar's interview seemed to be taking a long time. I felt as though an hour had elapsed since he had gone inside. It was getting late now. The sun had well and truly gone down.

I wish I could have said I wasn't nervous myself, but I would have been lying. Who knew what Carla was planning for us? Or how long any of us would last in that room with her.

Another fifteen or so minutes later, Max reappeared and asked Belle to follow him, leaving Chloe and me alone together.

'Balthazar was in there for quite a while,' Chloe said to me, alarm in her eyes.

'That could be a good or a bad thing, though, right?' I replied.

We waited a few minutes after Belle's departure to see if Balthazar would be joining us again. When he didn't come back, Chloe seemed even more agitated.

'Do you think he's gone?' she asked me.

'I doubt it. That guy seems to have nine lives,' I said.

Chloe went quiet for a minute.

'I think Belle will do great,' she said eventually.

'So will you,' I insisted.

'No thanks to everything that's already gone down this weekend,' she said.

I wanted to ask her what that meant, but wasn't sure how to do so without pissing her off. Instead, I tried to take her mind off things by asking her what she'd planned for the menu tonight.

'Who cares? I wasn't chosen.'

'I care,' I said. 'I think you have great taste.'

She looked at me thoughtfully, as if she was wondering whether she could trust me. *Why has she gotten it into her head that I'm the bad guy?* I asked myself in vain.

'So? Your menu?' I prompted with a smile.

Finally, she gave in and told me what she had planned.

'That all sounds amazing,' I said.

'But not as good as Monsieur Henri de la Fontaine's,' she said with a smirk.

'Did you add a cocktail to yours? I assume that's what got me over the line,' I said with a laugh.

'I did not. Nor did I think to include matching wines. I guess I'm not very experienced at orchestrating expensive dinner parties.'

I went to defend her, again, but I saw a smile on her face and realised she was joking. What a relief it was to see her relax a little. I was pleased to have finally figured out her soft spot: talking about food. Ingredients, dishes and flavours were her happy place. Her whole face lit up when she talked about the world of eating and dining, and even though I was stressed about what this interview would bring, just being with Chloe brought me some peace.

She asked me about the inspiration for my fish recipes and I told her about my trip to Nice with my parents when I was sixteen, and how we'd gone out for dinner and I'd had one of the most memorable meals of my life.

'I thought the food stuff came from your uncle,' she said.

Clearly, she'd done her research on me, too.

'Not all of it,' I told her. 'Occasionally, I've escaped his influence and managed to form my own opinions.'

'Is that why you're really here? To get away from him?'

How had she so quickly understood so much about me? How was she brave enough to talk to me so bluntly about something that everyone else seemed to dance around?

'Well, yeah. I want this job. I would like a fresh start without any of the baggage I have at *Le Cercle.*'

'I get it,' she said with a knowing look.

I heard footsteps and then Max appeared. I felt like Belle had only just gone in to meet with Carla, but when I checked my watch, I realised it had been almost an hour. I attributed the quick passing of time to the Chloe Effect.

'*À vous*, Henri,' Max instructed.

I gave Chloe one last look – *mon dieu*, was she lovely to look at – and then followed Max at his rapid pace down the corridor and into Carla's epic office.

Carla was sitting behind a huge desk, all wooden and luxurious.

There were two things in front of her: an iPad and a glass of Champagne.

She looked calm and serene, but less friendly than I'd been hoping.

'Well, Henri,' she said, her thick French accent rolling the 'r' almost aggressively in her mouth.

'Madame Duris,' I said, more nervously than I would have liked.

A pause, then a slight grin appeared in the corner of her mouth, followed by, thank god, a smile.

'Henri, I have known about you through your uncle for a very long time,' she continued. 'He and I go back many years, although due to the nature of his job, you will understand why we've never been particularly close. He was Paris's most revered critic in his day, and to be seen colluding with him would have shown people that perhaps ...' She paused and I waited. 'That perhaps his perspective could not be trusted. So, we were never friends, and I respected that. And it feels like you're following in his footsteps.'

I nodded slowly, unsure of how to respond.

She continued: 'You do many things like your uncle,

however, I feel like you are two very different people. Your personality is much harder to decipher than his ever was.'

'Hmm,' I murmured.

'What I'd like you to tell me tonight is who you are outside of your job – or should I say, your uncle's former job. Who is the Henri that chose to come down here for this interview?'

She sat back in her seat, indicating that she was finished talking. It was my turn now, and she'd led with what I considered one of the hardest questions to answer. Who am I? There had been no warm-up, no small talk. We were straight in at the deep end.

I thought for a moment and she tapped her fingers quietly on the desk, making the silence between us almost unbearable.

Who am I outside of my job?

I needed to buy myself some time.

'First of all, I wanted to say thank you for including me in this interview process. It was a huge honour to be shortlisted for this role, and I'm so grateful to you and Max for the opportunity.'

She nodded, clearly seeing right through me.

I swallowed. I could feel sweat prickling under my arms.

'I suppose what I'm getting at is that I'm grateful to be considered for such a role because it is so much more aligned with what I actually want to be doing.'

Okay, brain, now we're getting somewhere, I thought, relieved.

'Don't get me wrong. I love writing about food, more than

anything, but I hate the restrictions at *Le Cercle*. I hate having to follow the same boring format that my uncle upheld for years, just because of "tradition". I want to break free from this idea that all my thoughts on the French food scene need to fit neatly into certain columns. It doesn't allow for much creativity, or the exploration of ideas. Which is why, I suppose, the invitation to interview for this opportunity was so appealing.'

She was paying attention now, but it was hard to read if she was engrossed in what I was saying, or if she was bored by it.

'Carla, writing for you would allow me to escape the confines of traditional journalism and do something new. I'd love to get to know you more, to get to tell your story in the way you'd like to tell it to the world.'

I looked at her imploringly.

'So, you want to use *my* memoir as a way to "escape", as you say?' she asked.

Her eyes pierced into mine and I could feel the panic rising in my throat, but I tried to remain calm. She wasn't accusing me of anything; she was just trying to clarify my position.

'Not escape, I suppose, rather build upon. If I were to get this job writing for you, I'd be able to use all of my expert food knowledge and write you something that was steeped in the tradition of French food and culture, while at the same time being modern and chic.'

Here, I thought of Chloe, of her Australianness, of her foreignness. I shouldn't be highlighting that I would be better for this job because I was French, but I couldn't take that back now. Besides, I was here to get a job for myself, not for Chloe.

'Right,' she said. 'And tell me about the weekend so far.'

'It's been perfectly fine,' I said, trying to figure out what kind of answer she was after. 'The tennis was a wonderful way to kick things off, the boat ride was energising, the menu design was thought-provoking, and I believe I did quite well with it.'

Annoyingly, I could feel myself blush.

'And the lunch?' she asked.

'It was challenging being blindfolded, but it helped awaken the senses,' I said.

'And who do you think should be eliminated before the next round this weekend?' she asked, her tone matter of fact.

Mon dieu! I thought. *What a question!*

I paused only momentarily before answering, 'Balthazar.'

'And why did you hesitate?' she asked.

'Because it was hard to pick only one,' I replied, off the cuff. This obviously wasn't true – I believed that Chloe and Belle *did* have a right to be here – but I'd had to show some sort of resolve or she would have found me weak. The need for self-preservation was becoming more apparent the longer we spoke.

'Who else, then?' she asked.

'Belle,' I said, regretfully.

'Final question,' she said, and I panicked. The other interviews had gone on for much longer than mine. Was this a bad omen? Was she getting ready to dismiss me?

'How far are you willing to go to get this job?' she asked.

I took a deep breath. 'I'll do anything legal to get this job,' I said, with certainty.

'Nothing illegal, then?' she asked with an innocent smile.

I shook my head, then added as an afterthought, 'Well, I guess it would depend on the level of illegality.' Thinking about it, there were actually plenty of illegal things I'd be willing to do, and not just for a job, but it felt wrong to be admitting this aloud.

'You can go,' she said, and knocked on her desk.

'Can I ask you a question?' I said, annoyed by the reappearance of nerves in my voice.

'*Oui*,' she said, tilting her head as Max entered the room swiftly.

'Why are you choosing to write a memoir now?'

She looked at me intensely, as if weighing up whether, or how, to answer, so I continued. 'It's just that the public have wanted to read your memoir for years. Why now?'

'All will be revealed in the goodness of time,' she said. 'Now Max, take the lovely Henri back to his room, please.'

She paused, eyeing me carefully. 'Oh, and Henri, I'd like you to write a thousand words about this interview. Slip it in an envelope and leave it outside your door by midnight.'

I tried to keep my expression neutral, but I could hardly believe she was asking us to write an article at this time of day, after such an intense start to the weekend. The thought alone was completely overwhelming, never mind the lack of instructions, or information.

'Easy,' I said to her with a smile that was wide enough to hide my insecurities. 'It'll be done by 11.30pm.'

I could have kicked myself. *Why on earth did I just say that?*

'As you wish,' she said. 'Before you go, Henri, I trust you

already know that I will make this job financially worth your while, *oui*?'

I nodded, but honestly I hadn't actually considered the pay. Working with Carla would always be about more than just a figure on a pay cheque.

'And if you are successful, I'd like to invite you to lead my next venture, whatever it shall be,' she said.

I tried to match her collectedness, but I could feel a smile creeping across my face. This offer alone was a big deal.

'If there's nothing further, then,' Carla said, dismissing me. 'Max, collect Henri's envelope at 11.30. Good luck.'

Max led me back to my room, avoiding the terrace and any opportunity I might have had to see Chloe and give her a reassuring smile, to try to tell her that the interview wasn't as terrifying as she might have been expecting.

Returning to my room, I got to work on the article immediately. I had a near-impossible deadline to meet, and I hadn't left myself any wiggle room.

Chapter 27

The Interview – CHLOE

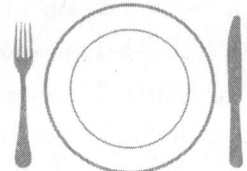

When Henri left for his interview with Carla, I found myself alone on the terrace. If I'd been nervous before, I swiftly moved to peak anxiety. I wondered if I might vomit. Then I wondered if that might help. Surely I wouldn't be evacuated (as I was now coming to refer to it) for having had one too many glasses of wine? But as Christopher and Juliette's departures had shown, there were no rules down here. I must have tried to picture my interview with Carla at least a hundred times since dinner earlier that week. Of all the ways I'd imagined it would play out, this had not been one of them.

In an effort to centre myself, I replayed everything that had unfolded since Carla had arrived – *in her helicopter!*

Almost immediately, the mood on the terrace had changed as we frantically tried to sober up. I wondered if Carla's plan all along had been to get us relaxed enough that we'd let loose, only to then reel us back in, like fish from the water, and show us who was boss.

I thought about Henri's words of reassurance, and

although I wanted to trust him, I still couldn't be sure of his intentions. He had openly admitted that he wanted this job, that he was ready to sacrifice pretty much everything he'd worked for in Paris to get it, so how could I believe a word he said? But then again, he'd felt so genuine, and been so kind.

I knew I couldn't let my guard down, but at the same time, I could feel myself growing more and more attracted to Henri. The timing was far from ideal.

I was surprised when Max reappeared and told me it was my turn. Henri's interview had been the quickest so far. Part of me assumed it was because he'd been able to charm her so quickly, but another part couldn't help wondering if he'd said something wrong and had been evacuated, too.

When I entered Carla's office, she was sitting on a plush white couch in the corner, sipping a glass of red wine.

She gestured to the couch opposite her, inviting me to sit, and asked me if I would like to join her for a drink. I accepted, and then immediately regretted it, wondering if Carla wanted her memoir writer to be more serious, or at least more sober, than I was in that moment.

At least the wine helped settle my nerves somewhat. I was sitting tête-à-tête with my cooking idol, so I guess it was only natural that I could feel my heart thumping in my chest. I just hadn't expected my stomach to feel like it had been left out there on the yacht on the Mediterranean Sea.

'If I am to believe your blog,' Carla said slowly, with a smile, 'you are a fan of me and my father.'

I giggled like a fangirl, unable to help myself. She'd read my blog!

'I am, yes,' I said. 'I've been following you since I started learning how to cook. You're a big part of the reason that I moved to France and began writing about food.'

'I am flattered, truly, but Chloe, you must tell me something,' she said, getting straight to the point.

I sat up a little taller. Even if I didn't feel prepared for this interaction, I had to pretend that I was.

'I need you to tell me if you have what it takes to write about some of the less flattering aspects of my life,' she said.

I thought of the rumours that circulated about Carla, about her private life, about her manner in the kitchen. 'This is your memoir. I will write whatever you feel needs to be included,' I said as resolutely as I could. I wanted to let her know that I was on her side, whichever side that might be.

'Chloe, I know that scandal sells,' she said with a glint in her eye. 'But I need this memoir to serve a different purpose.'

I looked at her, waiting for her to continue, but we sat for at least a minute in silence.

'You see, the rumours have not always been kind to me,' she eventually said.

'I can imagine that growing up in the spotlight must have been very challenging at times,' I said.

'Chloe, tell me if I'm wrong, but you grew up with a large family, *non*? Fishing, I believe?' she asked, steering the conversation away abruptly from herself.

'That's correct,' I said, almost nervously.

'And what did you learn from all of that?' she asked.

I thought for a moment about how best to summarise what my upbringing meant to me.

'Growing up with all that nature around me was like growing up with extra space in which to explore, to think, and to dream. Sure, I didn't have access to the same art and culture as the children who grew up in the city, but I feel that it was this same distance that left my mind free to understand who I was. At other times, I was bombarded with my brothers' energy, and growing up as the only girl in a family of boys taught me quickly that I had to fight for my right to be heard, but that talking loudly wasn't always the best way to do that. I guess that's why I love expressing myself through writing. Yelling was never my forte, but leave me alone with a pen and paper and I feel like I can take on the world.'

She nodded, almost approvingly.

'And what do you make of the weekend so far?' she asked.

'It's been a series of challenges,' I said.

'Very good,' she replied.

Emboldened by Carla's reaction, I went on. 'You've tested our strength, our agility, our determination, our ability to taste and discern, our resourcefulness.'

'Mmm,' she said, taking a slow sip of her wine. 'And where did you struggle?'

'I don't like not knowing the full picture, so the ambiguity of the tasks bothered me,' I said.

'This will make it difficult to begin writing a memoir, no?' she asked.

'It will only make it difficult if there is no chance to go back and edit things,' I said, practically.

'And do you think we can go back and rewrite history?' she asked.

'No, but I think you can mould it in a way that makes people understand the motivations behind certain decisions and allows for grace and understanding,' I said.

'I like that,' she replied, nodding.

I was feeling more hopeful, but then suddenly she drained her glass and knocked twice on the coffee table between us.

Max entered the room.

'One final thing, Chloe. If you get the job, this will be your remuneration.'

She handed me a card; it was the same stationery the initial dinner invitation had been printed on. I flipped it over and had to stop myself from gasping. Not only was the amount she was offering exorbitant in comparison to what I currently earned, it had the capacity to be life-changing.

'And I will give you an apartment in Paris when the job is finished.'

'Excuse me?' I said, sure I'd misunderstood.

'An apartment. Small compared to this place,' she said, motioning around her office with her hand, 'but I'm sure you'll enjoy it.'

I stuttered something unintelligent in reply and she just gave me one of her winning smiles, all serene and graceful.

'Max, see Chloe back to her bedroom, please,' she instructed. 'Oh, and Chloe, I'll need 1000 words about this interview, in an envelope outside your door by midnight, please.'

I picked my jaw up from the floor and managed a confident-sounding, '*Oui, bien sûr*, absolutely.'

I had no idea what I was going to write, but I'd make something work. I had to.

At least I am still here, I thought to myself as I followed Max back through the house. I listened carefully as we passed Henri's room, but all was quiet and there was no light on under his door.

Was there a chance he'd already been evicted?

Even though that would mean one less competitor, I didn't want to believe it could be true.

When I sat down to write my piece for Carla, I was overcome with doubt. I feared being asked to leave, I feared missing out on this opportunity and I feared the prospect of having to go back to my job at the hotel.

I paced the room, trying to focus. It was game on.

But how can I play the rest of the weekend to make sure I walk out of this villa with the job? What can I do to prove myself? I wondered.

The only thing I was sure about was that I wanted to work with Carla. I wanted to build my career in France, and I didn't want to return home to Australia. I loved my life in Paris. I loved writing about food and I wanted to keep doing it. Yes, it would mean a life on the other side of the world, away from my family, but they would understand. Besides, with the salary Carla had offered me, I'd be able to fly home a lot more often. I'd even be able to fly my parents to Paris, if they would agree to come.

But time was ticking, and I needed to write something down on paper if I had any hope of staying.

I pulled out a pen and began to write. I wrote about the interview I'd just had with Carla, but from the perspective of a much older version of myself, reflecting back on it as one of the most important moments of my life. A turning point, the moment everything fell into place for me. Perhaps it wasn't my most polished work, but it was good, and I felt confident putting the pages into an envelope and sliding it under the door.

After midnight, I got into bed but remained awake for a long time, staring at the shadows cast across my room and onto the very high ceiling.

I wondered whether Belle, Balthazar and Henri were still in the villa.

Eventually, I built up the courage to give a quick knock-knock on Henri's wall. Nothing bold or brash, more of what I hoped was a *Hey, are you still there?* knock.

My effort was met with silence, and I felt a familiar ball of anxiety in my stomach. Maybe he just hadn't heard me. I decided to knock again, a little louder this time. And then I waited again, my heart sinking at the realisation that he might actually have gone home.

Chapter 28

The Knock – HENRI

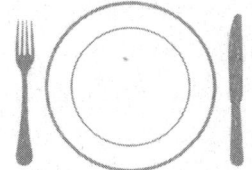

I'd been awake for what felt like hours, trying in vain not to overanalyse my interview with Carla (and failing), when I heard a knock on the wall between my bedroom and Chloe's.

I froze, unsure whether to trust my ears.

At first, I thought I'd imagined it. After all, I'd just been picturing Chloe in the interview with Carla, wondering if their conversation had gone well.

And then there was another, louder knock.

I felt my body relax. Chloe was still in the villa, and so was I. On that front, I guess, everything that evening had played out perfectly.

I knocked back softly, smiling like a fool even though she couldn't see me.

It meant a lot to me, her little knock. It meant that she cared enough to check that I was still there. It meant that she was thinking about me, too.

After our clandestine exchange, I finally relaxed enough to fall into something resembling sleep.

Chapter 29

The Painting Challenge – CHLOE

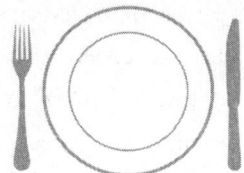

I woke up around 9am to the sun streaming through the curtains and felt momentarily peaceful – until I remembered where I was and what I was doing. I shot out of bed in a panic, rushing over to the bedroom door.

As I'd expected, there was a new note on the floor.

Breakfast in the garden at 9.30am
Dress casually

Relief flooded through my body. I must have passed the written component of the interview. We were onto a new day and, as terrifying as this prospect was, it was good news. Being here meant I still had a shot at getting the job. And after Christopher and Juliette's sudden departures and my late-night panic that Henri had joined their ranks, I wasn't going to take being here for granted.

I raced to get ready.

Stepping outside, I discovered it was another picture-perfect day in the south of France. The sun was bright, the sky a deep blue, and a few marshmallow clouds were dotted artistically across the horizon. It was going to be a hot day – the air hung thick and heavy. The grass was soft underfoot; it made me want to take my shoes off and sink down deep into it.

I wasn't sure what I'd been expecting to see in the garden, but it certainly wasn't four easels and painting stations set up in a wide circle. Having finally been told how much this job was worth – both financially and prestigiously – Carla now expected us to paint? It seemed surreal, but then again, what about this weekend so far had been normal?

A small breakfast table had been laid to one side, and Balthazar, Belle and Henri were standing around sipping coffee and eating croissants. Belle and Henri turned to me with huge smiles on their faces. My joy at seeing them still here was clearly mutual. Henri then looked bashful, as if remembering our late-night through-the-wall exchange.

'So, we're all still here,' I said to the trio standing before me.

'I hardly slept after that writing exercise,' admitted Belle.

'I always sleep like a baby,' said Balthazar.

'And you look like one too,' Henri sang quietly.

Nervous laughter escaped from me before I could stop it. It was a perfectly immature thing for Henri to have said, but the resulting scowl on Balthazar's face was comical. Henri gave me an eyebrow raise and a grin.

'Do we know what's with the painting equipment?' I asked.

'We haven't been told a thing yet,' said Belle.

'Is it a lesson, do you think?' I asked.

'We are writers. We are *créateurs*. Everybody here should know how to paint,' Balthazar said.

'Ahh ...' I went to object, but saw Max approaching and decided against it.

Max had exchanged his usual suit for linen pants and a linen shirt, all white. He looked like he was in some kind of artsy cult. The kind of cult that wouldn't actually be doing any painting.

'Good morning,' he said, giving us a micro-smile. 'Forgive me for skipping pleasantries, but we have a very full day ahead.'

I wanted to ask Max if he understood the definition of 'pleasantries', but thankfully managed to hold my tongue.

'Please, take an easel,' he barked, as if sensing my insubordination.

Balthazar strode around the circle inspecting each canvas, and then swiftly sat down at one.

I tentatively took a spot between Belle and Henri, perching on the little stool that had been set up before the easel, which held a startlingly empty, nerve-inducingly white canvas. The easels were positioned so we wouldn't be able to see what anyone else was painting. Whether this was a good or bad thing was yet to be established.

Max sauntered into the middle of our circle. 'As you all know, the south of France has been the inspiration for many of Europe's famous artists, particularly some of the finest painters – Picasso, Renoir, Matisse, Chagall ...' He paused, letting the weight of his list sink in.

As he did, my heart sank. I couldn't paint to save myself.

'Carla would therefore like to offer you the opportunity

to take inspiration from the air and the nature that surrounds you, and to paint a picture *of her*, in her beloved villa or its surrounds.'

Ah, what now? I thought. *Paint Carla?!*

'You have one hour,' he said, clapping his hands. 'And ... ready, spaghetti, paint.'

I looked at him and he smiled, obviously aware he was making a joke and revelling in our shock.

Then, he set a timer and walked off, leaving us in a cloud of worry and confusion.

I turned to Belle and mouthed, 'What the hell?'

She simply mouthed back, 'Farrrrrk!' and started frantically squirting tubes of paint onto her palette.

I stole a glance at Henri. He shared a name with Matisse, perhaps he also shared his aptitude for painting. We locked eyes and he shrugged slightly, then laughed; a hearty chuckle that I couldn't help but reciprocate. I guessed he was in the same boat as Belle and me then. It seemed that none of us – Balthazar excluded – knew how to paint.

I decided not to take the task too seriously, squeezing out paint and mixing colours in a haphazard way. I reasoned that an hour was hardly time enough to produce anything of great worth, so I tried to enjoy myself, hoping that injecting joy into my creation would somehow save me.

I looked over at Balthazar, who appeared to be fully invested in the task. He was standing up, flinging paint onto his canvas, looking more like a man gone wild than the arrogant guy I'd spent the last day or so with.

The sharp contrast between this activity – painting in the sunshine – and the one-on-one interviews last night had me feeling rattled. Making sense of this weekend was like trying to understand gravity in an Escher.

I wasn't sure exactly what Carla and Max were playing at, but it seemed like an attempt to throw us off guard. I mean, Carla was hardly going to kick somebody out for a bad painting, was she? *Was she?*

I heard Belle laugh next to me, and thankfully it broke the tension.

'How are you guys going?' I whispered.

Belle and Henri both shook their heads.

'What are you painting?' I asked Belle.

'Carla playing tennis,' she said. 'But it looks more like a unicorn vomiting while holding a racquet and a ball.'

I suppressed a giggle.

'Henri?' I asked.

'Carla in the kitchen,' he said.

Balthazar was still in some kind of genius zone and didn't even bother replying when I asked him.

'What are you painting?' Henri asked me.

'I'm attempting to paint Carla on her yacht, but the overall result seems to be getting more offensive with every brushstroke.'

'Are you including Christopher going overboard?' he asked, shooting me a devious smile.

I couldn't help a laugh. 'I don't think I have the technical capabilities to make that happen,' I told him.

'I bet you do,' he said, and turned back to his canvas.

Time at Carla's villa seemed to pass differently to time in Paris. We'd only been here for one day, but it felt like a lot longer.

From our group of six, two of us had already been asked to leave, and I got the feeling the next casualty wouldn't be far behind. In some ways, it was a shame, because I'd grown to like my fellow interviewees (Balthazar not included). If we'd all been down here for a weekend under different circumstances, I could imagine it being a lot of fun. But instead, we were all vying for the same job, the same ridiculous and life-changing opportunity to work with Carla. Now was certainly not the time to let my guard down.

I went back to my painting, attempting to make Carla more beautiful, or at the very least more human than the blob that was currently splodged on my canvas.

If I made it through this painting activity, it would be some kind of miracle.

Chapter 30

The Not-So Henri Matisse – HENRI

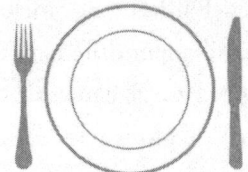

God, Chloe is a vision over there, I thought to myself. I was hardly able to focus on the task at hand with her sitting so close to me. A rogue drop of blue paint had dropped onto her leg, drawing my attention to the fact that that her skirt was ever-so-sexily riding up her legs.

I'd chosen to paint Carla in the kitchen, but the majority of the background was indistinguishable. Carla, however, had come out looking quite beautiful by some stroke of luck.

Thankfully, the timer was almost done and this painting challenge was almost over. I could picture Carla and Max falling about laughing while critiquing our efforts to recreate her. The whole artist thing was probably just for her amusement.

Max came back promptly on the hour and told us to put down our brushes. Four staff members came to collect our canvases and carried them off towards the villa, carefully shielding everyone's creations. While I would have loved to have seen the other paintings, perhaps it was a relief that nobody would see mine. Another little secret from this weekend that would remain well guarded, apparently.

'I shall return shortly with information about our next activity,' Max said, walking off in the direction of our canvases.

'What do you think all that was about then?' Belle asked, looking over at Chloe.

'Humiliation?' Chloe questioned.

'My painting looked like it had been done by a child,' Belle lamented.

'You mean it had a whimsical appearance,' Chloe suggested, waving her hand artistically in the air.

'And that's why you're the writer,' Belle told her with a laugh.

'You're very quiet, Balthazar,' I called over to him. 'Everything okay?'

'Henri, you should know that my grandfather was a painter. I take the craft very seriously.'

I heard a little snigger from Belle.

'And what did you paint?' I asked him.

'Carla, *à poil, nue*,' he said seriously.

'You chose to paint Carla naked?' I asked, baffled. 'Why?'

He nodded solemnly. 'I think she will approve.'

If Balthazar hadn't been taking all of this so seriously, I would have assumed he was joking. Painting Carla naked certainly wasn't a risk I would have been willing to take. Was he braver than me, or stupider? I guess we'd soon find out.

I watched carefully for Max's return. This weekend had me second-guessing everything, and I'd come to rely on Max to guide us. There was no denying there had been a weird shift in dynamic since we'd been at dinner earlier that week – he'd become like our leader in Carla's absence.

Instead, Carla walked out.

She was wearing a flowing beige linen dress that skimmed the grass beneath her, giving the impression that she was floating towards us.

'My darlings,' she said.

We waited for her to continue talking. Across from me, I heard Belle whisper a timid, 'Hello.'

I stole a glance at Chloe, who was sitting up straighter, giving Carla her undivided attention.

'Isn't painting the most wonderful way to express ourselves?' she asked.

I could see Balthazar nodding, but I remained unconvinced.

'Words can tell a very descriptive story, but sometimes it is through other mediums that I am really able to see into your soul.'

Merde, I thought.

'I have some artist friends inside who are now reviewing your work,' she continued.

Balthazar gasped, no doubt giddy with excitement.

'Each piece is helping me to get a better idea of your suitability for the task of working on my memoir, so thank you for your participation. Now, I must go and prepare for the rest of the day's activities. I will see some of you in the kitchens shortly. Please return to your rooms for the time being,' she finished, and floated away again.

'What does she mean by "some of us"?' Belle asked as we walked back to the villa.

'Surely a bad painting couldn't change anything,' Chloe said, in an attempt to reassure her.

'Of course it could,' said Balthazar with a snicker.

We went up to our rooms to await instructions on our next challenge.

When we reached our doors, Chloe turned to me. 'Henri, can I ask you a question?'

'Of course,' I said, moving closer to her.

'Do you think these activities are really necessary?' she asked me.

I wondered briefly if we were being listened to, if the microphones and cameras from outside the villa might also be concealed inside.

I took a calculated risk with my reply. 'Technically not, but then, Carla Duris isn't generally known for doing things the normal way,' I told her.

'I guess we've come this far,' she said with a half-smile. 'It'd be silly to pull out now, right?'

Was this a question or a statement?

'Just keep going. I'm sure it'll be worth it in the end,' I told her.

'I should probably just be grateful I'm still here,' she said.

I was about to say that of course she was still here, that she was probably the most talented out of all of us – except perhaps at painting – but she laughed in that Australian self-deprecating way and disappeared into her room before I could say anything more.

I wanted to warn her about the cameras, to not speak with anyone on the phone, or do anything that might jeopardise her place here, but I was worried that my advice would come across as controlling.

Chloe was right to question things. This was the most insane job interview I'd ever even heard of, let alone taken part in. Carla's methods were completely unconventional.

Just keep going, I repeated to myself.

Chapter 31

The Third Departure – BELLE

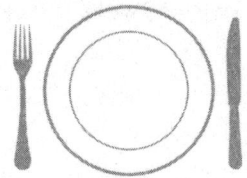

Holy crap, what the hell just happened? thought Belle as she packed her bags.

Never in her life had she imagined she would be excused early from a job interview because of her lack of painting abilities. But then, never in her life had she come across anybody quite like Carla Duris.

Belle had only just returned to her room after the painting challenge when there was a sharp knock on the door. Opening it, she had been surprised to find Carla standing there.

'Shall we talk?' Carla had said, brushing past Belle and sitting on the edge of the bed.

Belle agreed – what else could she do – and sat on the bed too, at what she felt was a respectful distance away.

'*Alors, ma belle, Belle,*' Carla purred.

Belle waited.

'You surprised me this morning,' she continued.

'Oh?' Belle questioned, unsure where their conversation was

going but feeling increasingly unnerved.

'Can I ask how you see me, as a chef and as a person?' Carla asked.

'I see you as a trail-blazing chef and an exacting person. You like the fine things in life,' she said, motioning around her, 'and you expect your employees to work to a certain standard, to be of a certain calibre.'

'Hmm,' Carla said, considering this. 'Do you feel like I'm too hard on people?'

'No, but you have high expectations,' Belle replied.

'Is that a good or a bad thing?'

'In your line of work, it seems important.'

'So, if you think I am a good boss, why did you paint me like some kind of rainbow troll?' Carla asked.

Belle laughed, thinking that Carla was joking.

'You think this is funny?' Carla questioned, her tone changing instantly.

'No, it's just that I can't paint. I'm so sorry; I'm awful at anything artistic,' Belle reasoned nervously.

'Clearly, you think I am someone I am not,' Carla said.

'No, I didn't mean to insinuate that you were a rainbow troll, obviously,' Belle replied.

'You are not taking this seriously!' Carla scolded.

Belle paused, unsure of how to proceed. 'Carla, this job would mean the world to me, you know that,' she tried.

'I don't give second chances,' Carla replied.

'*It was a painting*,' Belle said, panic making her voice catch.

'You have lost,' Carla said.

'Lost what?' Belle asked.

'Pack your bags and leave ... immediately.'

Belle stared at her in disbelief. This couldn't be the end of the interview. Especially not after the *actual* interview the night before had gone so well.

Carla stood and flicked Belle's suitcase onto the ground.

'You don't belong here,' Carla snapped. 'It's a shame, because I've seen you swim. You could have won.'

'Won what?' Belle asked. 'This is a job interview, not a competition!'

'*Au revoir*,' Carla yelled angrily, slamming Belle's bedroom door as she left.

Belle sat motionless, unable to believe what had just happened. The change in disposition between pre-painting and post-painting Carla was striking, scary even.

On the one hand, Belle was disappointed to leave on such a ridiculous note, but on the other, she couldn't help thinking maybe she had just dodged a bullet. Beyond the ridiculousness of what they'd been asked to do thus far, she had been rejected because Carla found her painting too colourful? Too troll-like? It was almost laughable. That was where the relief came in – she wouldn't have to waste any more time trying to please a woman as unpredictable as Carla.

But then Belle thought of Chloe.

'I have to warn her that Carla is unstable,' she said to herself quietly, remembering with a shudder the terrifying look on Carla's face only moments earlier.

Belle bent forward to retrieve her suitcase and pack. 'But first, I want to get as far away from this place as possible.'

Chapter 32

The Cooking Challenge – CHLOE

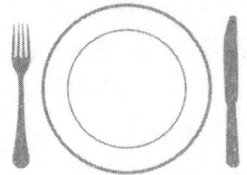

Back in my room, a little card had been left on my freshly made bed alongside a chef's jacket. I smiled, thanking the painting gods that I'd made it through to the next round, whatever that would turn out to be. I read the card:

> *Cooking challenge at 11.30am*
> *Theme: impress me*
> *CD*

I had to design a menu to impress Carla Duris? No pressure, obviously. Just something that would wow the socks off my cooking idol.

I couldn't help wondering why we needed to be able to cook to prove our suitability for the job of memoir writer, but at least cooking seemed more appropriate than painting. Carla's home was in the kitchen; maybe we had to prove that we could be at home there, too.

I needed to talk my menu through with someone.

My finger hesitated over the contact list in my phone before calling Drew.

'Hey, Drew,' I said when he finally picked up.

'You're still alive,' he said dramatically. I chuckled, but part of me was grateful that I was indeed still alive in the competition.

'I don't have long to chat,' I told him. 'But I was hoping to get some help.'

'Fire up, then,' he replied.

'I need to cook something to impress Carla,' I told him, in an attempt to be vague enough so that I wouldn't compromise the terms of the NDA.

'Just one dish? Sweet or savoury?' he asked, getting right to it.

'We've not really been given much direction,' I mumbled.

'You're also not chefs,' he unnecessarily reminded me.

'I guess she just wants to make sure we know our way around a kitchen.'

'Well, if it's a job in the kitchen you want, come back to Paris. I'll give you one,' he said.

'Ha, ha. I've made it this far. May as well see it through,' I said, not willing to get into the life-changing incentives of the job over the phone, not even sure that I legally could.

'So, what's your favourite thing to cook?' he asked.

'Any Carla Duris recipe,' I said without hesitating.

'Cooking other people's recipes for them, especially in a kitchen you're not familiar with, sounds a little risky. Why don't you cook her something Australian?' he suggested.

'I'm meant to *impress* her,' I said with a laugh. 'You want me to serve her up a meat pie? Throw another shrimp on the barbie?'

'You know Australian cooking is more than that,' he scolded, even though he knew I was joking.

'I wouldn't know where to start,' I said.

'A Tasmanian speciality? What about a scallop pie? Like that one you cooked on my birthday.'

'It's not too simple?' I asked.

'You could add hake. Double the fish, double the fun?' he suggested.

'That could work,' I said, the plan starting to buzz through my head.

'Good, glad to help,' he said, clearly getting ready to hang up.

'Hold on,' I said. 'Should I make something sweet?'

'What do you think?' he asked.

'I did wonder if she'd enjoy a lamington. Or would that be lame?' I asked.

'It'd be cute! And what kind of deranged person wouldn't love a lamington?'

'Right!' I agreed, glad to be on the same page.

'Just keep things simple, don't overcomplicate it,' he instructed.

'Look at you giving amazing advice,' I said.

'Well, you know what they say about people who give great advice: they can never follow it.'

'You're doing just fine,' I told him.

'Will I see you again in Paris at some point, or should I start looking for a new flatmate?' he asked.

'I'll probably be back tonight. Maybe earlier, if I get kicked out after the cooking challenge,' I said.

'Right, well, text me if you need anything else.'

'Thanks, Drew,' I said.

'Oh, and did you hear Carla is looking for a new head chef?' he asked.

'Umm, no! What the hell?' I asked.

'Does she seem worried?' he asked.

'Not in the slightest,' I said, wondering what had happened with her old head chef. Was this the reason she'd decided to write her memoir now? Was she trying to get ahead of something?

I had to put those thoughts aside to focus on the cooking challenge that lay ahead.

I thanked Drew and hung up, searching for recipes and making a plan for my time in the kitchen. I wasn't sure how long we'd have to cook, and I wanted to be economical with my movements.

My menu was simple, but everything needed to go off without a hitch if I had any hope of impressing Carla.

Chapter 33

The Chef's Jacket – HENRI

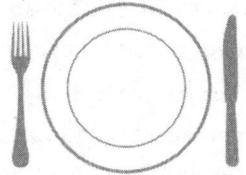

After the near-miss that was the painting activity, I returned to my room to find a note and a chef's jacket on my bed:

Cooking challenge at 11.30am
Theme: impress me
CD

I had work to do.

I thought about Chloe next door and wondered what she was going to cook. Chloe revered Carla's food, and I could imagine her panicking at the 'impress me' instruction. Even though we were competing, I still wanted to see her succeed.

I sat down at the little desk by the window to plan out a menu simple enough for me to execute well, but that would also impress Carla Duris. Shortly after, my phone rang, making me jump. I answered before I had time to consider if it was normal to be so on edge.

'*Oui,*' I said, clearing my throat.

'Hey big brother, still snoozing?' Lucy's voice sounded sprightly but also a little too sweet, like she had a confession to make.

'Not all of us have the luxury of a weekend off,' I said, waiting for her to get to the point.

'You are in the south of France on a free holiday!' she squealed with indignation.

'You don't know the half of it,' I said.

'Anyway, I was wondering ...' Lucy paused and my mind started racing. What kind of chaos could she have gotten herself involved in?

'Mmm?' I said.

'Well, I was wondering if could borrow your scooter?'

I thought of her crashing my shiny red Vespa and my heart sank.

'Lucy, have you already borrowed my scooter?' I asked.

'Ah, maybe ... But hear me out.'

'Lucy, you'd better not have had an accident,' I said.

'I'm fine,' she said.

'And the scooter?' I asked, nervously.

'It's just a little scratch. Cosmetic, really. I could probably patch it up with nail polish.'

I looked out the window, trying to draw composure from the beautiful view.

'Don't even try it. I'll get it fixed and you can give me the money,' I told her.

'About that,' she said.

'I know, I know. You're poor right now, but you promise to

pay me back one day. Look Lucy, I should probably go. I need to prepare ...'

'Oh yeah,' she said, sounding grateful for the change of topic. 'How's the interview going?'

I didn't really want to recount everything that had happened so far, because I felt like it wouldn't make sense to anyone who hadn't actually been here, plus there was the NDA to consider, but I told her about our yacht trip, because I knew she'd find it entertaining.

As I was getting to the best part, where Christopher fell off the boat, she interrupted me: 'Oh, I nearly forgot to mention. Papa said he saw Carla slipping out the Senate's back door and into Luxembourg Gardens the other day. Apparently, she's been having meetings with one of the senators, I forget who.'

I froze. *Why was Carla meeting with a senator?*

'Anyway ...' Lucy said, breaking my silence. 'When will you be back?'

'Oh, um, tonight, I assume. Maybe tomorrow morning.'

'What's on for the rest of the day?' she asked.

'Cooking, apparently,' I said.

'What kind of interview is this?' she asked.

'I'll let you know once I figure it out.'

'So, what are you going to cook?' she asked.

'Something French?' I questioned, thinking aloud.

'Why not make her a really amazing beef burger? She looks as though she hasn't eaten anything fatty and delicious in years. Or why not cook Mom's buttermilk-fried chicken? Show her your American side.'

The mere mention of our mom's chicken made my mouth water.

'You know what? I think that could be perfect,' I said. Carla probably hadn't eaten any good fried chicken since she left the States.

'Right, well, now that I've saved the day, enjoy!' she said, ending the call with a lightness that I wished I felt.

I made myself a shot of espresso, my mind coming back to Carla's visit to the Senate. *What had she been doing there?* One of the wilder rumours about Carla was that, a few years earlier, she'd been dating the President of the French Senate, a man old enough to be her father. People had often claimed she had a thing for men in positions of power. Maybe she'd gone back for more? A possible affair *could* be the impetus for her memoir. Did she want to publish her side of the story first? Or was there something she was trying to cover up?

Chapter 34

The Heat in the Kitchen – CHLOE

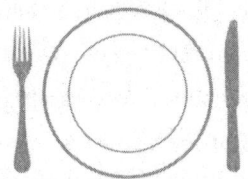

I walked nervously down the stairs, unsure of where to go or who I'd see as I tried to make my way to the kitchen. It was a weird feeling, being in somebody's house when you didn't really know what was going on with any of the other guests.

I was wearing my chef's jacket – quite cute, actually – and had a little cooking cheat sheet tucked neatly into the pocket of my jeans. I felt ready to go. Sort of. I took a deep breath and told myself that things would be okay, even if today didn't go well. Life *would* continue beyond the confines of Carla's villa. There was, in fact, a world outside of this interview weekend, and it was a life that up until a few days ago I'd quite enjoyed. But now, a Carla-shaped carrot had been dangled in front of me and I felt determined to get it.

Max met me at the bottom of the stairs and escorted me towards the kitchen. Walking in, I saw the backs of two other people in chef's jackets.

Two men. No women. No Belle.

No Belle!

Carla was at the front of the room, also wearing a chef's jacket. There was a hint of excitement in her eyes. She smiled at me as I took my spot beside Balthazar and Henri.

'Now that everyone is here,' Max said, joining Carla, 'I shall give you three important pieces of information about this morning's cooking challenge. 1. You will have two hours to complete the challenge. 2. No questions. 3. No holds barred. Your workstations are named, you can begin.'

I chanced a look at Henri to see if he was as surprised about Belle's absence as I was, but he was looking straight ahead.

Carla smiled and clapped her hands. 'May the best cook win!' she called out amid the chaos as the three of us began setting up. I started by checking out the tools I had to work with. Flustered, I started grabbing mixers and bowls. When a spoon clattered to the floor, drawing everyone's attention, I knew I needed to calm down.

I took a second to regroup. Two thoughts were racing through my mind: 1. Where the hell was Belle? and 2. What the hell did Max mean by 'no holds barred'?

Under the workbench, I discreetly whipped out my phone and opened Instagram. I found Belle's profile and sent her a message asking what had happened, then I shoved my phone back into my pocket and started to gather everything I needed to mix the batter for the lamingtons. I figured the sponge base would need about half an hour to cook. I'd easily have enough time to make the fish pie while the sponge was in the oven, if all went smoothly.

I hadn't been overly ambitious with my menu planning, but

I felt that if I could execute these dishes well, I could impress Carla, as per the theme of the challenge. I *had* to execute these dishes well – there was no plan B.

My heart was pounding as I looked around to see what my competition was cooking up. Henri had an extraordinary number of ingredients out on his bench and Balthazar was getting out some weird cooking implement that I'd never even seen before, let alone used.

Maybe I needed to step it up a little? I rushed to the pantry and fridges to look for some more luxury ingredients. Perhaps I could make an entrée? I spotted a jar of caviar, but it didn't really feel like me. My head was brimming with possibilities, but I only had two hours. I just needed to stick to my plan, I decided.

'*You okay?*' Henri whispered to me as I checked the oven settings.

'I guess. Just not sure if I'm doing the right thing,' I replied quietly.

'How do you define "right thing"?' he asked.

'Something to impress Carla,' I said.

'You've impressed *me*,' he said, and I couldn't help a little laugh.

'You think now is a good time to tell me that?'

'When I get stressed, I have this horrible habit of telling the truth,' he said with a smile.

'What about you? Are you okay?' I asked him, in reference to both his cooking and his mental state. It was the first time I'd actually seen him sweating.

'Absolutely not,' he said. 'If I make it through this, I'll be very surprised.'

'May the best cook win,' I said.

'May the best cook win,' he returned, mimicking Carla's accent and making me laugh again.

I shook myself back into the moment. If I had any hope of pulling this off, I had to stop getting sidetracked. Besides, what if Henri was distracting me intentionally? Was going on a charm offensive his idea of 'no holds barred'?

Once I started to smell my sponge cake baking, my thoughts calmed down. My mouth was watering. That was a good sign. Lamingtons were simple yet delicious. Perhaps I was in with a chance yet.

I felt my phone vibrate in my pocket. *A message from Belle?*

With everything that was going on around me, I didn't feel brave enough to check. Any slip-up at this point could be the difference between getting the job and going home. There was too much at stake.

Chapter 35

The Jump Out of the Frying Pan – HENRI

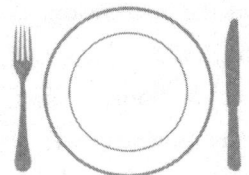

I was feeling pretty positive about the cooking challenge. Sure, I would have liked more time in the kitchen, but two hours actually felt pretty generous. Especially knowing Max could easily have decided to squeeze the task into twenty minutes.

What had surprised me was Belle's absence. She'd been there at the painting activity this morning, so full of joy and excitement, and now she was gone. Either her painting had been truly awful, or something else had happened. Honestly, it felt a little off. Not that I let my thoughts show; not in front of Carla. Still, it was a shame. Belle had been a breath of fresh air in this competition, and it would have been fun cooking alongside her now. From what I'd seen on her YouTube channel, she was the first to admit that being behind a stove was not her forte – accidents would follow her like lost cats on the island of Corfu. She would have lightened things up, for sure.

With only three of us left, there really was nowhere to hide. Things felt very serious. And I didn't really *want* to beat Chloe at this point. I didn't want my last ally to go home, particularly if it left me here alone with Balthazar. I chanced a look over at him, calm and collected, but noticed he only had ingredients for a dessert on his workbench. It would be a bold move to not cook anything savoury, I thought, but who was I to guess his intentions? Besides, I felt he would always do things his own way, regardless of the instruction. And surprisingly, Carla seemed to enjoy his antics.

Chloe was racing about, looking panicked. I tried to make sure she was okay, to reassure her that the cooking challenge was only one part of the interview, but who was I to promise such things? Especially considering Max's comment about there being no holds barred. Was he openly encouraging us to mess with each other? It seemed a little out of place, but perhaps Carla wanted to test our ruthlessness. I guess I could imagine myself sabotaging Balthazar, watching his smug face turn sour after realising I'd swapped his sugar for salt. But if anything, I wanted to help Chloe, not hinder her. Besides, the smell of her cake baking in the oven had put some kind of spell on me.

Allez Henri, *focus!*

I'd settled on making Mamon's fried chicken with a saffron aioli dipping sauce, in a little nod to Provence. I wasn't sure I could pull it off, but the one time I'd made fried chicken for Lucy, she'd spontaneously told me she loved me, so I felt like it had the potential to be a winning dish.

I started to marinate my chicken and fell into the cooking zone.

Later, on my way back from the pantry, I walked past

Chloe's cooking station, noting her absence. Passing her oven, I thought I smelt something burning.

'Hey Balthazar, what are you burning now?' I asked him jokingly.

He pulled his headphones out of his ears. 'You need my help?' he asked smugly.

'Seriously,' I asked, 'is something burning?'

'Check with your girlfriend,' he replied.

I looked at him. Did he know something about me and Chloe that I didn't?

'What's up with you, dude?' I asked.

'May the best cook win,' he said, and placed his headphones back in.

I went to find Chloe, who had disappeared into the pantry. 'Hey, I think I smell something burning.'

She looked at me like I'd just told her someone had died. And then she relaxed.

'I double checked all my timings and temps, so it's not anything of mine.' She shrugged, then added with a laugh, 'You sure it's not coming from your oven?'

We stood in silence for a moment and then Chloe paused, taking a long, deep inhale.

'You're right! Something's burning,' she squealed and ran back to her oven.

I watched as she pulled out her sponge cake, burnt, a look of complete defeat on her face. And then she checked the oven.

'Who turned up the temp? Who turned on the grill?' she yelled.

I looked at Chloe helplessly as Balthazar ignored us.

'Could you have made a mistake?' I asked.

'No,' she said with certainty, throwing her cake in the bin. 'I don't make mistakes like that.'

'I'm so sorry,' I said, which she seemed to take as me admitting to the sabotage.

'Please, just let me concentrate. I have to make another cake,' she said, grabbing the flour and turning away from me.

I had to draw my eyes away from her because I felt like she might attack me if I didn't – she was clearly stressed, and I wasn't helping.

Could Balthazar have messed with her oven settings? I vowed to keep an eye on him from then on. Meanwhile, he was playing it way too cool. He appeared to be filling choux pastry balls with *crème pâtissière*. *Is he making a goddamn croquembouche?* I wondered. *How will he even have time to finish it?*

There was a weird vibe in the kitchen, which made it hard to focus on my own cooking. I forced myself back to work.

Chapter 36

The Sabotage – CHLOE

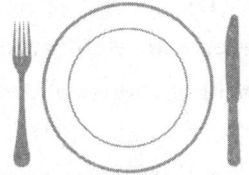

My beautiful, perfect sponge cake was burnt.

And I don't mean lightly singed. The whole thing was scorched. Unsalvageable.

And I knew it wasn't my fault. I'd checked the oven dials at least ten times between putting it in and it burning because I'd been feeling paranoid. I needed the sponge to cool completely before cutting it into squares and finishing the lamingtons. Maybe, just maybe, I'd have time to make another, but I could already picture the sponge being too warm and the chocolate and coconut coating sliding off into a big, messy puddle.

Which is exactly what *I* felt like doing: disintegrating into a big puddle. Tears were welling in my eyes but I blinked them away. Now wasn't the time to get emotional. I had another cake to bake.

The whole time I was sifting and mixing, I kept replaying the moments before I'd raced back to my oven to pull out the ruined sponge.

Henri had come to find me in the pantry. If he'd thought

my cake was burning, he could have just taken it out of the oven rather than wasting time by coming to *ask* me if it was burning. Perhaps he'd even flicked on the oven's grill setting as he'd walked past. Maybe he and Balthazar were in cahoots somehow.

This wasn't the first time I had questioned Henri's intentions. I thought back to how he'd released Balthazar's fish on our yachting adventure, how he'd encouraged me to have a drink with him on the train. Maybe the nice guy façade was all for show.

If growing up with three older brothers had taught me anything, it was that some people just couldn't be trusted when it came to competitions. I didn't want to believe it, because I'd grown very fond of Henri. He'd been so supportive since we'd arrived at the villa, particularly before my interview with Carla. But then again, I knew he was as desperate for this job as I was.

Once I'd managed to get another cake in the oven, I went back to making my fish pie. Even though things might not end up being perfect, I was still on track to get everything done.

I tried to breathe.

At that moment, Max and Carla entered the room.

The first thing Carla did was smell the air – *my burnt cake!* I thought, my face reddening – but even though the scent must have lingered, she acted as though it was inconsequential.

She and Max circled the room quietly, watching what we were all doing, analysing and appraising.

While I tried to focus on my own tasks, I couldn't help overhearing them praise Balthazar, and then encourage Henri to work a little faster.

And then they came over to me.

'Hello, Chloe,' Carla said.

I tried to act calm, but couldn't ignore the fact that this moment would be life-changing. Carla Duris watching me cook had the potential to be my happiest memory or my most miserable, depending on how everything turned out.

'*Bonjour*,' I said nervously.

'Are you finding everything you need?' she asked.

I had to fight back a laugh. Not even Drew's work kitchen and pantry was as impressive as Carla's 'home kitchen'.

'It's lovely here,' I said.

'So, tell us about what you're cooking,' Max asked.

'My mum's fish pie and lamingtons ... if all goes well,' I said. I wished I could have sounded more self-assured, but the burnt cake was sitting in the bin mere centimetres away from my leg. I couldn't forget it.

'And is that your most impressive dish?' Max asked. Clearly, he'd been assigned the role of bad cop.

'I think there will be beauty in the simplicity,' I said.

'How charming,' added Carla.

'Chop, chop,' said Max sharply.

And with that, they sauntered back out of the kitchen.

I took another breath, grateful to have at least received some positive feedback from Carla.

Chapter 37

The Second Coming – HENRI

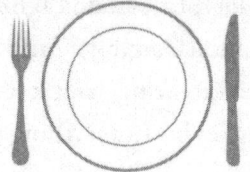

We had forty minutes remaining before we were required to present our dishes to Carla and Max.

I was frying golden hunks of chicken while trying – and somewhat failing – to make my aioli. My first attempt had split, and it had left me feeling flustered.

Seeing the calibre of dishes Chloe and Balthazar were creating, I'd felt the need to step up my own efforts, so I'd also made a chocolate and chilli crème brûlée that I would blowtorch at the last second. It was tasty, but perhaps a little too spicy. When I'd told Carla what I was attempting, she'd said it sounded 'interesting', which I took to mean good, but then again, Max had said I'd set myself a very large challenge. *Mon dieu!*

Balthazar, on the other hand, had started to assemble his croquembouche. I couldn't believe he was actually going to pull it off. He had to have cheated at some point along the way, surely? But since Chloe's burnt cake disaster, I'd been keeping an eye on him and hadn't seen him do anything untoward.

Chloe had been checking on her second cake religiously. She'd also been doing a lot of nervous tapping of her wooden spoon on the benchtop. I'd watched her taste something on her stove earlier and she'd almost melted in pleasure. Her lips over that spoon were almost enough to make me want to throw in the towel and wave a white flag, but I'd somehow managed to keep it together. I was relieved things seemed to be going better for her.

Time was ticking away when I saw Chloe run off to the pantry for something.

Out of the corner of my eye, with one hand prepped and waiting to pull my chicken out of the fryer, I saw Balthazar scurry towards Chloe's oven.

When I saw him turn the temperature dial, I gave him a wild look.

'What are you doing, Balthazar?' I called out, trying not to burn my chicken.

He winked and placed a finger in front of his lips, telling me to 'shh.'

I actually couldn't believe what I was seeing. He *had* been behind her first burnt cake, and now he was attempting to do the same thing again.

I stood frozen, watching him return to his goddamn perfect dessert, not knowing what to do.

My chicken would be ruined if I pulled it out too early, or too late, so instead I just called out, 'Chloe! Burning!'

It had only been a minute, but Balthazar must have turned on the grill and maxed the heat, because in the time it took for

Chloe to run back and remove her cake, the top had already started to burn.

'Oh my god,' she said, pulling the cake out. 'What the actual hell?'

Balthazar had conveniently disappeared into the pantry and Chloe shot me an angry look.

'I promise I had nothing to do with it,' I told her.

'You're the only one here,' she said.

'It was Balthazar, I swear. He left the room right after doing it.'

'Why didn't you tell me sooner?' she asked. 'Cakes don't burn in seconds.'

I tried to explain, but Chloe looked so wounded that I realised there was no apology in the world that could make this better.

'You're as much to blame as Balthazar,' she said.

Two burnt cakes in less than two hours. I could feel her disappointment radiating across the room.

She turned away from me to inspect her cake.

I couldn't stop watching her, despite my own fried chicken starting to burn. Her cake actually seemed all right, apart from the top, which was obviously overcooked and far too dark. She was in a panic, though, and while she probably could have covered the damage with some icing sugar, time was against her.

With a wild look in her eyes, she grabbed a knife and lifted it into the air.

Chapter 38

The Shit Hits the Fan – CHLOE

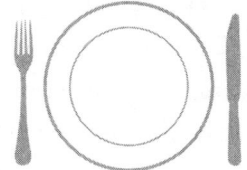

Oh my god, I'd messed it up ... AGAIN!

I had one job: to not burn the cake (again ...).

I'd failed. Or, more accurately, somebody had made me fail.

Inspecting it, I figured the only thing left to do was to slice off the burnt parts, salvaging enough cake to cut into the lamington squares. They wouldn't be tall and perfect, but after I'd drizzled over the chocolate and coconut coating, hopefully Carla and Max wouldn't notice.

With my knife in the air, I avoided any thoughts or hesitations, and just cut off the top layer.

I thrust the burnt crust aside and was relieved to discover that what remained smelt divine. The beautiful aroma of butter and flour weaved its way into my brain and, for the second time that day, helped calm me down. I was transported back into Mum's kitchen as a kid, waiting, waiting for her to finally announce that the sponge was cool enough for us to make the lamingtons. Honestly, I think part of the reason she made us wait was to teach us patience. Or perhaps she knew that once she gave my brothers the go-ahead, anything she cooked would be devoured in minutes.

At this point in the cooking challenge, I had no time to waste. Thankfully, the cake wasn't as monstrous as I had feared – step one complete. I shoved it into the freezer so it would cool quicker and turned back to my pie.

Once assembled, I slid them into the oven, checking the temperature and vowing not to leave my workstation until I pulled them out. With that done, I started to prepare the icing and the bowl of coconut for the lamingtons. A taste test told me everything was perfect. I wanted to wait until the last minute to finish everything off and plate up, which gave me a moment to pause.

I surreptitiously watched Balthazar and Henri moving around their workspaces, Balthazar calmly stacking up his ridiculous profiteroles, and Henri grabbing a bloody blowtorch for his crème brûlée. I felt well out of my league. There was a part of me that wanted to go and bump into Balthazar, send those cream-filled balls spinning onto the floor, but I just didn't have it in me to ruin somebody else's work. Even looking at Henri didn't bring me any peace. I really thought he'd had my back, but clearly he was as ruthless about winning as Balthazar, he was just more discreet about it.

But I wasn't going to waste another second thinking about Henri or Balthazar. Instead, I removed my sponge squares from the freezer, touched them to see if they had cooled, and then started to ice each square and fling them into the bowl of coconut. Honestly, they looked a mess, but there was nothing

I could do at that point to improve them. We only had a few minutes left. I'd just have to call it rustic and hope for the best. There was a world in which Carla might not notice the slightly burnt flavour of the sponge, but I was pretty sure it wasn't the world I was actually in.

Oh god, let this taste test go well!

Carla and Max returned to the room and Max started a quick, staccato countdown.

Ten, nine, eight ...

And then Henri dropped a plate with a loud clatter.

I turned to see chocolate crème all over the floor and his face a mix of horror and panic. My feelings of anger towards him were instantly replaced with sympathy. Annoyingly, it turned out that I still wanted him to do well.

And then I saw that Henri had another plated dessert and I realised that he'd be fine. People like Henri de la flipping Fontaine were always fine.

He looked up at me with an embarrassed grin and mouthed, 'Thank god that's over.'

I couldn't help but agree.

'Congratulations, my darling chefs,' Carla said, clapping her hands together. 'You've all proved to me today that you know your way around a kitchen. Bravo! Being comfortable while cooking is obviously very important to me. The person who helps write my memoir will need to understand more than simply the basics of cooking and preparing food – they need to understand the dynamics of a kitchen, the stress of working to time constraints and the difficulties of functioning within a team – often the most challenging aspects of being a chef. Despite what I've asked you to do today, my work as a chef has never been a solitary pursuit. Supporting each other is important. But for now, let's get to tasting,' she said.

A tall table was brought out and placed before Max and Carla. I felt like I was in some kind of reality TV show. If I didn't feel ill with nerves, it would have been rather exciting.

'Balthazar, please bring us your creation,' Max instructed.

Balthazar walked his croquembouche to the table.

'Not an easy undertaking,' said Carla, eyeing the dessert from various vantage points.

'I wanted to make something worthy of you,' he said.

She appeared to swoon, and I couldn't help a little eye roll. *Kiss-arse,* I thought.

Max went to hand Carla some cutlery, but she shook her head and grabbed one of the little pastry balls between her fingers. She bit into it with gusto and then closed her eyes.

'*Délicieux,*' she said with reverence.

Max served himself a profiterole and cut into it using a little gold knife and fork. He took a tiny bite, chewed thoughtfully and nodded once at Balthazar.

'You can return to your workstation with your dessert,' Max said.

Balthazar turned and faced us, the smile on his face as dazzling as the sun reflecting off the Mediterranean Sea. There was a bounce to his step. I could tell he felt like he'd secured himself the job.

'Chloe, please bring forward your dishes,' Max instructed. My heart was pounding as I approached the table with my modest-looking fish pie and haphazard stack of lamingtons. I looked at the plates apprehensively as I set them down. I couldn't see how this was going to end well.

'Tell us about what you've chosen to cook today,' Carla said.

'Fish pie and lamingtons – two of my mother's specialities.'

'You know I love a family recipe,' Carla purred.

Of course I know you love family recipes! I wanted to shout, but I simply nodded, too nervous to say anything more.

Carla dug into the pie with a spoon, fished out a steaming scallop and slipped it into her mouth, sauce splashing onto her chin. She looked at me wide-eyed and, for a second, I panicked. And then she burst out into a huge smile.

'It is really wonderful,' she said, with a hint of surprise in her voice.

I sighed in relief.

Max also seemed to approve of the pie, and while I would have loved to bask in the glory of my savoury success, Carla then turned her attention to my lamingtons.

'Now, if I am correct, these are an Australian speciality?' she asked, eying them dubiously.

'A fan favourite,' I told her.

Carla grabbed a lamington with her fingers and bit into it. She chewed thoughtfully and then took another large bite.

'Hmm, interesting,' she said.

Max sampled in silence.

Carla then whispered something in his ear.

Panic took over, and I felt as though my luck had run out.

'Chloe, please return to your workstation,' Max said.

I had no idea if Carla had liked, loved or loathed the lamingtons, but at least she'd enjoyed the pie. And at least I hadn't been asked to leave on the spot.

Henri gave me an encouraging look as I passed him, which I was unable to reciprocate. If I'd just lost this cooking competition because of his and Balthazar's antics, I would never forgive them.

'Henri, last but not least, bring forth your creations,' Max said.

Henri confidently took his plates up to be sampled.

While Carla and Max were busy being presented with Henri's dishes, I pulled out my phone and snuck a look at my messages.

Nothing from Belle, but a good luck message from Drew.

I reasoned with myself that Belle was probably still in transit and hadn't had time to reply. I just had to hope she was all right.

Chapter 39

The Taste Test – HENRI

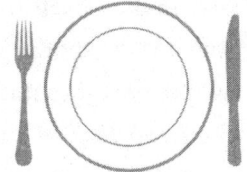

I'd been putting on a brave face as I'd carried my dishes up to Carla and Max, but I'd been petrified.

The cooking challenge hadn't gone very well for me. Chloe was pissed off that I hadn't managed to save her cake in time, and I'd dropped one of my crème brûlée dishes moments before Max told us to down tools.

I was anxious that Carla would think my fried chicken was too basic, and that my chilli dessert was too spicy. And perhaps most of all, I was anxious to get out of the kitchen and convince Chloe that Balthazar had been behind the cake sabotage, and that I'd warned her as soon as I could.

After I'd introduced my dishes, Carla served herself a piece of my fried chicken, dipping it into the saffron aioli. As she chewed, her face remained neutral.

'Hmm,' she said.

Perhaps I'm in more trouble than I realised.

She didn't say anything else, but finished the piece of chicken and then moved the plate aside.

Carla then grabbed a spoon and, with a flick of her wrist, broke the surface of the brûlée, which let out a very loud and very satisfying crack. I couldn't help a grin, but quickly wiped it off my face. There was so much tension in the air; I didn't want to celebrate too soon.

Carla and Max each took a small spoonful of the chilli crème – there wasn't much there, given the other serving had fallen on the floor – and brought it to their lips.

Carla let out an 'Ooo' and Max let out a quick exhale. I'd tasted it before plating it and while it *was* spicy, I didn't think it was *too* spicy. Max's face suggested I was wrong. His eyes began to water and he wiped his lips with a napkin. The only silver lining to perhaps failing at this cooking challenge was seeing Max lose his composure.

My heart rate shot up at the same time as my hopes were dashed.

Carla and Max had put down their spoons, seemingly unwilling to have a second bite.

I walked back to my workstation with a lot less confidence.

Carla and Max told us to finish cleaning up and then meet them on the terrace.

The mood in the kitchen was sombre, at least for Chloe and me. Balthazar, on the other hand, was humming to himself joyfully.

It was the first time since arriving at Carla's villa that I actually felt like I might be sent home. I prayed that Carla would forgive me for being heavy-handed with the chilli, but I knew it was futile. All control was out of my hands, and my whole future seemed to depend on a plate of fried chicken and a spicy bloody crème brûlée!

Chloe, Balthazar and I congregated on the terrace shortly after. We were instructed to sit down on the three chairs opposite Max and Carla's.

I sat on one end, Chloe on the other, and Balthazar ended up in the middle.

We sat in silence. Things suddenly felt very serious.

Carla spoke first. 'I'm quite impressed with your enthusiasm for the cooking challenge today. I know you are all writers, and not chefs, but I have asked myself: how can you possibly write about my life if you don't understand how kitchens run?'

Max nodded along seriously beside her.

'I know I have a reputation for being a demanding leader, *n'est-ce pas?*' Carla continued, her words hanging in the air.

She had a reputation for being a lot more than demanding. Cold-blooded was the term more often used to describe her.

She paused, and then said in a strong and emotional voice: 'I am many things, but ruthless I am not. I value integrity above all else. We are humans, after all. A kitchen team needs to run like a well-oiled machine, but occasionally there is a cog that gets loose, and somebody needs to step in to make sure everything doesn't fall apart. I assume you all understand what I'm talking about?' she asked, fixing us with an expectant gaze.

I tried to keep the expression on my face neutral. I was lost.

Another long pause.

'Right, well, all things considered, Balthazar, you can leave. I didn't expect you to fall into the trap of actually sabotaging a fellow chef, but seeing as you tried to multiple times, I cannot have you work for me.'

'But ...' he began to say.

'Balthazar, go and pack your things,' Max said, standing up and ushering him out.

It was one of those moments when you think things are almost too good to be true. Balthazar had been named and shamed. His true character had shone through, and now, he was leaving.

I could hear him protesting as Max escorted him away, but he was mostly spouting threats about how Max and Carla were going to pay for wasting his time, and how he'd never wanted the job anyway.

All I could think was that I was grateful Chloe and I were both still in with a chance. That she was by my side. I looked across at her with a smile, but she was staring straight ahead, watching Carla unwaveringly, clearly awaiting instructions on what was to come next.

What that might be was anybody's guess.

Chapter 40

The Next Steps – CHLOE

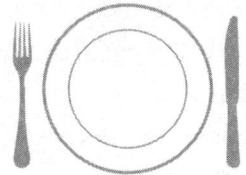

Carla was looking at us intensely. She was smiling, but it wasn't a reassuring smile – more of a wicked one. I was too nervous to take my eyes off her, even though I felt Henri looking at me.

Balthazar had just been booted out of the interview for messing with my oven. While I felt a tiny bit sorry for him, I mostly felt validated, relieved that Carla knew I hadn't messed things up on my own accord, reassured that I was still in with a chance, buoyed by the fact that my chance still involved Henri, and elated that he'd had nothing to do with my burnt cake. The closer we got to the finish line, the more I knew I wanted this job.

'I have one last surprise for you both,' Carla said, suddenly joyful.

For some reason, my stomach dropped. I wasn't sure I could handle any more surprises. I forced myself to rally, though, because if getting through one last surprise meant getting the role, I would be ready. I sat up straight and waited to hear what awaited us.

'This evening, I shall throw a party to celebrate your success thus far and to get to know you both in a social setting. You will have the remainder of the day to prepare a speech, and tonight, I would like you to regale my guests with tales of this interview weekend thus far,' she said.

My mind was racing. I couldn't believe that the interview would continue into the evening, or that we would need to give a speech in front of Carla's friends.

'Max will give you the rest of the details,' she said, standing. 'I'll see you both later.'

She strode off into the garden, leaving us both frozen in shock as we waited for Max to return *sans* Balthazar.

'Are you okay? You look worried,' Henri whispered. His voice was kind, making me feel even more embarrassed about the way I'd spoken to him earlier. If only I could turn back the clock for a do-over.

'I'll be alright. I just need some down time,' I said quietly.

'It has been a busy morning,' he said breezily. 'On and up.'

The fact that he could be supportive after I'd all but accused him of ruining my cake left me speechless. I tried to apologise, but the words got stuck in my throat.

Max finally returned and sat down with his clipboard.

'Right,' he said. 'Carla mentioned you are to give a speech this evening. Two minutes max. You should discuss what Carla, and this weekend, means to you. The party shall be on Carla's other yacht. You have the rest of the day to prepare.'

A familiar knot of anxiety returned to my stomach. Another deadline for the weekend. Another hurdle to jump.

Max continued: 'There will be fifty guests. Suitable attire will be delivered to your rooms one hour before we are set to depart. There is lunch for you in the dining room.'

Walking into the dining room, I saw that a table had been set for Henri and me. Just the two of us.

I sat down opposite the man I'd been ready to assassinate for not saving my cake only an hour earlier and attempted a smile.

'I'm sorry about how I reacted in the kitchen,' I managed to say after a few moments of hesitation.

If Henri held a grudge, he didn't show it. 'Don't mention it,' he said, smiling widely as if he didn't have a care in the world.

A waiter arrived with a large tray.

'Your creations,' he said, putting plates down in front of us.

I couldn't help but laugh. We were being served the food we'd cooked for the challenge. I guess it was good that it wouldn't go to waste, but for some reason I felt as though Carla was playing some kind of joke on us.

I picked up a piece of Henri's fried chicken and dipped it in the accompanying sauce. Although it was now stone-cold, it was good. The chicken was tender, elevated by the added flavour kick from the saffron aioli.

'This is nice,' I said, not wanting to give him too big of an ego.

'It was hard to know what to cook for a famous chef,' he confessed.

'Yes! Obviously you want to impress her, but there's a limit to what you can do in two hours – or at least, that was how I felt.'

Next it was Henri's turn to try my pie. He lifted a forkful to his mouth with reverence.

'This is fantastic,' he said, pleasure reverberating through his voice.

My cheeks flushed. 'Thank you,' I managed to blurt out.

There was something about getting praise from Henri that was particularly heart-warming.

'Is it a Tasmanian speciality?' he asked.

'It is!' I said, impressed by his knowledge. 'Did you ever go there?'

'Unfortunately, no. I never really had much money to travel. Plus, there was always so much going on in Melbourne that I never felt like I had the time. I regret it now, obviously.'

'It's so beautiful. There's this little island off the south coast. I swear it has the best oysters you'll ever eat in your life. There's even a cheese shop there. I think you'd love it.'

'Maybe one day you could show me around.'

'Henri, it's on the other side of the world.'

'And?'

'Well, you seem pretty busy in Paris. Are you about to drop everything for a trip to Tassie?'

'Are you inviting me?' he retorted.

Thankfully, we were interrupted by the waiter carrying the remains of my stack of lamingtons.

I looked at them, remembering what had happened in the kitchen with regret. 'Again, I'm sorry for blaming you over this,'

I said, motioning to the lamingtons. 'It seems like a ridiculous thing to have gotten worked up over now.'

'It was a stressful challenge. I think we were all feeling the pressure,' he said, placing his hand over mine. The intimate gesture took me by surprise, mostly because of the shock of electricity that his touch sent coursing through my body. After a few moments, regretfully, he removed his hand to grab a lamington.

He bit into it.

'*Mon dieu,* this tastes like Australia!' he said joyfully.

I smiled in relief, grabbing one and taking a bite.

'It tastes so burnt!' I squealed.

'Oh, not so much,' he said, but I could tell that he was just being kind. The burnt flavour was unmistakable.

The shame I felt at having served Carla Duris a burnt lamington was almost crushing.

'The icing is really good,' Henri said.

'And the sponge is really bad.'

'You're still here, which goes to show that the dish didn't really matter,' he consoled.

'But I forced Carla Duris to eat a burnt lamington. I've brought shame on my country! How do I come back from this?' I asked.

'At least we don't have to taste the crème brûlée that I dropped on the floor. Did you see Carla and Max's faces? They hated it!'

'But the top of it cracked so beautifully,' I offered.

'Right!' he said excitedly. 'I guess that proves I'm good with a blowtorch.'

We shared a smile and then fell into silence, the burnt lamingtons sitting between us like a cruel reminder of the stressful situation we were still in.

'How are you with speeches?' Henri asked, changing the subject.

'Not great,' I said. 'You?'

'I've given a few in my time,' he said.

Of course you have, I thought. I could only imagine how beautifully he must speak in public. His voice all deep and smooth as honey, his face all handsome and charming.

'It should be fun, right, out there on the yacht,' he said, sounding genuinely excited.

'Sure,' I lied.

I just couldn't reciprocate his enthusiasm. There was something about the events of the morning that was making me second-guess Carla's intentions. The activities and challenges she and Max were setting us were becoming increasingly intense, and had very little to do with writing. Plus, our group had now been whittled down to two, with Belle's dismissal still a complete mystery.

'What do you think happened to Belle?' I asked quietly.

'No idea,' he admitted.

'Do you think it had something to do with her painting?'

'I'm sure something else must have happened. Perhaps the interview didn't go well last night and the painting was the last straw?' he suggested.

'But she would have let us know, right?' I asked.

'Maybe she just didn't get the chance to. I'm sure it's all legit,' he said.

'I don't know. Things have been a little unpredictable since Carla arrived last night,' I said nervously, looking around to make sure no waiters were lurking.

'Stick by me tonight if you're worried,' Henri said quietly. 'I'll make sure everything goes well.'

'What about the job?' I asked, knowing how much we both wanted it.

'Some things are more important than a job,' he said.

I was finding it hard to imagine going to a party on Carla's yacht in the Mediterranean Sea. We'd been through so much since arriving at her villa the day before, I wondered what else she could have planned for us. Would it really all be over after the speeches? I was desperate to know when Carla would be making her decision.

The waiter returned to escort us back to our rooms to prepare for the party. As we reached our doors, I said a regretful 'See you soon' to Henri, wishing we could spend the afternoon together, but knowing that we both had work to do in preparation for the evening ahead.

Chapter 41

The Fourth Departure – BALTHAZAR

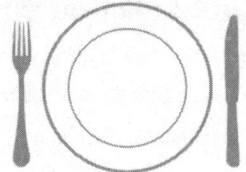

Clearly there's been some kind of mistake, Balthazar told himself as he was packing his bags.

Max had most definitely instructed the interviewees to approach the cooking challenge with a 'no holds barred' approach. Could it really have just been a test to catch him out? He hadn't considered Carla to be such a stickler for the rules. He'd thought she'd had more gumption than that.

And what a boring way to leave the villa, he lamented. *After such a successful interview, and such a beautiful painting, too. They'll come to their senses eventually,* Balthazar reasoned, unable to imagine Carla actually choosing to work with either Chloe or Henri. How dull they would both be. *She's setting herself up for disappointment with those two,* he told himself.

At least now he'd be able to go back to Paris and call Juliette. A date with her almost felt like adequate compensation for everything Carla had put them through. Or maybe he'd even call Lucy while Henri was still stuck in Antibes. That'd show him who had the upper hand.

Balthazar set off for Paris feeling like it wouldn't be long before Carla came running back to him, begging him to accept the job ...

Part Three

Carla Duris's Yacht

The Mediterranean Sea

Chapter 42

The Suiting Up – HENRI

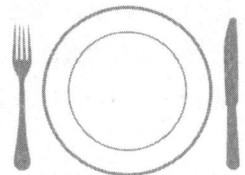

Back in my room, I lay on my bed thinking about Chloe, imagining all the fun we could have been having if we hadn't been banished to our rooms to write a speech for Carla's rich friends and associates. We could have been lazing around in the sunshine, by a pool somewhere, sipping rosé. She'd seemed nervous when she'd found out about the yacht party, and I wanted to be the one to console her.

Get the girl! The phrase kept interrupting my thoughts, distracting me from what I was here to achieve. I wasn't sure when my motivations had swung away from Carla and towards Chloe, but I had to force myself to focus on the task at hand.

I reluctantly got up, made myself a coffee, showered to clear my head, and got to work on the speech. How could I sum up everything that had happened this weekend in two minutes? How could I spin it into something that would make Carla want to hire me?

At 5pm on the dot, there was a knock on the door.

One of Carla's numerous staff members – different from

the ones I'd seen this morning, but equally stony-faced – was holding a black suit bag and a shoebox. He handed them to me wordlessly.

I said a quick '*Merci*,' and then he retreated. I wondered what kind of spell Carla had put on these guys. I wondered how easily I would fall under it if I were to get this job.

I placed the suit bag on my bed and unzipped it, wondering what kind of dress code was in store for the evening.

Black tie. *Bof!*

It wasn't that I minded wearing a suit and bow tie – it always looked good – but it wasn't the most comfortable outfit. It also meant we were in for a formal evening, which made me question some of the jokes I'd tried to incorporate into my speech. It was probably too late to rewrite it, so I'd have to settle for a few omissions.

I dressed, surprised to find that the tuxedo and dress shoes fit me perfectly, and made a vague attempt to tame my hair.

My thoughts briefly diverted to what Chloe would be wearing, but I reined them in. I needed to focus. I needed to prove to Carla that I was right for the job. I'd come this far, and the offer she'd laid on the table was too good to pass up. Writing this memoir would open so many doors. I needed to give this last part of the interview everything I had.

To motivate me, I pictured myself back at my desk at *Le Cercle* responding to another email from Uncle Michel about why I'd chosen to review a certain restaurant instead of another, more important one. The thought alone was enough to gee me up for the evening.

Sliding my speech and phone carefully into my jacket pocket, I went downstairs. I walked slowly, hoping to run into Chloe, listening for her footsteps, but the house was eerily quiet.

A black car was waiting for me outside. Max met me on the steps and ushered me quickly into the back seat.

'Where's Chloe?' I asked him seconds before he shut the door in my face. His expression had remained neutral, as per usual, giving nothing away.

The car sped off, with me the only passenger, down Carla's driveway and towards the port.

'Is another car coming with the others?' I asked the driver, at this point starting to worry.

'I drive. I do not answer questions,' the driver replied, shutting down the prospect of any further conversation.

I could feel my heart racing. Was I out of the running for the job? Was I being escorted to the train station? But then I reasoned with myself: *You are in a very expensive suit, heading towards the port. Your bags are still at Carla's villa. Unless the driver suddenly veers off in the opposite direction, all is well.*

I managed to maintain my composure, but I knew I wouldn't be able to properly relax until I was on that yacht. Probably until after I'd given my speech and could settle in the knowledge that I'd done everything I could for this interview. When the driver finally turned towards the port, I breathed a little easier.

Chapter 43

The Dress – CHLOE

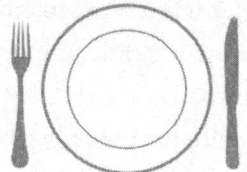

Geez, this outfit doesn't leave much to the imagination, I thought as I looked in the mirror one last time before heading downstairs.

As Max had foretold, I'd been sent a dress for the evening, and my god, was it a Dress with a capital D!

When I'd slipped it out of the bag and spied the tag (price removed, of course), my mouth had almost hit the floor. It was a Celine dress, something I normally couldn't even afford to *look* at, let alone wear. It was the colour of Champagne, with glistening diamond straps. I slipped it on, not entirely surprised to find that it fit perfectly. *These people don't do things by halves,* I thought to myself.

What did make me gasp, however, was the cut. The dress fell gracefully to the floor, was backless and had a neckline so daring I wondered if I was now competing with my own chest to get the job.

I pulled out the accompanying shoes, relieved to find that the heels weren't *too* high. They were black, red soles, soft as butter, the perfect height so the dress wouldn't drag across the floor.

The outfit wouldn't have looked out of place on the red carpet at the Cannes Film Festival. *Do all Carla's potential employees get this kind of treatment?* I wondered.

I noticed a smaller fabric bag inside the garment bag and pulled it out. Another gasp. Like a small child on their birthday, I removed a Chanel evening bag with giddy excitement. It was the colour of pink Champagne – bubbles were obviously *in* this season – and it sparkled like a freshly poured *coupe*.

I normally steered clear of luxury for obvious financial reasons, and this outfit felt like a power play from Carla. If I were ever to get rich, a Chanel bag would probably be one of my first frivolous purchases. I ran my hands over my hips, taken aback by the softness of the gown, enjoying the weight of it against my skin. I understood how people could get sucked into this kind of lifestyle – it was intoxicating.

Inside the Chanel bag was a note on one of Carla's signature embossed business cards:

A small gift to thank you for your dedication so far.
CD

I mean, come on! My idol just gifted me Chanel. Was I even still alive? Had Balthazar actually killed me in the kitchen and I was now living out some kind of dreamlike fantasy?

I slipped my speech, phone and lipstick into my new bag. It was time.

Actually, I was one minute late.

I rushed downstairs, fearing any potential repercussions from Max.

As I walked out the main door, I saw a black car speeding down the driveway. I was certain that I saw Henri's beautiful head of hair in the back seat, which annoyed me. By being late, I'd missed the opportunity to drive to the port with him. Or had it been Max's intention to keep us apart?

Thankfully, another car quickly pulled up. Max opened the door and ushered me in.

I ignored the nerves plaguing my thoughts and tried to enjoy what had turned into a Cinderella moment for me.

When the driver pulled into the port, we drove towards a black, glistening superyacht that looked like something a villain would escape on in a Bond movie. It was all sleek lines and chrome, lights twinkling. It was nothing like the beautiful – much smaller – fishing yacht we'd been out on the day before. In fact, it was beyond anything I could have actually pictured Carla owning.

I ran through what I knew about the evening ahead. Carla was hosting a cocktail party and we were the guests of honour. She was probably going to introduce us to her friends and colleagues so we'd get a sense of the life we'd be living if we were to win the job of writing for her. We would give speeches, and then she would decide whether Henri or I would be better suited to write her memoir. *No pressure,* I kept trying to tell myself.

White-shirted staff members were waiting on the dock to escort guests onto the yacht. I could hear the happy chatter of people – many people, by the sounds of it – and I found the prospect of being at a party somewhat calming. There was always an element of risk, taking a boat out on the water at night. Safety in numbers, isn't that what people say?

A waiter escorted me up to the top deck and handed me a glass of Champagne.

I hung back for a moment, trying to establish the lay of the land. Beautifully dressed people were lounging around the space, drinking and eating, with the lights of the port starting to glisten around us. *Perhaps we won't even leave the dock,* I thought.

I caught sight of Henri and found myself momentarily short of breath. In his tuxedo, he looked beyond perfect, a slight ruffle of the hair showing his rebellious side, but his suit impeccable. He was chatting with a small group of people, completely at ease.

I dragged my eyes away from Henri as Max appeared to run through the program for the evening. By now, I didn't even question the logistics of Max putting me in a car at the villa and then seemingly arriving at the boat before me. I'd come to accept that he was just everywhere.

'We will sail in five minutes,' he said sharply.

'And the speeches?' I asked.

'Later,' he said.

I looked at Max, waiting for him to elaborate, but it appeared that was all the information I was going to get. The nerves bubbled away in my stomach like the Champagne that I'd been sipping too quickly.

'And Carla?' I prompted. 'She'll be introducing us, I assume?'

Max shot me a look that warned me not to try and anticipate his plans.

'Carla is organising a surprise for you and Henri in the main cabin. For now, enjoy the party.'

Please, no more surprises! I begged the universe.

Max, out of the blue, attempted a smile, but I think we both knew it didn't suit his usual demeanour, so he resumed his serious look and left me to mingle.

As I heard the motors fire up in preparation for the yacht to leave the dock, I stood awkwardly on the precipice of the party, wondering who the other guests were, unsure to whom I was meant to talk.

My phone buzzed.

Finally, I thought in relief when I saw it was a message from Belle.

'Chloe, I feel like I should warn you. Carla really turned on me after that whole painting challenge this morning. Honestly, I worry she might be insane. Please be careful if you're still at her villa. I think this interview has gone to her head. You and the others need to watch out.'

My stomach dropped at the same time as the yacht started moving.

Shit, I thought, terrified by the knowledge that I was about to be stuck at sea with these people. If the warning had come from anyone else – from Juliette or Balthazar – I would have taken it with a grain of salt, but the fact that it came from Belle, the most down-to-earth and honest of us all, had me very worried.

Chapter 44

The Getting Off the Dock – HENRI

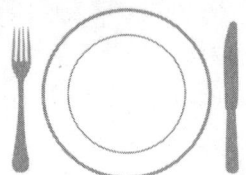

Chloe was a vision! An absolute vision.

As soon as I could, I extricated myself from a boring rich lady who claimed to have met me when I was a child – and who now, rather shamelessly, seemed to find me old enough to flirt with – and approached Chloe.

'You look incredible,' I said.

She blushed, and smiled, and I felt like I might melt right in front of her, a puddle of devotion.

'Do you know what's going on? What the plan is for this evening?' she asked, a hint of panic in her voice.

'It's a party. Try and relax,' I told her, wishing I could take my own advice.

She gave an unconvincing laugh.

'What is there to worry about?' I asked.

'I just got an odd message from Belle,' she said. 'But let's talk about it later.'

'Sure, whatever you want,' I said, trying to put her at ease.

'So, do you know who all these people are?' she asked.

'From what I can tell, they're mostly well-heeled Parisians down for the weekend,' I told her.

'And they're nice?' she asked.

'Of course,' I said, which was part lie, part truth. They *were* nice, if you were one of them. But who knew what Carla had told them about us? Who knew what they'd been prepped to believe?

I saw Chloe's shoulders soften and I couldn't help glancing at the plunging neckline of her dress. I wondered if Carla had chosen it. Had she done so to distract me or to test my loyalty? I forced myself to look away, taking a long sip of Champagne, the cool bubbles exploding on my tongue like pop rocks. The sensation helped ground me and took the edge off my own nerves.

I thought back to my upbringing, trying to draw strength from the memories of all the black-tie events my parents dragged me to as a teenager and beyond. If there was one thing I could do, it was fancy parties. I'd certainly been to enough of them in my lifetime. Small talk was almost as natural to me as breathing. It was just a shame that, unlike breathing, I hated it.

Among the crowd were chefs, painters, gallery owners and philanthropists. There was plenty of old money on the boat. I could only imagine the havoc that would be created among the insurance brokers, bankers and executors of wills and estates if Carla's yacht were to sink. It would be mayhem.

Chloe and I made the rounds, introducing ourselves to Carla's friends. We hadn't been briefed on what to say, so I ad libbed that we were writers helping Carla with a project.

Chloe immediately jumped on board with this idea and began repeating the same spiel. I couldn't help noting how well we worked together. Even though we didn't know each other particularly well, things between us felt easy.

Time seemed to pass quickly as we sampled canapés of caviar and sea urchin, and had our Champagne glasses refilled from large jeroboams. Carla certainly knew how to throw a party – the joy on that yacht was infectious.

But where is our generous host? I kept wondering. Max, in his usual ominous way, had told me she had a last-minute issue to resolve and would join us shortly. *Whatever,* I figured. She and Max were probably watching our every move, deciding which of us to get rid of next. I had to remain on guard, but the lack of information was starting to frustrate me.

As Chloe and I continued on, we did our best to chat and charm. At one point I even gave her hand a squeeze, as if to say, 'You're doing great.' She reciprocated the gesture and *mon dieu*, if I could have made everybody else on the yacht disappear in that moment, I would have. There was just something about her that reeled me in like a fish on a hook.

Eventually, the nerves and anticipation of the evening caught up with me and I began feeling extremely tired. I wanted to get these speeches over and done with so I could properly enjoy myself. The idea of knowing that the final decision would soon be shifted into Carla's hands was a welcome relief. *One last hurdle*, I kept telling myself.

Shortly after, Max appeared in front of Chloe and me and asked us to approach the bridge. I was happy to finally be doing something proactive, something other than talking and pretending everything was totally normal.

I pictured Carla at the helm of the yacht, waiting to talk to us. What did she have in store? I figured she'd be steering the yacht or doing something else to throw us off guard, but as we approached the bridge, I was surprised to find she wasn't there at all.

Instead, a captain met us at the door. It wasn't Gregorio, the captain of Carla's smaller boat, but an older man. He was short with small, dark eyes and a forehead forged with deep wrinkles.

He welcomed us in accented English, but I couldn't put my finger on where he was from. He didn't ooze charm like Gregorio had. He was serious, almost a little shifty in his quick, staccato movements. Like he was showing us around against his will, as if his boss was watching.

Chloe smiled at the captain. 'Hello,' she said affably. Chloe seemed to be more comfortable here at the helm of the yacht than at the party. She looked around at the equipment that lined the bridge with curiosity.

'I wanted to show you the shoreline,' he said.

I'd hardly registered that we were now quite far out at sea.

He pointed out the window to a lighthouse and explained that it was at the tip of the Cap d'Antibes, which meant we were heading in the direction of Cannes. The famed Hôtel du Cap-Eden-Roc was not much further inland, flanked by the rocky coastline with tiny inlets.

'How charming,' Chloe said.

'And what is the reason for the tour?' I asked the captain, my patience starting to wane.

'Carla asked me to show you the sights,' he replied with a forced smile. *The boss is watching,* I thought to myself.

'And what's that over there?' Chloe asked, pointing to an island off the shore.

'That's Île Sainte-Marguerite, about two miles off shore from Cannes,' he replied, and Chloe nodded attentively.

After a few more questions, I nudged Chloe as if to say, 'What's going on?' But if she registered my confusion, she didn't acknowledge it.

Instead, her focus was on the captain, and her gaze was fixed on the controls of the boat. She seemed to be taking a great interest in the array of dials and screens. The look on her face had me worried.

Chapter 45

The Whiteboard – CHLOE

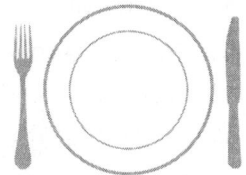

Gazing at the controls, I quickly tried to gather as much information as possible about our position, the winds and our distance from shore. I had the most awful feeling in the pit of my stomach that Carla was plotting something dramatic for this final part of the interview.

Belle's message had hit me like a hammer. Yes, her warning about Carla was vague on details, but there was a part of me that could clearly picture Carla turning on her after the painting activity. And Belle knew how important this job was to me. She wouldn't exaggerate. In a way, her warning had given me a necessary reality check, making me question the normalcy of this whole weekend. Carla's offer of remuneration had blinkered me to some of the red flags that had been raised since we'd arrived at the villa, and I felt like my brain was now struggling to piece everything together.

To make things worse, on the way up to the bridge, I'd seen a whiteboard with timings for this evening:

18.30 – guest arrival

19.00 – set sail

21.30 – fireworks

21.40 – water challenge

I'd tried to reason that perhaps I was reading too much into Belle's message, but Carla's absence was unnerving. The fact that there'd been no mention of when the speeches would take place also had me concerned, and the detailed tour of the bridge the captain was giving us further unsettled me. In fact, everything about the evening, if taken out of context of the weekend so far, could be considered a little strange. The outfits, the extravagance, the absence of the host, the whiteboard ...

The captain had welcomed us in with a curt smile but he didn't seem like a typical captain. He didn't have that salty, seaworthy grit to him that I would have expected. To be fair, he was a yacht captain, not the captain of a fishing boat, but still. This guy seemed more like a caricature of a villain than somebody responsible for such an immense vessel.

'And could somebody easily swim ashore from this position?' I asked.

'A strong swimmer, yes,' the captain replied, giving me a knowing look.

'Even in the evening?' I asked, wondering if I was perhaps onto something, and hoping like hell I wasn't.

'It may be slightly more challenging, but yes, I should think so,' he said, not giving anything else away.

Next to me, Henri was shifting about, seeming agitated. Maybe he was just keen to get back to the party. He placed a hand on my bare back, which forced me to take a deep breath. He was a reassuring presence regardless.

Out of the corner of my eye, I spied a small leather journal – the captain's logbook, maybe. Perhaps it had information about what Carla was planning, or how the hell this 'water challenge' might unfold.

My mind was reeling with ways I could 'borrow' it undetected.

For the first time that evening, I cursed my beautiful new Chanel accessory. *Damn impractical bag!* It would be far too small to conceal the logbook.

Where else could I put it?

I could slip it into Henri's suit jacket, but I was worried he would give us away. Sure, he felt comfortable at a cocktail party, but would he feel as comfortable as a thief? I found it hard to imagine.

Time was ticking. If I was going to make a move, it had to be soon.

When the captain turned to show Henri something out the port side, I grabbed the book and slipped it down the back of my dress, into my underwear. It felt bulky, cumbersome, especially compared to how gently the fabric of the dress draped across my skin, all smooth and luxurious.

Suddenly, Carla appeared beside us.

Crap! I moved to stand with my back to the wall.

'Don't you two look divine,' she said.

I scanned her eyes for any hint that she was onto me, but her expression remained neutral.

'Please, come with me,' she said, moving out of the bridge and bidding farewell to the captain.

I walked behind Carla and Henri uncomfortably, knowing that at any second the logbook could fall out of my dress.

Carla walked us through the boat, avoiding the deck where the majority of the guests were still enjoying the party. Their voices seemed to follow us, so close yet one step removed.

'Come and watch the fireworks with me,' Carla cooed. 'I have the perfect spot.'

My heart was racing. I nervously fingered the captain's book, trying to secure it. If only I'd worn something more practical for thievery, or opted for shape underwear – the tight fabric would have been perfect for concealing something, or at least would have stopped it from falling out completely.

Carla led us out onto the swim platform.

The sun had just set and the sky was nothing short of magical. Under different circumstances, I would have been swooning.

The water lapped at the sides of the swim platform, gently rocking us back and forth. Carla invited me and Henri to sit on a low, white leather couch opposite her.

We did as we were told.

I wasn't sure how Henri was feeling, whether he was beginning to share my suspicions, whether he was worried about the evening ahead. He was quiet, probably more so than usual, but perhaps I was reading more into his demeanour because I was so on edge. I feared the impending fireworks might well shatter me into a pile of anxious pieces.

I looked at Carla and she returned my gaze with a smile.

'Relax, my darlings,' she said, and I unclenched my jaw in an effort to at least appear at ease. It was harder than expected, and I'm not sure I succeeded. I forced a smile but it felt more like a showing of teeth. I went back to a neutral expression and hoped for the best. The logbook was digging into my spine and I moved slightly to reposition it. I was desperate to find an opportunity to flip through it, to look for any kind of clue as to what was happening. I just needed a moment by myself. But how was I going to get it?

Chapter 46

The Swim Deck – HENRI

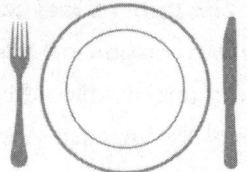

Chloe seemed restless, wiggling around in her seat uncomfortably. She'd gone from being very focused with the captain to now seeming entirely ill at ease. I couldn't figure out what had made her so nervous. She was smiling like she had a gun to her back and was pretending that everything was fine. What did she know that I didn't?

The swim platform was bobbing about in the water, making me queasy. Given the size of the boat, and the extensive deck space where we could have sat to watch the fireworks, I was surprised she'd taken us to the back of the boat. But then, with Carla I knew to expect the unexpected.

Eventually, after a minute or so in complete silence, Carla called out, 'Champagne!'

Until this point, I'd assumed that the three of us were alone on the platform. A waiter appeared swiftly with three glasses and then scuttled off, retreating out of my line of sight as quickly as he'd come into it.

Carla took an unhurried sip and looked out over the water.

I tried to relax.

'So, here we are ... my final two,' she said.

Chloe and I sat, waiting for her to continue. I could feel the anticipation building about what would happen next.

'You've made it this far. Congratulations,' she said. 'You know, I've been wanting to write this memoir for quite some time, but have struggled to find the right person to help me craft it. Such a job requires a certain mix of finesse and creativity. It requires a writer who is loyal, understanding, but also somebody who could fleetingly inhabit my life and what I stand for.'

All of this felt like old news. We already knew that Carla was fussy with her staff, we knew the type of person she was looking to hire. What was with the preamble?

I just wanted to get our speeches over and done with and find out which one of us would get the job.

Enough with the theatrics, already! I felt like shouting.

Chapter 47

The Fireworks – CHLOE

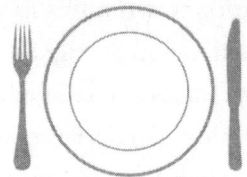

I was beginning to feel like a sitting duck, stuck out on the Mediterranean Sea, wondering what my fate would be. If I were to die out here, like this, I could only imagine how disappointed my father would be. *I taught her everything she needed to know to survive even the wildest days on the water, and then she goes and drowns off the back of a yacht in France. That's what you get for trusting the frogs ...*

Carla's eyes bored into me.

I wasn't sure if it was the situation, or if I'd just never noticed it before, but her stare – when not softened by her talking, or moving about – was terrifying.

She continued. 'So, this final aspect of the interview, you see, needs to prove to me that you are committed, that you are fearless.'

There was a foreboding in her tone that was making me nervous. Blood was pounding against my temples. I didn't *feel* fearless. I wondered if Henri did.

All of a sudden, Max walked out, bent down and whispered something in Carla's ear.

'Excuse me for a few moments,' Carla said. 'A technical issue with the fireworks.'

Together, she and Max retreated, leaving us on the swim platform. Alone. Exposed.

Darkness was descending quickly around us, lending a sinister quality to the water that only an hour earlier had looked so inviting.

'What the hell is going on?' I asked Henri in a whisper.

'I have no idea,' he said. His voice was light, seemingly unconcerned. 'Do you think we will do the speeches soon?' he asked me.

'I don't think we'll be doing the speeches at all,' I said.

'What do you mean?' he asked.

'I think the whole speech thing was a ruse, to lull us into a false sense of security and make us come out here on the yacht.'

'Huh?' he asked.

I pulled out the captain's book. 'I took this from the bridge. It's the captain's. I think it might give us a clue to what's going on.'

'You're not serious,' he said, looking at me like I had two heads.

'Henri, on our way to meet the captain, I saw a whiteboard that said there was going to be some sort of water challenge at 21.40.'

'Slow down,' Henri said. 'What are you talking about?'

'I'm not sure, but I don't think we're safe out here. Perhaps if we could get back to the party, surround ourselves with people ...' I trailed off, trying to figure out a plan.

Henri's face went from relaxed to slightly concerned. *Still handsome*, I thought to myself distractedly.

'What do you mean we're not safe? You don't think Carla's going to leave us out here in the water, do you?' he asked.

'At this point, I think anything is possible. I'm not sure I trust any of these people.'

He grabbed my thigh. In different circumstances, I would have found the move incredibly sexy. But in that moment, I was legitimately scared of what was about to happen.

'Has the stress of the weekend got to you?' he asked, looking at me with concern. 'You don't seem like yourself.'

'I know I'm coming across as crazy, but I just have this hunch. And after what Belle said in her message, I'm even more concerned.'

'Belle?' he asked.

Of course, I hadn't told him about Belle's message yet. No wonder he was acting like everything was fine. But there wasn't time to explain that now either.

I flipped frantically through the logbook, looking at the last entry for today. There were the coordinates where we were currently anchored, the distance back to shore and a few scribbles, which had to be about the currents. Nothing certain, but I wondered why our position tonight had been so specific. Why was the evening's timing so important?

Suddenly, I heard someone approaching.

In a moment of panic, I flung the book into the water, hearing it land with a light splash.

As Carla returned and sat once again opposite me and Henri, a wave of nausea washed over me. The water felt too close, Carla too ominous. I was worried I might faint, which seemed even more dangerous, so I focused on my breathing and tried to stay calm.

I took solace in the fact that Henri seemed at ease. He surely had a better read on Carla than I did. If he wasn't worried, maybe I shouldn't be either. But then, he hadn't received Belle's warning.

I heard the motors fire up once again and realised that we must have hauled the anchor. I wondered why we'd be doing that before the fireworks. Wouldn't the captain want to stay in the one place for that part?

'Now, where was I?' Carla asked.

'I think you were about to tell us when we'd be giving our speeches,' Henri said.

Clever, I thought.

'Ah, yes. So, I have decided that tonight is not the night for speeches. No, I think I need to understand a little more about your willingness to go the extra mile for me, as they say. I am obviously having a terrible time trying to figure out which one of you would be best suited to this role, and I can't for the life of me decide.'

The malice I'd seen in her eyes earlier had been replaced by a look of kindness. *Have I read this whole situation wrong?* I wondered, almost hopeful.

'Tell me, Henri. Why do you deserve this job over Chloe?' Carla asked.

'Excuse me?' he said, the directness of the question clearly throwing him off guard.

'You heard me. Now, talk,' Carla instructed.

There it was. The wickedness I'd been anticipating descended over Carla's face like an evil mask.

I looked around for something that might be useful if we were about to be flung off the yacht. There was a lifebuoy nearby, and I could see seabobs just inside the stern doors.

I tried to consider my options but felt trapped in my seat, panic overwhelming me.

Henri stuttered and mumbled for a few seconds, clearly trying to find his voice, and then said: 'Chloe would be a fantastic person for the job. I honestly think we're both worthy contenders. It comes down to your preference for our writing styles. Chloe is more poetic, and I am more to the point,' he said.

It was an adorably diplomatic response. I couldn't help a little blush, despite the gravity of the situation unfolding around me. There was something about Henri that just made me swoon.

'And?' Carla probed.

'I guess I have more connections in France, which may suit your requirements, but I believe that's the only potential advantage.'

'Are you telling me I should hire Chloe?' she asked, seeming almost annoyed.

Henri didn't respond.

'Never mind then,' she said, clearly exasperated by his lack of resolve.

She turned her attention to me, and her gaze made the hairs on my arms stand on end.

'Chloe, tell me why I should give you the job,' she barked.

'Because Henri doesn't appear to want it,' I said.

I felt him whip his head around to face me. I knew what I'd said sounded harsh, but I had a rough plan. I hoped that *if* I was offered the job, Henri would be asked to leave, and *if* he got off the boat safely, he would know to raise the alarm. I tried to avoid thinking about all the 'ifs' in this scenario. I just hoped that Henri had faith in me.

'I believe I'm more in touch with your sensibilities, that I could better explain your perspective than Henri,' I continued.

Carla smiled at me as though I'd just won.

'Good,' she said. 'Now we're getting somewhere.'

Oh my god, the relief I felt. She'd clearly been waiting for us to turn on each other.

But the respite was short lived.

Seconds later, as we were motoring along, Max appeared, holding the dripping captain's book in front of him like it was a dead animal.

'I believe we have a traitor,' he said theatrically, walking over to hand the book to Carla. He was clearly enjoying himself. It was the most genuine smile I'd seen from him.

Carla looked at Henri and me in disbelief.

'Which one of you felt you needed to take this?'

I anxiously waited for Henri to rat me out, particularly

given what I'd just said about him, but we both remained silent.

'Do you not trust me?' she demanded, scowling angrily. I'd never seen this side of her. I hadn't even imagined it could exist. Was this what Belle had witnessed?

'Tell us why we're really out here,' I said quickly, panicked. 'What is the water challenge you're planning?'

Carla squinted, assessing me. The wind whipped about me, blowing my hair, the hem of dress, even my nerves.

Max stepped in and touched Carla's arm in what appeared to be an attempt to silence her, or perhaps to calm her down. It seemed to work. Carla quickly regained her composure, taking a deep breath, followed by another slow sip of Champagne.

'Enough about me, my darlings,' she said. 'I have one last little challenge for you both. It's quite simple really, because you're both wonderfully determined and athletic.'

As if on command, fireworks started exploding above us.

Carla took this as her cue and stood up.

Henri shuffled towards me on the couch and gripped my hand in his. His closeness was intensely reassuring, despite the situation.

'Whoever makes it back to shore first gets the job,' Carla said, raising her voice to be heard over the cracking of the fireworks.

Henri took a sharp inhale. 'Carla, please. You know who my uncle is. If he finds out about any of this, it's all over for you.' He was on his feet now.

'*If!*' Carla snapped and then laughed. 'I'm not sure you're in a position to be throwing your weight around.'

I looked over at Max, hoping in vain for some sign that this was all a joke. Instead, I saw him mouth the letters 'NDA'.

Henri moved forward in what I can only assume was an attempt to grab Carla and try to stop her. He was cut off by Max, who stepped in front of him and patted his pocket with a look that said: 'Don't try it.'

Oh my god, does Max have a GUN? What the actual hell is happening? My brain was screaming.

While Max and Henri faced off, Carla gracefully untied a knotted rope, releasing our small section of the swim platform from the yacht.

We were adrift.

I jumped to my feet, thinking I could easily swim back to the yacht – but where would that leave me? Back on board with a woman who was clearly insane and her armed accomplice.

Plus, the boat was picking up speed, and the partygoers were all focused on the fireworks exploding in the opposite direction. My stomach dropped as the full reality of Carla's well-orchestrated stunt hit me.

'May the best writer win!' she called out, giving us a final wave as she turned away, following Max back towards the party.

Henri sat back down on the little couch and watched, stunned, as Carla's yacht rapidly floated away from us.

As the initial shock wore off and the vulnerability of our situation began to sink in, my mind moved towards action.

The first thing I did was to check my clutch for my phone. Gone.

'Henri, quick, call the coast guard or the police,' I said.

Henri sat very still, as if quietly contemplating the drama exploding around us.

The only movement he made was to pick up his glass, lift it to his mouth and scull the remainder of his Champagne.

'Henri!' I half-shouted, surprised he could think about drinking at a time like this. But he was one step ahead of me.

'They've got my phone too,' he said resignedly. 'Not much else left to do.'

Chapter 48

The Journey into the Drink – HENRI

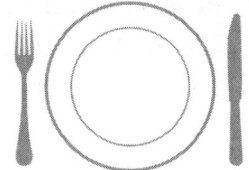

Under different circumstances, being marooned in the middle of the Mediterranean Sea with Chloe would have been a dream come true. In our current predicament, however, it was far from desirable.

The fireworks had stopped now, but they were still ringing in my ears, the sparkling lights still flashing in my field of vision.

I was trying to come up with a plan to get us safely back to land. All I could think of, however, was the very obvious answer, which was to swim.

Once Chloe realised that Carla and Max had taken our phones, she really started to panic. Honestly, I felt like joining her, but I knew it would be a waste of energy. Besides, I didn't want her panicking and jumping off the swim platform.

I was still in shock. I'd always had the feeling that Carla was a little off kilter, but I'd never expected her to pull a stunt like this.

We could actually die out here, under the guise of her testing our stamina.

But it wasn't the time to be dramatic. I wasn't the only one stranded out at sea; I had Chloe to think about. I had to stay calm.

'I think we should swim,' I said.

'And give up this floating platoon? No way,' she replied.

'We can push it with us,' I told her. 'Take rests on top of it when we need to.'

'This can't be real,' she said. Obviously, I wasn't the only one in shock.

'Try not to think about it,' I told her. 'Let's get to land first, and then we can deal with Carla.'

'How can I not think about what she's done? I mean, she's psychotic, right? This stunt has got to be illegal.'

'I think it's best to try and keep our heads clear. Focus on the task at hand. It feels like we're drifting further away from the shore, so I think we should start swimming.'

'I'm really not sure we can make it,' Chloe said. The self-assuredness she'd displayed earlier in the yacht's bridge had disappeared.

'I'll swim first,' I said, scanning the coastline for the closest section of land.

'But you agree this is mental, don't you?' she asked.

'Fully,' I told her.

'I knew something was wrong when the captain was pointing out all those landmarks. Do you think he was in on her plan, too?' Chloe asked me.

I didn't even want to think about the implications of what had just happened, nor did I want to consider the repercussions.

I took my suit jacket off, followed by my shirt. I hesitated before removing my pants, but figured the less weight we had dragging us down, the better.

Chloe was watching me, apparently still in shock.

'Are you okay?' I asked, hoping she wasn't about to freeze up completely.

'Yep,' she said, shaking her head as if to clear it. 'Let's get to it. We'll swim the first leg together.'

She put her bag down gently and removed her heels. She, too, hesitated before removing her clothes. In the end, she turned and asked me to help her with the clasp on her dress. She stepped out of the luxurious fabric and placed her dress next to her bag. In the moonlight, in her underwear, she was a vision. I had to force myself to focus on getting back to land safely.

'We should ditch the couch,' I suggested, realising how ridiculous it looked on the swim platform now that we were detached from the yacht.

She looked at me quizzically.

'Extra weight,' I said.

'Ah, right. Good idea,' she said, grabbing her dress and bag from the couch and then helping me push it into the water. It floated momentarily and then sank ominously.

With that done, I slid into the water. Fortunately, the evening was warm and the water temperature was bearable.

We started swimming in silence, neither of us mentioning how far we were from the shore.

Thankfully, Chloe was a strong swimmer, and by the time she said she was ready for a break, we'd covered a good distance.

I helped her onto the platform and she paused before using her dress to dry herself, looking at the fabric as though mourning the loss of something dear to her.

'You can put on my jacket, if you like,' I told her. She was clearly cold. Shivering, she gratefully accepted. *Focus*, I told myself, forcing my eyes towards the shore.

'Could Carla go to jail for this stunt?' Chloe asked, stretching out her calves.

'She's pretty well connected,' I replied gently, knowing there was very little chance that Carla would take the blame for putting us in danger, even if the truth about the situation came out.

'But you're well connected, too, right?' she said to me.

'I guess so, but my gut tells me there's something in that NDA that gets her out of any major drama.'

Chloe looked enraged. 'You can't be serious!'

'There's a reason her memoir is so coveted,' I said, still swimming, beginning to tire. 'People are desperate to know more about Carla's private life.'

'You don't think it's all part of her plan, do you? I mean, you wouldn't accept the job now even if she offered it to you, right?' she asked.

'God no,' I said, already dreading returning to *Le Cercle* – assuming we made it back to Paris.

'I don't even want to see her again, let alone work for her,' she said, her voice catching.

I swam until my legs felt like jelly and then told Chloe I needed a break. It was exhausting pushing the platform, and although I would happily risk the swim without it, I was worried about Chloe. One leg cramp could take us both down, and at that point, I didn't have it in me to get us both back to shore without some kind of safety net.

We lay on the swim platform side by side. I could feel my heart beating hard in my chest, and did my best to slow my breathing.

'Did you ever expect the weekend to end like this?' she asked.

I laughed. 'I wouldn't be here if I had,' I told her.

'I had my concerns after we got on the yacht, and when Belle texted me, I think I started to see things for what they really were,' she said. 'But in no way did I envisage Carla actually putting us in danger.'

'How badly did you want the job?' I asked her.

'Very. But now I know her offer was too good to be true,' she said.

'What did she offer you?' I asked.

'An enormous salary plus an apartment,' she said.

'She offered me a stake in her next business,' I told her. It was clear Carla had been playing us differently.

'How badly did you want it?' she asked me.

'I can't keep doing my uncle's old job,' I admitted.

'Yeah, I understand that,' she said.

'But maybe it isn't so bad after all. At least reviewing a few restaurants isn't a matter of life and death,' I said, attempting a joke.

I heard Chloe start to cry, and grabbed her hand.

'Hey, worse things could happen, right?' I said.

She looked around us, at the expanse of water, and said, 'Really?'

'You could have been out here with Balthazar. Or even worse, Christopher ...' Despite the precariousness of our situation, we both laughed.

'Let's just keep swimming,' she said.

The sky got darker as time slid away and we slowly edged our way closer to the shore. How long had it been? An hour? Two? At times I felt sure we were going to make it; at others, I began to doubt everything, but thankfully we were both still strong enough to keep swimming.

'I'm so thirsty,' Chloe said at one point.

'To be surrounded by water with nothing to drink is a cruel twist of fate, isn't it?' I replied. And then I remembered my hipflask. 'I have some whisky.'

'Seriously?' she asked. 'How are we only finding out about this now?'

I reached for my trouser pocket, pulled out the little flask and offered it to her. 'My lady,' I said in an exaggerated English accent.

'You're more ridiculous than I first realised,' she said, taking the flask with a smile.

'You're more beautiful than I first realised,' I said, watching her take a sip. I couldn't help myself. Even among all this chaos, Chloe was perfect. There was nobody I would rather be marooned with.

She looked at me, as if on the verge of saying something more, but held back.

'We should keep going,' she said, taking one last sip and passing the flask to me. 'I feel like we're getting close.'

Chapter 49

The Swim – CHLOE

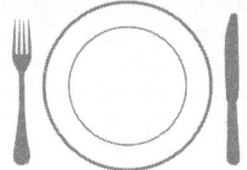

How ridiculous, to be flirting with a guy in the middle of the Mediterranean Sea when my former idol had just set me adrift off her yacht.

Well, that was the current state of affairs.

As Henri and I swam and pushed the stupid swim platform towards the shore, I kept wondering what would happen next. I dismissed thoughts of sharks and daydreamt about passing boats, but neither of those things appeared. It was just me and Henri out there, and a whole lot of dark, foreboding silence.

While kicking through the seemingly endless water on what I hoped would be our last big push to the shore, Henri and I talked about the weekend and compared our experiences. He even told me how he couldn't bear catching fish from the ocean. I admitted I'd thought he'd been sabotaging us, and he just laughed.

Perhaps it was the shared near-death experience, perhaps it was just our heightened emotions, but I found myself having to repeatedly force my focus back to the shoreline and away from Henri's beautifully sculpted body, or his wonderfully adorable face.

When he'd pulled out that flask of whisky, I could have kissed him.

But there would be time for that later. Right now, we had to swim.

I had to admit, the closer we got to the beach, the more of the load Henri was bearing. I felt like I had no power left in my legs.

'I don't know how you're still going,' I said to him.

'I won't let anything happen to you,' he replied.

'You're kind of amazing,' I told him. As soon as the words came out of my mouth, he appeared to refocus his efforts and speed up.

Eventually, we could hear the faint sounds of chatter and music coming from a nearby restaurant. The realisation that we were almost there gave us both the final push we needed.

'I think we can leave the platform now,' Henri said.

'You don't think we should keep it as evidence?' I asked, nervous to let go of the only thing that could prove what Carla had done to us.

'Fuck Carla,' he said. 'You're the only one out here that I care about.' He smiled at me and I grinned back.

We thrust the platform aside – including our clothes and my beautiful Chanel bag – and started to swim freely, spurred on by the knowledge that we were going to make it.

As we dragged our exhausted bodies onto the shore, I heard voices on the beach nearby. We were saved.

'Please help us,' I called out weakly. 'We came off a yacht and we've been swimming ...'

The sound of clapping swiftly put a halt to my pleas.

Oh god, I thought, grasping for Henri's hand as I tried to slowly haul myself into a standing position. My legs were like jelly.

Henri moved towards me and clung to my side. I could feel his entire body trembling from exhaustion.

'Bravo, my darlings,' came a woefully familiar voice only metres away.

The relief I'd felt moments before was replaced by a wave of nausea.

Suddenly, a light illuminated the space around Henri and me. Max appeared behind us, wrapping towels around our shoulders and handing us each a bottle of sparkling water with a wedge of lemon sticking out of the top. *Ridiculous man,* I thought.

'What the hell is going on?' I said, furious, teeth chattering.

'We've been tracking your progress with our scuba team but you made it back in record time,' Carla said, sounding genuinely pleased with us. 'The only problem is that you made it back together. I guess the two of you are less competitive than I realised. Never mind that, though. You both did exceptionally well.'

My brain tried to catch up with whatever logic Carla had created.

'We could have died out there,' I choked out.

'It was all part of the test,' Carla said.

My mind was reeling. This was actual insanity.

'Come back to my place,' Carla said. 'Let's get you cleaned up and showered, and then I will explain the next steps. I've had the most perfect idea.'

I looked at Henri, who was shivering and shaking.

Too exhausted and emotionally drained to do anything else, we let ourselves be escorted back to Carla's.

In the car, I held tightly onto Henri's hand as we were driven away from the beach by the same people who'd left us stranded at sea hours earlier.

I must have fallen asleep during the drive, or maybe I'd fainted in the wake of all the stress and adrenaline.

I vaguely remember being guided back to my room, and the relief I felt when my body hit my bed. My brain wouldn't let me consider anything beyond sleep. Shutting my eyes felt dangerous, but I was incapable of doing anything else. I quickly succumbed.

I woke to find I was wearing a set of incredibly soft, sand-coloured silk pyjamas. I looked around the room, half expecting to see Carla or Max, but everything was peaceful. The balcony door was ajar, letting in a light breeze and the sound of the sea. My body ached intensely and I felt as though I hadn't slept long enough, despite the clock telling me it was nearly midday.

The thought of Henri made me sit bolt upright.

I had to go to his room. I had to make sure he was okay.

I opened my bedroom door to Max.

My heart sank.

'*Bonjour*, Chloe,' he said, sounding surprisingly cheery. 'Carla is ready to see you now.' My mind raced with fears over what she had cooked up now. What kind of mayhem should I expect from her, given everything she'd put us through the night before?

'Where's Henri?' I asked, trying to keep my voice level. Trying not to show Max how distressed I felt.

'Be patient,' he said. 'Please follow me.'

I'd had enough of following these people around. *Something better give soon or I might lose my mind*, I thought. Perhaps that was Carla's plan.

Afraid of what might happen if I didn't listen to Max, I followed him out of my room, still dressed in the pyjamas. I'd clearly stopped caring about what was appropriate – if that word even existed in Carla's vocabulary.

Max led me to a bright dining room I hadn't seen before, where a generous breakfast had been lain out on a white marble table. Max directed me to sit, and I found a pot of coffee waiting before me. Going from standing to sitting, I felt the muscles in my legs groan in exhaustion. How anyone thought a swim like that could be considered a normal part of an interview process was beyond me.

I took a croissant and devoured it quickly, suddenly realising just how famished I was. I took another.

'I see you are hungry,' said Carla, appearing from out of nowhere.

I jumped at the sound of her voice. I hadn't had time to process everything that had happened yet, but my anger towards Carla was red-hot.

The night before, she'd claimed that they'd been tracking us while we were swimming, but who knew if that was true. I wasn't sure what to believe anymore.

'I thought I was going to die out there,' I told her through a mouthful.

'There was no way I would have let you die,' she said with a light laugh.

'How were we supposed to know that?' I snapped back.

Carla sat down and poured herself a large cup of black coffee. She took a slow sip, as if contemplating her next move.

'Is this all a big game to you?' I asked her. 'Because it's not to me. This is my life you're messing with. My future.'

'Your life was always safe. But I can see you are angry. Eat, you'll feel better.'

We sat in silence as I ate eggs and bacon, toast and lobster tails.

When I finally felt like I was getting close to feeling replenished, I stopped chewing and took a sip of coffee. Carla asked me if I was ready to talk, and I nodded.

'I'd like to offer you the job,' she said.

I was shocked. Shocked that she could still think I would want the job, and shocked that she'd offered it to me when clearly, I was furious.

But if I was to get out of Carla's villa in one piece, I knew I'd have to play my cards carefully. Provoking her at this point didn't feel wise.

'And why not Henri?' I asked, trying to buy myself some time.

'Henri has also been offered a job,' she said. 'You have proven yourself to be excellent candidates. I don't want to let either of you escape.'

She spoke these last words lightly, as though she hadn't considered their implications, but I was sure she had ...

I smiled, treading carefully. 'Can I think it over?' I asked.

'Why of course. I will have Max draw up an official offer while you pack your bags to return home.'

Home. The idea of returning to Paris filled me with relief. I wanted to get away from Carla's villa as quickly as possible. I summoned all of the energy I had left to reply.

'That's wonderful. Thank you, Carla, for this incredible experience, for everything you've taught me.' I swallowed hard – my nerves, my anger, my fear all threatening to come exploding out of me.

She smiled and gave me a nod of acknowledgement.

'*À bientôt,*' she said, swooping out of the room.

'I'm not so sure about that,' I said quietly in her wake.

When I got back to my room to pack, my phone was on the freshly made bed next to a brand-new Chanel evening bag. No explanation, no apology.

I packed as quickly as I could, desperate to get away from the villa, desperate to get home to Paris, desperate to find Henri.

Chapter 50

The Return – HENRI

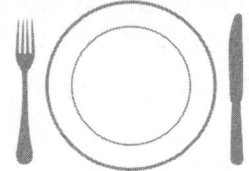

Carla had pulled me aside the moment we got back to her villa.

Despite the fact I was still wrapped in a towel, she instructed me to sit with her in her office, where she'd given me a large glass of whisky and had offered me a job working for her. I'd been exhausted, emotional. All I could think about was getting Chloe away from the villa safely before anything else happened.

Chloe and I hadn't had the opportunity to talk about what to do next, and I had no idea how she was feeling about everything. I just wanted her back beside me. She'd been so exhausted after the swim that she'd fallen into a deep sleep in the car, and had been taken straight to her bedroom when we'd returned. I'd wanted nothing more than to stay with her, to protect her, but Carla Duris had summoned me. And now that I knew what Carla was capable of, upsetting her seemed almost as crazy as this whole weekend.

I accepted Carla's job offer on the condition that Chloe and I could return to Paris the following morning. Carla had looked at me like I was mad. She laughed and said: 'Of course you will be returning to Paris. I have a business to run. And you have a job to resign from.'

Apparently, she'd never planned on holding us hostage, although I wouldn't have put it past her.

She told me she'd instructed Max to draw up a job offer and that I would have it by morning. We parted on affable terms, but really, I'd just been biding my time until I could get away from her.

That night, I slept in fitful bursts, my whole body aching and my nerves on edge. I couldn't wait to leave this weekend behind. I just had to make sure I could take Chloe with me.

I slept late and woke to a breakfast tray being delivered to my room. On the tray sat a note telling me to pack my bags for a quick departure.

I sipped my coffee with a deep pleasure that was amplified by having narrowly escaped drowning, and then I packed as fast as I could.

Waiting by the front door with my overnight bag slung over my aching shoulder, I looked back inside the villa with a very different sensation to the one I'd had when we'd first arrived. Had we really only been there for a weekend? It felt like it had been weeks.

Chloe descended the stairs, the sight filling me with relief. The fact that she was okay, that we were both okay, after going through something so insane was almost overwhelming.

When she saw me, she gave me an enormous, relieved smile. She quickened her step and pulled me into a hug.

'We'll talk when we're out of here,' she whispered almost inaudibly into my ear. During our swim, I'd told Chloe what I'd heard about microphones during our blindfolded lunch. She was right to be cautious. Who knew who was listening?

I nodded, giving her a little squeeze, then took her by the hand.

Max appeared and led us towards a car that was waiting in the driveway. He handed us our tickets and an envelope each, which I assumed contained Carla's job offers. 'You're on the 2pm flight back to Paris. See you both soon,' he said.

In the car on the way to the airport, I grabbed Chloe's knee. 'We did it,' I said, but she wouldn't reply, instead giving me a quick look that I interpreted to mean, 'Not here.'

We spent the next few hours in silence. The only thing that gave me hope that Chloe wasn't angry or upset with me was our physical contact, which was hardly broken for the entire trip. She was holding onto me like we'd held onto that swimming platform. I just had to hope she wouldn't cast me aside as soon as we got back to Paris.

Once we stepped off the plane, I turned to her. 'Are you okay? What's with the silence?'

'Not here,' she said, firmly.

'Come back to my apartment?' I suggested.

For a second, she looked surprised, but then she accepted the offer with a brief nod of her head.

We caught a cab, again in silence, and when I finally slid my key into my apartment door and we went inside, the floodgates opened.

'Honestly, I don't know if we can trust anyone anymore. It feels like everyone is in on this stupid interview process and I feel like everyone is listening, and that Carla and Max are going to appear at any second and throw daggers at us or something. I'm so on edge. I was terrified the pilot was going to crash the plane, just to see if we'd survive.'

I pulled her into my arms and she burst into tears.

She sobbed and I tightened my grasp, reassuring her that everything was okay now. That we were home. That it was all over.

'Are you sure?' she asked.

'It's done, now. Come sit,' I instructed, clearing a space for her on my couch.

I wasn't thinking about the fact that she was seeing my apartment for the first time, or about the fact that Lucy could be home. When it dawned on me that she could be, I went to check her room and was relieved to find it empty. Chloe and I needed to talk. We needed to keep this between us.

'Can I make you a cup of tea?' I asked.

More tears from Chloe. 'That would be perfect,' she sobbed.

I made tea and also grabbed a bottle of red wine and two glasses. I was in this for the long haul. Whatever she needed from me, I would be there for her.

'That was fucked up,' she said.

I was surprised by her language, but there really was no other way of putting it. What had happened that weekend really was fucked up.

'Do you really think she had a scuba team following us?' she asked.

'I have no idea what is true anymore,' I replied. 'But I'd like to think she wouldn't have let us die out there.'

'I'm not so sure,' she said. 'It all feels surreal now. To think that I could have spent the weekend in London with my dear friend Hazel. Now, I almost wish I had. It would have saved me a lot of anxiety.'

'But then we wouldn't have got to hang out,' I said with a grin that I hoped she'd find endearing.

'Well, I'm glad you can still find the positives,' she said, softening into a smile.

'Carla offered me a job,' I admitted to Chloe.

'Me too,' she replied.

'Have you read the offer? Have you opened that envelope?' I asked her.

'I was too scared to do it on the plane in case somebody was watching,' she admitted.

'Shall we do it together?' I asked. 'Compare notes?'

'Is there an offer you'd be tempted to accept?' she asked.

'God no. You?' I replied.

'Obviously not, but at the same time ...' She hesitated before saying, 'I desperately want a better job in Paris. And I want to be writing about food full-time. This was meant to be my big opportunity, to get me out of the back office of that crappy hotel. Something big enough that my parents will stop asking me when I'm moving back to Australia.'

The idea of Chloe leaving Paris hit me like a punch in the stomach. I couldn't let her go. But could I be reason enough for her to stay? I had to at least find out.

'I don't want to write for the paper anymore,' I told her.

'Why not?' she asked.

'I want to do my own thing, make my own way,' I said.

'I can understand that,' she said, giving me an empathetic look.

'I had an idea on the plane,' I said, trying to conceal the excitement in my voice.

'Go on,' she said with a smile.

'Why don't we start something together?' I suggested.

'I thought you didn't approve of blogging,' she said to me sceptically.

'I love your blog,' I told her. It was the first time I'd said it and I couldn't help blushing. 'I think I've read every post.'

'Seriously?' she asked with a laugh. 'All this time I was under the impression you thought I was a hack.'

'You deserved the job with Carla more than anyone.'

'I'm not sure that feels like a compliment anymore,' she told me.

'No, I guess not,' I said. 'Sorry.'

We were silent for a moment.

'So, why don't we turn *Eat Me, Paris* into something a lot bigger? I've got the money to get us going, and I could certainly drum up a lot of advertisers. We could both write; we could even ask Belle to help with video content.'

'What do you mean?' she asked me.

'A printed monthly food magazine distributed all around Paris. I'm sure between us we've got the connections. We could do things our own way, not have to worry about pleasing other people,' I told her.

'It'd be a risk. There are no guarantees we could even make enough money to break even,' she told me.

'I think I'm okay with that,' I said.

'I'm not,' she replied.

'Don't worry. I won't let you starve or become homeless,' I assured her. 'I want to invest in us.'

Chloe mulled the idea over for a minute and then smiled. 'Obviously, you'll get all the crappy jobs,' she said with a laugh.

'So, you're in?' I asked.

'Well ...' she said, hesitating, but then unable to resist a smile. 'Honestly, it sounds like a dream come true.'

'And you're sure you want us to work together?' I asked her.

'After what we've just been through, I would trust you with my life,' she said.

'And you'd be happy to stay in Paris? At some point we're probably going to run into Carla,' I said nervously.

'True, but at least on our turf we have the advantage, right?'

'You're right. Let her come after us if she dares,' I said.

'What a wild weekend,' she said. 'It's almost hard to believe it even happened.'

She looked at me, tears welling again, and in that moment Carla and her memoir ceased to matter, because now I had something much sweeter – Chloe, and the prospect of working with her and creating something that had the potential to be incredible.

'Chloe,' I said, moving towards her and wrapping my arms around her waist, 'I think we can build something brilliant, you and I.'

She smiled and pulled me closer, no more hesitation or second-guessing what we were doing. Everything finally felt right. This was where we were meant to end up.

And then she kissed me until the memory of Carla releasing that swimming platform had drifted into insignificance.

Chapter 51

The Reckoning – CHLOE

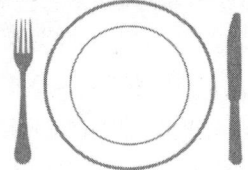

I woke to see a pretty young woman staring at me. I was disorientated for a moment, before realising I was on Henri's couch.

Who the hell is this? my brain yelled at me.

I went to jump up, but Henri pulled me back gently. 'It's just Lucy, don't worry,' he said sleepily.

'*Just* Lucy!' the girl squealed. 'Is that how you introduce me?'

Slowly, I remembered that Lucy was his much younger sister. I felt my body relax.

'Nice to meet you,' I said, sitting up and disentangling myself from Henri. I was still a little jumpy and on edge, but I tried not to appear unhinged in front of Henri's sister.

Henri, meanwhile, sat up a little, rubbing his eyes and stretching his neck.

'Good to see you made it through the weekend unharmed,' he said to Lucy.

'Ha, ha,' Lucy said sarcastically. 'So, how was the rest of the interview?' she asked, looking between us.

'Ah ...' I started.

'It went pretty well,' Henri said.

I looked at him, wondering why he wasn't telling her the truth.

'Did either of you get the job?' she asked, perkily.

'Nope,' Henri answered. 'Shame, really.'

I choked back a scoff. In different circumstances, perhaps with a little more distance from the whole weekend, I might even regret not getting the opportunity to work with the one-and-only, very crazy Carla Duris. But that certainly wasn't now.

'Where have you been all night?' Henri asked, concern obvious in his voice. 'Not with Balthazar, I hope,' he said, and I shot him a confused glance.

'Why would I be hanging out with that little dweeb?' Lucy asked, and I chuckled. 'I was studying at a friend's house. Anyone fancy coffee?' she asked, pulling out her phone. 'I'm ordering Starbucks.'

'I'll take a flat white,' I said gratefully.

'A flat white,' Lucy repeated in an Australian accent. 'Adorable!'

'Put your phone away, Lucy. I'll make us all breakfast,' Henri said.

'I was hoping you'd offer, because I've actually run out of cash,' Lucy said, sheepishly but with a grin. 'I'll go have a shower.'

After she'd left the room, I gave Henri a questioning look.

'Why didn't you tell her what really happened?'

'The NDA,' he whispered, and I had my own moment

of reckoning. I knew that technically we weren't allowed to discuss what had happened this weekend, but even with our closest friends? Henri couldn't continue hiding such a life-changing event from his sister. Lucy was bound to guess that something was up eventually. Or could he just keep pretending? Could I?

I nodded slowly as the weight of this sank in.

Henri was the only person who would ever understand what Carla had put us through, the extent of her madness. Even the people who had been evicted before us had no idea what had happened. In a way, I guess they were lucky, getting out when they did. They probably just thought Carla was spontaneous and perhaps a little ruthless. The extent of her demands and whims would have to remain our secret.

I grabbed Henri's hand, nervous that it was Carla who had brought us together, while also being relieved that he had been with me throughout the weekend. It might have been a messy beginning to a relationship, but hopefully it wouldn't dictate how things developed between us.

Slowly, Henri kissed the top of my head and got up from the couch. I felt cold the minute his body moved away from mine, and I wasn't sure I was ready for him to leave my side.

'Get back here,' I said, pulling his arm until he succumbed.

'If Lucy doesn't get coffee she turns into a gremlin,' he said and I laughed.

'Right, well, off you go then,' I said, eventually releasing him.

My phone lit up with a message from Drew: *'You alive?'*

Crap! In my exhaustion, I'd forgotten to tell him I was

back in Paris. I hurriedly sent a reply: *'All is well, I'll fill you in in person. Coffee later?'*

I thought again of the NDA and wondered how much I could actually tell Drew. I was sure I wouldn't be breaking any rules if I said that things had gotten weird and that I had rejected the job offer. I mean, the interviewees who had left before me would probably say the same thing, if not worse. I thought of Juliette getting busted for public urination and had to suppress a laugh. I suppose there had been warning signs that Carla was perhaps a little nuts, but then there had been the beautiful Celine dress, and the offer of a Parisian apartment, and the goddamn Chanel evening bag ... I was a fool, but could anyone really blame me?

'Well, I'm just glad I don't have to look for a new flatmate,' Drew replied, and I had to stop myself from saying he'd almost needed to ...

I was looking forward to seeing him, to things going back to the way they had been before I'd been invited to that stupid dinner at Chez Duris, to erasing memories of all the antics from this past weekend – except Henri, of course, and perhaps my growing friendship with Belle, and our new magazine. These were things I wouldn't mind holding onto. Silver linings, for sure.

When Henri came back in with a breakfast tray, I was fingering the envelope Max had given me. Part of me was desperate to see what I'd be missing out on, but I also knew it was probably better for my sanity not to know.

Henri gave me a questioning look and I said, 'I think we

should burn these. Avoid the temptation to look at them, in case we regret turning her down.'

'I couldn't agree more,' he said, pulling his own envelope out and giving it to me.

'You really don't want to see what life could be like on the other side?' I asked.

'That's a hard no,' he said, and I smiled.

'Did Carla ever tell you why she wanted to write the memoir?' I asked. 'Not that it matters anymore, but I still want to know.'

'Nope, and by the time I met with her after the swim, I didn't even want to know,' he said.

'Do you think she's trying to cover something up?' I asked.

'I have no doubt she is,' he said, grabbing a box of matches from above the fireplace and handing them to me.

'Who do you think will write the memoir now?' I asked.

'Hopefully someone who can match her level of crazy,' he said.

I lit the corners of our envelopes and watched them slowly go up in flames, only letting them fall into the fireplace at the last second, leaving nothing of Carla's offer but a pile of ash.

When it was done, I wasn't sure how to feel, but when I turned to see Henri opening his arms to me, I knew I'd made the right decision.

He kissed me and, in that moment, I realised where my future was: by his side.

Our phones both flashed with an alert showing we had a new email from Max.

Ignoring it, we turned back to each other.

'We're going to have to let him know eventually,' I told him.

'After what they've put us through, let them wait until we've properly caught our breath,' he said, kissing me again.

Chapter 52

The Offer – BALTHAZAR

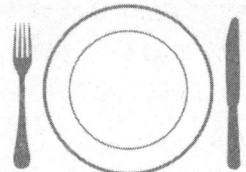

I was not surprised when Carla called me to offer me the job. I had known it wouldn't take long for her to realise the error of her ways.

Honestly, I considered not answering my phone when Max called, just to prove a point. But at the last second, I changed my mind.

'*Bonjour*,' I said, confident that I now had the upper hand.

'Balthazar ... Max.'

'*Et alors?*' I asked, regretting it immediately when Max went quiet. As much as I wanted him to beg me to come back, I did not want to piss him off.

'Please clear your calendar for the foreseeable future. Carla would like to offer you the job of writing her memoir. I've booked your travel to Antibes this evening to come and sign the contract and go through the planning for the year. I'll email you the tickets shortly.'

'Of course,' I replied.

'One last thing. Carla is currently on board her yacht and

will meet you there to sign the papers. Pack your swimming things,' he instructed, before hanging up.

I walked to my fridge and opened a bottle of Champagne.

My only regret was having felt sorry for myself after being sent home mid-interview. What a waste of time. I should have known things would work out. They always did.

And to think that neither Henri nor Chloe had been good enough to get the job, and that Carla had come back to me, recognising her mistake. Not that I cared *how* I got the job – what was important was that I *had* the job. I'd scored the jackpot. I would be writing Carla's memoir, and finally I would be at the top of the top of the Parisian food scene, far above all those other idiots who were not good enough to seal the deal. Not only had I been offered the job, but apparently it was to start with an evening on Carla's yacht! In his email, Max had told me to 'await a night of adventure ...' Could life get any sweeter?

Sipping on my Champagne, I went to pack.

I grabbed my phone to message Henri.

'*Guess you missed out this time, old friend,*' I messaged, pretending to give a shit but really just wanting to rub it in.

His reply made me laugh. I had never imagined him to be the spiteful sort.

'*You're the perfect man for the job, Balthy! Enjoy getting to know Carla.*'

What an idiot, I thought, texting back: '*Eat your heart out, Henri!*'

Epilogue – CHLOE

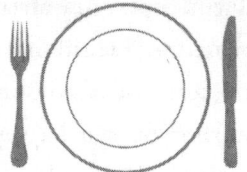

One year later ...

I woke to my phone buzzing.

Lazily, I rolled over and silenced it.

Henri and I had been out at a new wine bar last night and it had been late when we'd finally fallen into bed. Judging by how intensely my head was throbbing, I figured I'd need a few more hours of sleep.

My phone buzzed again, this time with a text.

Leave me alone, I thought, flipping it over to see who it was. *What in the world could be urgent enough for this cruel wake-up?*

A missed call and a message from Drew. *'Turn on your TV. Carla!'*

I shook Henri's shoulder to wake him up.

'Carla is on TV,' I said, leaping out of bed.

'Huh?' he asked sleepily.

'Drew just messaged me. Let's go!'

We rushed to the couch, hunting for the remote, and finally

switched on the TV. Henri flipped through channels so quickly that it was hard to register what was going on.

And then, there she was: Carla Duris.

Seeing her face set my heart racing. Memories that I'd managed to repress from our weekend in Antibes began resurging, and I could feel my palms starting to sweat.

I'd actually grown used to a world that didn't contain Carla – at least not for me. Since discovering the Duris's cookbook a decade earlier, Carla had been a huge part of my life. But following my brush with death after her yacht party, I'd gone cold turkey on anything and everything Duris. I hadn't watched Carla's TV appearances, hadn't cooked her recipes, hadn't even thought about her or her influence on French food. I'd found a way to live in Paris and write about the city's food scene without mentioning Carla or Jean. It had been surprisingly easy – so much so that I wondered if I'd had Carla on too high a pedestal.

Obviously, Carla had tried to shut down *Eat Me, Paris* after Henri and I had rejected her job offer and instead begun working together. But Henri's family had their own team of lawyers, and thankfully, they'd made Carla's threats go away. There had been extensive meetings between Uncle Michel and Henri about Henri's future, of course. But it had been worth it. After the dust had settled, we had been able to continue living as though Carla didn't exist.

But now, here she was, exploding into our lives on the screen in front of us.

The news report showed a clip of Carla, handcuffed, being walked out of her villa to a waiting police car. She was in her chef's jacket, which was blood-stained, and looked deranged as she shouted to the policeman: 'I am innocent. You will regret this.'

But what had she actually done? What had she finally been busted for?

The damning images of Carla were replaced by a familiar, more composed-looking face. Belle's.

'Crossing now to our cultural correspondent, Belle Williams, who has previously spent time at Carla's famed Antibes villa and has been following this breaking news story since earlier this morning,' the anchor said. 'Belle, what can you tell us about the events that led to Carla Duris's arrest?'

I grabbed Henri's hand. Our eyes were fixed on the screen.

'On the eve of Carla Duris's hotly anticipated memoir release, an ambulance was called to her famed villa to attend to an alleged stabbing. The details of how the accident or injury unfolded are still to be confirmed. However, footage from Antibes this morning show Carla being removed from her south of France home and being taken into police custody.'

'Oh my god, she stabbed someone!?' I asked Henri.

He looked at me, speechless.

'Belle, do we know anything about the events prior to the knife incident?' the anchor asked.

'According to a staff member who wishes to remain anonymous, it is believed that Carla was hosting a pre-release party for her memoir and was mid-cooking demonstration when things apparently turned sour. Shouting was heard from the kitchens, followed by the alleged stabbing. The police have now entered her villa, confiscating video footage and pulling staff in for questioning,' Belle continued.

Max appeared briefly on the screen, getting into another police car, looking completely at ease, almost smiling, before the camera flashed back to Belle.

'Our anonymous source has also sent through the following video footage of the man who was injured.'

The footage cut to a blurry video of a man on a stretcher being carried towards an ambulance in the dark of the night. His body was covered by a blanket, but the wails escaping him were deep and guttural. I recognised Balthazar's face immediately; his eyes were skittish and afraid.

'Some very confronting scenes, indeed,' said the anchor. 'So, what's next for France's best known female chef?'

'The incident has caused a cascade of other staff members to step forward, accusing Duris of ill-treatment that often bordered on abuse. The influx of claims against Carla Duris make it difficult to anticipate how long it will take for her to go to trial. I imagine the police will have their work cut out for them, trying to contact former employees and going through what is said to be thousands of hours of video footage that has been found in the villa. For now, Duris will be held in police custody awaiting bail.'

'And what of her memoir that was due for release?'

'I've been in contact with Duris's publisher, who has said the memoir will not be released until after the trial. They were unwilling to comment further.'

'Belle, you have had first-hand experience dealing with

Madame Duris. Does this news come as a surprise to you?'

'Frankly, no. From the moment I met Carla Duris, I knew there was something more going on with her businesses than the polished final product would suggest. I could tell by her secretiveness, her ruthlessness, and her adoration of power that she was somebody who didn't believe in boundaries and was prepared to go to any length for her own fame and fortune.'

'And what do we know about the man who was injured?'

'We have an unconfirmed report that it is Balthazar Baillairgé, the former *Le Monde* food writer who was employed by Duris to co-write her memoir. Despite being the alleged victim, Baillairgé's innocence in this sordid affair is yet to be proven.'

When saying this, Belle's eyes seemed to sparkle a little, almost like she was telling me this juicy bit of gossip in person, over drinks.

'And do we have any idea of Duris's motive for allegedly stabbing Monsieur Baillairgé?' the anchor asked.

'At this point, no,' said Belle. 'However, rumours have been circulating that he was too close to Madame Duris, was too embedded in her life and knew too much. Unfortunately, all we can do at this point is speculate.'

The news report ended and I sat there, stunned.

'Wow,' said Henri. 'I knew she had it coming, but I hadn't realised it would be such a public fall from grace.'

'I actually can't believe it. And they've pulled her memoir, too. Balthazar must have written a puff piece after all. If it was a tell-all, the publishers would have run with it, right? The publicity would have been huge for them. And now she's gone and stabbed him!'

'I know we've all thought about hurting Balthazar, but to actually go and do it ...' Henri replied.

'Clearly we got off lightly with Carla,' I said.

'A swim sounds almost pleasant compared to a stabbing,' he said with a half-laugh.

'What do you think this means for us?' I asked.

'Nothing much,' he said. 'We remain silent for now. If the police ask to speak with us, I'll get us legal support and we can finally tell the truth about what Carla put us through. Trust me, we've done nothing wrong – other than signing that NDA, perhaps.'

'Should we post something about her arrest?' I asked. 'Some kind of statement on *Eat Me, Paris*?'

'I think the less we say, the better.'

'You're right,' I said.

We sat in silence for a few minutes, digesting the news.

What else was there to say?

'Fancy going for lunch?' Henri said suddenly, as if it were any other day. 'I feel like eating something delicious.'

'Why not?' I said, feeling surprisingly calm about the whole thing, and a little like we had something to celebrate. 'I'll give Belle a call. See if she can spare some time for us after her busy morning.'

'She's so great on TV, isn't she?' Henri said.

'A natural,' I agreed.

Henri put his arm around my shoulders and gave me a squeeze before getting up to go shower.

Drew called me shortly after. 'Spill the beans, Chloe,' he said as soon as I answered.

'I signed an NDA. I've been dying to tell you everything,' I admitted.

'Are you mad?' he asked.

'Everyone was doing it,' I said, attempting some humour.

'Chloe! Come in for coffee, now! You have some explaining to do,' he instructed.

'Okay, calm down. Henri and I will be there soon,' I told him.

That day, between coffee, lunch and a bottle of Champagne, I kept an eye on the headlines.

Celebrity chef's fall from grace.

The knives came out on the eve of Carla Duris's memoir release.

France's culinary goddess cutting off more than she can chew.

Daughter of French culinary god crumbles under pressure of running father's restaurant.

I cringed, thinking about how much Carla would have hated that last one. She'd spent her life trying to move out of her father's shadow and the media were putting her right back there.

Her face was suddenly everywhere. On every news report, on every newspaper and all over social media. It was the

310

additional fame she seemed to have craved, but the format had betrayed her. She'd stumbled at the last hurdle, and her true and terrifying nature had finally shone through.

In the weeks that followed, I was surprised I didn't feel more about Carla's arrest. I'd expected to feel relief, maybe validation, but life went on much as it had before. Henri and I ate out, we drank, we wrote article after article. The police never called us in, probably because Max had already destroyed any evidence from our insane weekend at her villa. And maybe that was for the best.

I knew I should hate Carla Duris, but there was a small part of me that would always be grateful to her. Yes, she was batshit crazy, but she was also one of the reasons I came to Paris, the reason I was now a full-time food writer and the reason I'd fallen in love with Henri. Would I do it all again? In a heartbeat.

Acknowledgements

I had the idea for this novel towards the end of a six-year stint living in France, but it took moving home to Australia to start getting it down on paper. While I was drafting Chloe's and Henri's chapters, I felt so part of their world, so ensconced by the surrounds of Carla's villa, it was as though I would spend half my day swanning around the south of France and the other trying to readjust to life in Australia. Writing became a great remedy for my homesickness. Thankfully, some other amazing people also loved this story, which allowed me to keep re-entering my faux-French life in order to share it with you now. To them, I am so grateful.

So, thank you to all of the following people.

First, to my dedicated and hardworking agent, Gregory Messina. It has been quite a few years now since our first coffee in Paris. I'm so glad we met.

To Kelly Doust and Martin Hughes. Within five minutes of meeting you both, I knew that I wanted to work with you – and what a dream year it has been. A particular thanks to Kelly; your guidance, support and encouragement have meant so much to me.

To my editor, Kevin O'Brien, thank you for your patience and careful work during each editing phase. You were always willing to make another change if it improved the manuscript, and I'm beyond grateful for that.

To the incredible Affirm Press team, in particular to those with whom I've had the pleasure of dealing personally: Julia Kathro, Dana Anderson, Alistair Trapnell and Susie Kennewell. It's been wonderful working with such a kind, talented and dedicated crew. Thank you!

Thank you to Andy Warren for the fabulous cover design; to Vanessa Lanaway for the thoughtful copyedit and to Libby Turner for the incredibly detailed proofread. After so long working alone on a manuscript, it's a relief to have such talented people contribute to making it print ready.

Outside of the book team, I want to say thanks to my husband, Jamie. You are the most wonderful support person and the most terrifying reviewer of my early drafts. Your idea for a little weekend on the Mediterranean led me to this story, and I'll be forever grateful. When's our next trip?

A huge thanks also to my sister Jules, who always answers my calls and devotes hours to reading my drafts and discussing the fictional lives of my made-up characters. Writing books would be a whole lot lonelier without you.

To my kids, Clementine and Hugo, thank you for being so amazing. You've skipped between countries, schools, holidays and new houses with a grace and insouciance that I can only try to replicate.

To Dad and Lorns, thank you for always being encouraging of a good adventure. The travel bug runs deep in our family.

To Mum, thank you for reading and proofreading and

pre-ordering copies of this book. You're my number one hype girl and I'm so grateful for that!

Thank you as well to my extended family, friends and the many people who have supported me and my writing along the way. From university lecturers to creative writing teachers and to the incredible *Time Out Shanghai* team. My experience as a dining critic certainly wasn't as dramatic as Chloe's, but it taught me so much about the world of dining and chefs and the complexities of these industries. I loved every minute.

And finally, and perhaps most importantly, to all my readers, thank you for choosing this book. I hope you've enjoyed the ride.

With love,
Victoria

Reading Group Questions

1. Why do you think Chloe misjudged Henri in Part 1 of the book?
2. At what point did Chloe and Henri's dynamic begin to shift?
3. Who was your favourite supporting character?
4. Who did you want to get the job at first? Did this change?
5. Do you think the characters got what they deserved?
6. Do you think Carla's intentions were ever good?
7. Which challenge do you think you would have enjoyed the most during the interview weekend?
8. Which dish from the novel would you most like to try?
9. Who would you cast as the leads in a movie adaptation?
10. What would you do on a dream weekend in Paris or on the Côte d'Azur?